The Dark Worlds of Joe P̶

The Vermilion Book of the Macabre

"Ranging from stories of evil curses, unfortunate circumstances, and harrowing monsters Pawlowski unravels a narrative where the characters are the anchor point, the setting is undisputed, and the darkness of these stories settles uncomfortably in the mind of the reader." — Irish horror writer Gloria McNeely

"Joe Pawlowski is an artist. With words as his medium, he paints his dark tales so realistically you will have nightmares. This book is a 'must read' if you enjoy the macabre." — Barbara Taylor, Amazon reviewer

"Just have to say: I bought it this week and I love it. Scary and beautiful." — Emanuel Mayer, Facebook

Dark House of Dreams

"The story had me drawn in from the start. The book is well-written and creepy. — Heather Bane, Goodreads

The Watchful Dead

"Pawlowski possesses the talents of a classic great writer, and this reader found myself pulled to the page as 12-year-old Ring Gargery experiences loss, brutality, friendship, and love. Behind the dark title lies a spellbinding, outstanding story. I suspect — and hope — we'll hear more of Pawlowski's Ring Gargery tales!" — Lissa Carlson, Wisconsin editor/publisher

"In the city of Hastur, Ring's family are slavers, but his father and uncle have loftier ambitions. Political ambitions, which they hope to attain by some fairly sneaky, roundabout methods involving pirates and a captured island witch with the power to awaken the dead. ... All in all, it's a gutsy, ambitious, skillful exploration of cosmic/epic dark fantasy that brings something new to both facets of the genres." — *The Horror Review*

The Cannibal Gardener

"A quick and gory read with a surprise ending I did not see coming," — *Worth a Read*

"This is an interesting book that takes the reader on a twisted journey through the minds of some warped people." — Amazon Reviewer

Why All the Skulls Are Grinning

"*Why All the Skulls Are Grinning* ended up being a fantastic read for me who generally does not read or watch the horror genre. The short stories were descriptive and drew you into the story so you could picture where you were, who you were with and what they maybe thinking. Being caught up in story telling, I found many of the endings were a surprise but made sense with the masterful way the story was weaved. I would say Joe honored his craft by successfully scaring the hell out of me with a couple of nightmares especially after reading 'Alien Eggs' and 'Uncle Morven!' — Tammy Severe, Amazon Reviewer

Pleasant dreams,
Joe Pawlowski,

In the Heart of the Garden Is a Tomb

Joe Pawlowski

Glint Media

NEW HOPE, MINNESOTA

Also by Joe Pawlowski

The Watchful Dead
Dark House of Dreams
The Vermilion Book of the Macabre
The Cannibal Gardener
Why All the Skulls Are Grinning

Joe Pawlowski/Glint Media
New Hope, Minnesota
www.joepawlowskiauthor.com

Publisher's note: This is a work of fiction. Names, characters, places, and incidents are a product of the author's imagination. Locales and public names are sometimes used for atmospheric purposes. Any resemblance to actual people, living or dead, or to businesses, companies, events, institutions, or locales is completely coincidental.

***In the Heart of the Garden Is a Tomb*/Joe Pawlowski**
1st edition
ISBN: 979-8-9857407-0-7

For William Boyle, my English teacher and "B" Squad basketball coach at Algonquin Middle School, who turned out to be one of the greatest influences on my life.

Contents

"Alas! in the heart of the garden is a tomb—a tomb so trellised and embowered with vine and blossom, that the sunlight reveals the ghastly gleam of its marble to no careless or incurious scrutiny. But in the night, when all the flowers are still, and their perfumes are faint as the breathing of children in slumber—then, and then only, the serpents bred of corruption crawl from the tomb, and trail the fetor and phosphorescence of their abiding-place from end to end of the garden."

—Clark Ashton Smith, "The Garden and the Tomb"

Gunplay

"The old gods of war are wakened by this loud clamour of the guns."
—Arthur Machen, "The Bowmen and Other Noble Ghosts"

I t would be wrong to say Corbin Grimwood was ever a man without faults. That before he found the gun, he was anybody's idea of altruism personified. But if Corbin was a curmudgeon from the get-go, most would have regarded him as a harmless, fair-natured one. As one of those guys who always grumble about having to pony up for the taxman and who sometimes go on about how creeping socialism will be the death of democracy, but who wasn't averse to tossing an occasional coin into a bell-ringer's kettle during the holidays or buying a box of cookies to help out the Girl Scouts.

He wasn't a heartless man, not by any means.

"Martha," he said to his long-enduring wife as he stared glassy-eyed at the talking head on Fox News, "the country is going to hell in a handbasket."

"Yes, Corbin," she said, carrying a steamy bowl of Campbell's vegetable soup out to the living room. She set this on the TV tray in front of him, along with a soup spoon and a napkin. "Eat your lunch before it gets cold."

The years had been kind to Martha Grimwood. Or at least as kind as she might have hoped. Her plump and supple features softened her laugh lines and crow's-feet, her cheeks maintained their rosiness, and she never lost the clear-eyed quality of her hazel eyes. Her post-menopausal figure had transformed from pear-shaped to more apple-ish, and when her ankles swelled up in warm weather, she walked with a sort of hobble, but she still had her original knees and hips. Though she colored her hair, she always instructed the girl at the beauty shop to leave a bit of gray at the temples.

She walked back out to the kitchen, then returned with a second bowl of soup, which she placed on the coffee table in front of the sofa, then she placed herself on the sofa. "Corbin, would you mind changing the channel? All this talk about the president is giving me a headache. Isn't the man trying to get us free of this Covid business?"

"Covid shmovid. The only reason I got those vaccination jabs was to keep you from harping at me. For all we know, the whole thing was invented by the government to keep us in line."

Nonetheless, he changed the channel. The Minnesota Twins, who'd been on fire before the pandemic, but who were now trying desperately to battle their way out of last place in the American League, appeared on the screen. Matt Shoemaker was winding up on the mound. Matt Shoemaker, with an ERA of 7.28.

"You don't believe that business about Covid being a government conspiracy, Corbin. Minnie Price from St. Alfonzo *died* from it. Your cousin Darlene was in the hospital for a month on a *ventilator*. Ask her if it was a government plot."

Matt Shoemaker delivered his pitch. Strike one. Well, that was something.

"I'm not saying there isn't some truth to it. Sure, many people have died from it. But maybe it's just a little overblown. And what if it's the next step toward socialized medicine? What would happen then?"

"Then everyone could afford to go to the doctor, and wouldn't that be terrible?"

He started to say more, but Martha leveled the stink eye at him. That was his cue to drop the subject.

He scooped a spoonful of alphabet pasta and square-cut chunks of carrot from his bowl, blew on it, and shoveled it into his mouth. "After lunch, I'm going to go to Two Stooges. Shoot a little stick. Get my mind off things."

"That's a good idea. Maybe you'll run into one of your drinking buddies and have a little fun."

"You could come along if you like." His eyes took on a sheepish quality.

"Tell you what, Corbin. You go to the pool hall and let me get at my garden for a few hours, then we'll have dinner tonight at the Olive Garden. How does that sound?"

Matt Shoemaker rifled one out of the strike zone, but the batter chased it anyway and missed. Strike two.

"Sounds like a plan," Corbin said. He dug into his lunch with renewed vigor.

Wednesday was garbage day in New Hope, so by Tuesday night, plastic trash receptacles stood sentry at the end of every driveway on Decatur Avenue. Corbin figured, why wait till later? He pulled the wheeled bins out of the garage and down the cracked pavement to the curb.

The neighbor's front yard looked a bit weedy. He frowned at it.

The neighbor's name was Tanoh Ridley, which Corbin judged as a perfectly ridiculous name. Tanoh did something with computers; Corbin wasn't sure what. A thirty-something Black man with somber brown eyes and a vaguely impatient air about him, Tanoh lived with a girlfriend known only as Bunny. She smoked cigarettes in the wire-fenced backyard.

They were Biden people.

Tanoh and Bunny's frequent lovers' spats had earned them dubious fame in the neighborhood, but most of the time they seemed to get along. Some couples require the occasional flare of anger to keep fonder passions simmering. Secretly, though, Corbin wondered how much longer Tanoh and Bunny would stay together.

Back in the garage, still musing about Tanoh's weedy front lawn, Corbin unlocked the driver's side door of his 2015 Jeep Patriot. That's when a ruckus in the street drew his attention.

A pair of lanky, stringy-haired teenage girls in cutoff jeans popped into view. The taller one, the one with the nose ring and the cowboy boots, looked nervously up and down Decatur Avenue and said something to her friend.

They appeared agitated.

The shorter one, the one with the Band-Aid above her eye and all the tattoos, nodded excitedly. This one opened the brown plastic lid on one of the trash receptacles Corbin had just wheeled out and dropped in a small, white paper bag.

They hurried out of sight, neither looking up at Corbin, who watched them quizzically from the shadows of his garage.

"Hey!" he called after them.

By the time he walked the length of his driveway, they were already down the street, running at full speed, looking left and right like a couple of fugitives. Running, Corbin judged, as if their lives depended on it. They rounded the corner onto Bass Lake Road.

He studied them for a minute, then studied the cockleburs rising like sinister totems from Tanoh's longish grass. *The country was definitely going to hell in a handbasket.*

He walked back to the garage, started the Patriot, threw it in reverse, and rolled down the driveway. He was about to back onto Decatur when curiosity struck him.

What had those girls tossed in my garbage, anyway?

He put the Patriot into park and climbed out. Lifting the lid on his receptacle, he peered in.

Atop his twist-tied Hefty bags sat the paper sack, oily as if it had once contained maybe french fries. He picked it up. It was heavy. Opening the mouth of the bag, he looked inside.

A coldness seized in his belly.

It was a gun. A revolver, steely blue. He closed the bag, closed the lid on his garbage, and carried the bag back to his car, determined to take it immediately to the police department where he would report the two girls who left it.

With the bag in his lap, he slipped the transmission into reverse but kept his foot on the brake. *The hell with it.* Reaching down, he slid the bag with the gun under his seat. He'd drop it off at the police department *after* he shot some pool at Two Stooges. After all, what's his hurry? Those girls were probably halfway to Brooklyn Center by now.

TWO STOOGES SPORTS BAR & GRILL, established in 1988, sits on University Avenue in Fridley, Minnesota. Something of a mecca to area pool shooters, it features forty-three playing tables, a bar, a restaurant, six dartboards, twenty-five flat screens and three projection TVs, all conveniently located in a squat, twenty-five-thousand-square-foot brick building with Kermit-green awnings.

Having driven the fifteen minutes from New Hope to Fridley, Corbin was ready for a cold one. Leaving the revolver under the seat, he crossed the parking lot and swung open the pool hall's door.

Inside, the last of the lunch crowd occupied tables near the bar.

Toiling at individually lit pool tables were maybe two dozen shooters, most in groups of two or three, but a few loners. The smack of resin balls filled the air as a long-haired biker type delivered an opening break in a far corner of the building. Corbin ordered a tap beer, then carried it from the bar to a counter near the pool table where his friend Fast Benny Santiago leaned over the felt.

All the regulars knew Fast Benny, and he knew most of them by name. Benny seldom forgot a name.

"Corbin," he said as he snapped his wrist with just enough velocity to send an orange five-ball spinning into a side pocket.

"How's it going, Benny?"

"Can't complain."

"Want to shoot?"

"Ten bucks a game?"

"Let's make it five. My Social Security check doesn't come in till next Wednesday."

"Five it is." Fast Benny was a hundred and twenty-five pounds of ageless Latino poured into an ever-present tan suit and topped with a pork-pie hat pulled down over his eyebrows. "You rack, I'll break."

"Alright." Corbin arranged the fifteen billiard balls within a triangle rack, alternating stripes and solids. "You seen Maxie around lately?"

"Not lately. Seems to have dropped off the planet."

"Maybe he's sick or something."

"Maybe." Having chalked his stick, Benny set the cue ball off-center, adjusting it slightly for what he considered to be the optimal angle.

Corbin lifted the racking triangle, hunted up a pool stick, and carried it back to the table. "Let me ask you something, Benny. You get around, right?"

"Sure," he said, whacking the balls solidly, sending a yellow one ball into a corner pocket. "Looks like you've got stripes."

"What I mean is ... do you know anything about guns?"

"I know enough to duck when somebody pulls one out, if that's what you mean."

He told Benny about the gun he'd found, but not about the girls. "What would you do?"

Benny whistled. "First off, I'd have left it right where I found it. Right there in the garbage, where it belongs. I've known a lot of big shots who messed with guns and wound up on the wrong end of one." He sank the purple four-ball.

"You don't think I should take it to the police?"

Benny looked up from the felt. "You can do what you want. But me, I'd just get rid of it. No sense getting mixed up in gun business and the police and all that. But that's just me. I'd get rid of it and get rid of it quick."

Corbin nodded. Benny was right about getting the police involved. Corbin envisioned a lot of questioning and forms to be filled out and whatnot. *But just get rid of it?*

"What if providence wants me to have the gun?"

Benny's green six-ball caught the edge of a side pocket and rolled back toward the center of the table. He squinted one eye at Corbin as if he was having trouble focusing.

"Now you want to *keep* it?"

"I don't know. Maybe. It's a scary world out there."

"You don't know where that gun's been. Maybe someone killed somebody with it. You don't know. You get caught with it, and maybe the po-po think you killed the guy."

Corbin looked away from Benny's piercing gaze. He solemnly chalked the tip of his stick. "Yeah. Maybe you're right."

BUT CORBIN didn't get rid of the gun. Nor did he turn it in to the police. Instead, he left it in the bag under his seat and tried not to think about it. He didn't need to decide what to do with it just then.

That evening, he and Martha enjoyed a delightful dinner of pasta, salad, and breadsticks at Olive Garden in Maple Grove. They talked about that time years ago when they visited Custer State Park in South Dakota on vacation, and the wild burros had gathered about the car looking for something to eat. Martha had fed them popcorn from her hand. Their tongues had tickled her palm, and she'd laughed uncontrollably.

"It's been a long time since I laughed like that."

"We need to laugh more," Corbin agreed.

On the drive home, with the pasta and breadsticks cooling in his belly and Martha riding in the passenger seat, he thought again about the gun. He didn't know much about guns, but he knew they generally had some kind of safety switch. He wondered now if the revolver had one and whether it was turned on. *What if I hit a bump and the damn thing fires?* He eased off the gas a bit.

New Hope is about seven miles northwest of Minneapolis. A modest burg of 21,000 souls of assorted races, ages, and temperaments, it's home to mostly middle-class dwellings, subsidized apartments, and shopping areas. And eighteen city parks, always kept neat and trim. Corbin and Martha lived in a section of town that consisted chiefly of one-story ramblers interspersed with an ungodly number of trees.

"It's like living in a jungle," Corbin would moan whenever faced with clearing branches and leaves from his backyard. "I keep expecting Tarzan to come swinging in on a vine."

They arrived at their doorway, the car (and the gun) safely tucked into their garage for the night. The gun never did go off, and all his worrying was for naught.

Across the street, Mrs. Chan, who lived alone, cheerfully waved to them as Corbin fumbled with his house keys. The Grimwoods waved back. It was the neighborly thing to do.

Corbin knew nothing much about Mrs. Chan other than that she enjoyed having her front door painted a scandalous shade of red. Her never-ending cheerfulness niggled at him. But at least she had the good sense to avoid pestering him.

Inside, the Grimwoods watched some game show featuring Elizabeth Banks, had mugs of hot cocoa, and then called it a night. Two Tylenol PMs and Martha was out like a light, but Corbin lay awake on his pillow, staring at the ceiling and thinking about his gun. Yes, he now thought of it as *his* gun. Wasn't he an American with the God-given right to own a firearm?

It might be good to have a gun around the house, in case home invaders struck in the dead of night. He imagined himself springing from beneath the covers with the revolver in his hand, gunning down thick-necked criminals in the dark. *How heroic.*

Sitting up, he stepped into his slippers, tiptoed through the bedroom, into the living room and out the front door. In his pajamas, with his hair swirled wildly from lying in bed, he skulked around the side of the house to the freestanding garage.

The lights were still on at Tanoh Ridley's. In Tanoh's backyard, Bunny sat on the back steps, partially hidden by Tanoh's trash receptacles, puffing on a cigarette and crying softly. Another lover's quarrel, no doubt.

"Tomorrow's garbage day," he wanted to remind her, but that would just invite a conversation with a crying woman. That was one bear he didn't want to poke. Besides, it was none of his business whether Tanoh got his garbage out in time for pickup.

She didn't look over as Corbin punched in the code that engaged the automatic door opener, allowing him to enter his shadowy garage.

Reaching under the front seat, he removed the oily bag and tucked it in his waistband under his pajama top. Its coldness licked through the paper.

He carried the gun back to the house and into his den, then turned on the light and closed the door.

He carefully emptied the bag onto his desk.

It was an older pistol, judging by the wear, but it appeared to be in working order. The glossy-blue finish and wooden grip panels earned it an air of integrity. The barrel, which was about two inches long, was stamped with the manufacturer's name: SMITH & WESSON. The company's trademark appeared on the flat surface behind the trigger on the left side, and in gold on both grip panels. The right of the barrel bore the inscription .38 S&W SPL.

He flipped a little switch on the left side. Doing so released the cylinder.

He popped the cylinder open, and the butt ends of five bullets looked back at him. He emptied them onto his desk. He spun the cylinder, snapped it shut, and clicked the release latch back into place.

A thing of beauty, that's what it was. Truly fascinating. How it settled compactly into his grasp, not as weighty as he would have imagined, but solid, like a piece of machinery used in heavy industry. He held it up and sighted down the barrel. A mechanical phallus? Perhaps, but one that gave him a feeling of power beyond anything he'd ever before felt.

He held it for the longest time, relishing the sensation.

Eventually, he returned the revolver to the bag, then inspected the rounds, which were jacketed in gold. One had been fired. The fired cartridge had mushroomed into a glob at the firing end and still held a faint scent of gun smoke. The other four—maybe an inch-and-a-half apiece—sported bronze tips.

That one of these tiny projectiles could snuff out a human life astounded him.

He placed the bullets in the bag and stuffed the bag into the bottom drawer of his desk.

Was he *really* going to keep this gun?

Well, he'd decide tomorrow.

He turned off the light as he left the room. Climbing into bed, he could still feel the revolver in his grip. It was a warm feeling.

THE NEXT DAY, he and Martha drove to the library in Golden Valley, Martha to gather a cache of mystery novels and he to page through select newspapers and magazines. They usually went to the library once a month or so, now that it had reopened after having closed during the first wave of Covid. Facemasks were required inside the building—as they were inside all Minnesota government buildings—which chafed at Corbin a bit, but he went along with it.

He was thumbing through the *National Review* when a man he thought he recognized sat down across from him in the periodicals section with a copy of *American Handgunner*. It was hard to tell for certain who anyone was with facemasks on, but Corbin had become surprisingly adept at half-face recognition.

For instance, he was willing to bet he knew this man from way back, from Robbinsdale High School—which was later repurposed as a junior high, then a rec center, then finally, in 2005, was reduced to a dusty pile of bricks, demolished to make way for the Parker Village

> 11

Townhouses. At Robbinsdale High's all-class reunion nine years ago, he'd exchanged phone numbers with this man, though neither of them had followed up. *What was his name again? Walt something or other. Walt ... Shipman. Yes, that was it.*

"Walt?" Corbin said.

Walt looked up as if startled from a daydream. Now a wiry old man with liver spots and thinning gray hair, Walt was once the placekicker on the Robbinsdale football team and had been pretty good at it, Corbin recalled. They'd teamed up as lab partners in a junior chemistry class and had hit it off at once.

Walt's face lit up with recognition. "Corbin Grimwood!" He rose to his feet and extended a shaky hand. "How the heck are you?"

"Great. Surprised you recognized me with this mask on. And how are you?"

"Can't complain."

Corbin motioned with his head toward the front door. "Let's go outside for a minute and catch up."

Walt, who was something of a ladies' man in his youth, had married Angie Strangis after graduation. Angie was quite the catch, a cheerleader, diminutive but well-endowed, with a mouthful of pearly whites and dark, flashing eyes. It may or may not have been one of those "convenience" marriages, but Angie'd had a noticeable bun in the oven on their wedding day. Still, Corbin had to give them credit: their union lasted thirty-some years, produced two exceptional children, and only ended when cancer handed Angie its calling card.

Meanwhile, Martha was wife number two for Corbin, though he had definitely traded up.

"How are your kids doing these days?" Corbin asked as he pulled their masks off and stood with bare faces overlooking the library parking lot.

"Walt Junior is an anesthesiologist at Chester County Hospital in Philadelphia. Makes almost two hundred thousand a year! And Eliza is a dentist in private practice in St. Paul. So, they're both doing very well. Their mother would be proud of them. Altogether, they've given me four beautiful grandchildren."

"That's great. You still have that collie? What was her name?"

"Coco. No, Coco gave up the ghost a year ago. I miss that dog."

Corbin allowed a solemn moment to pass. "I seem to recall you collected handguns, Walt, isn't that right?"

"Yes. I have twenty-seven now. I kept them in a gun safe when the kids were little. Angie insisted on it. But now they're grown up with families of their own, so I display them in a glass case in my den. You should come by sometime and see them."

"I think I might." He looked behind him at the library's front door to make sure Martha wasn't sneaking up on him. He lowered his voice: "I've recently come into possession of a firearm. A Smith & Wesson .38 Special. You know anything about the gun?"

"Sure. A wheel gun, J frame. Smith & Wesson started manufacturing them in the 1950s. How much did you pay for it?"

"Nothing. A, uh, friend gave it to me." He looked behind him again. "Martha doesn't know. She's not a gun person."

"I see." Walt ran fingers through his wispy hair. "Tell you what. Give me a day or so to do a little research on it, and bring it over. I'll tell you what's what."

"That sounds great, Walt. I'd really appreciate your expertise on the matter."

Walt smiled and nodded, and Corbin for an instant saw a trace of the former high-school placekicker in the old-timer's features.

WALT LIVED in a blocky little, two-story house on St. Claire Avenue in the Macalester-Groveland neighborhood of St. Paul, just down the street from St. Claire Diner where, years ago, Corbin would occasionally stop in for a steak sandwich and fries. This was, of course, before Corbin'd had that health scare and the doctor had told him to lay off red meat. At least lean poultry wasn't off the table and, luckily, he discovered that some of the plant-based fake meats weren't half bad, but that didn't keep him from grumbling about the unfairness of fate and the general folly of doctors.

Walt glad-handed him at the doorway. "Corbin! Come in, come in. I can't tell you the last time I had a visitor."

It was hard to believe a family of four had once lived here—with a collie. Must have been tight quarters. But the house had a homey, lived-in feel with comfortable furniture, wood floors, and tastefully curtained windows. Family photos covered most of one living-room wall, and in the corner sat an end table with a framed picture of Angie, a vase of plastic carnations, and a pink floral cremation urn. The urn featured a canary-yellow band with a gold heart inscribed in cursive letters: *Angie.*

Corbin felt a touch queasy in the presence of human remains, even cremated ones.

He pulled the Smith & Wesson .38 Special from his pocket and laid it on the coffee table in front of the couch while Walt fetched a couple of bottles of Moosehead from the fridge. Returning, he held one out to Corbin.

It had been almost a week since Corbin met Walt at the library in Golden Valley. Since then, Corbin had made a habit of slinking from bed after Martha was asleep, to go sit in his den, toying with the gun, feeling powerful. He wondered how many others had clutched the wood panels of the handle. *Who were they?* He imagined a lawman, a criminal, a jealous husband pulling the trigger and sending a bronze projectile crashing into someone's chest. He wondered what it felt like to end someone's life.

These nocturnal fantasies were just good fun, he told himself.

"That's the wheel gun, eh?" Walt said, nodding toward it.

"Yep."

Walt looked at it like a Doberman eyeing a meaty soup bone. "Let me show you my collection."

Carrying their beers, they walked past the stairs into a hallway that led to Walt's den. In it were plaques and posters and all sorts of gun paraphernalia: military insignias, militia flags, tin lunch boxes of the Lone Ranger and of Paladin from *Have Gun Will Travel*, a reproduction of a newspaper page featuring an ad for Colt pistols, a placard for an Arizona gun show, a shelf of gun-toting figurines, and, of course, the glass display case with Walt's twenty-seven handguns.

"This one," Walt said, pointing through the glass, "is a Nighthawk Custom Enforcer .45 ACP. One-piece mainspring housing and magwell. The serrated top eliminates glare when sighting down the barrel. Cost me three-thousand dollars. Want to hold it?"

"Sure."

Walt swung the glass open, reached in, and handed the Nighthawk to Corbin.

"It has a nice grip," Corbin said, unsure what to do with the weapon in his hand.

"This one is a .45 Smith & Wesson Schofield revolver, the kind of gun Jesse James used. It's known for its top-breaking action. Look. It still has some of the original blue. Seven-inch barrel, walnut grips, a little pitting but not bad. Walt Junior bought it for me for my fiftieth birthday. Can't imagine where he got it or how much he paid for it. This one, I believe, was part of a batch of three hundred produced years ago for the U.S. Army."

Corbin nodded, handing the Nighthawk back to Walt.

One by one, Walt gave him a guided tour through his personal stockpile: the Ruger Mark IV with its distinctive lightning cut; the blunt little Bond Arms pocket pistol; the gold Colt .45 Tribute with the Second Amendment etched into its wood panel grips; the sleek, art-deco designed Mauser HSc pistol with its European heel-style catch; the fixed-barrel, single-action Walther PPK; and so on. It took Walt almost a half hour to get through his whole collection, and Corbin got to hold several different models.

Finally, Walt said, "Now let's take a look at that .38 of yours." He chugged the last of his beer (mostly foam) through the bottle's green-glass neck. He pointed toward his empty. "Want another?"

"Why not?" Corbin replied.

In the living room with their fresh Mooseheads, Walt bent to pick up the .38. "This truly is a marvelous weapon," he said, holding it flat in the palm of his hand. "This is a Model 36 Chief's Special. It was created especially for detectives and off-duty police officers. The weight is a little under twenty ounces. Just under seven inches long. Carbon-steel cylinder and barrel. They're known for being easy to use and reliable. They're accurate and have manageable recoil. Used mainly for target shooting, defense, and hunting small game." He arched an eyebrow. "You're not a hunter, are you?"

"No." Corbin chewed the inside of his cheek, wondering once again what he was getting himself into.

Walt extended his arm unsteadily and looked down the pistol's sight. He cocked the hammer. "Is it loaded?"

"Yes."

Walt hefted the .38 in his hand, looking on with pure admiration, the weapon still cocked. "There's something genuinely alluring about this revolver. When I was a young man, my father told me once about old-time gun enthusiasts who said certain guns 'called' to you. It was as if they hummed in your hand, but barely perceptively, as if they interacted with your hand on almost a molecular level. I never understood what he was talking about, but now I do. That's how this revolver feels. Does it feel that way to you?"

"Yes. Yes, it does."

"How much would you take for it? How does eight-hundred dollars sound? That's a fair price."

Corbin held out his palms. "I don't know that I'm interested in selling it, Walt. I've only just got it."

"How about a thousand dollars? Would you take a thousand dollars for it?"

Suddenly Corbin got the feeling that Walt wasn't going to hand the .38 back to him. "I really don't want to sell it, Walt."

"Twelve hundred?" Now Walt held the weapon in his open hand close to his chest. "You're a reasonable man, Corbin. For twelve-hundred dollars, you could buy yourself another one of these and still have money left over."

Corbin's nerves tightened. "Just give it back, Walt." He reached out to take it.

Walt pulled the gun back higher on his chest, until the barrel rested just below his larynx. "Hold on. Not so fast." He took a step backward.

Corbin wasn't sure how it happened. It occurred so fast. The pistol roared, filling the living room with sound and smoke. A flame leapt from the barrel, entered the soft underside of Walt's jaw, then exploded through the top of his skull, splattering blood and flecks of bone and brain tissue onto the ceiling. His eyes rolled.

Then Walt's legs collapsed under him, and he fell to the floor, still clutching the .38.

This horrible accident could have offered Corbin an excellent chance to get rid of the gun. He could contend that the weapon was Walt's. That the old fellow had brought it out to show him, and it discharged in his hand. Just another fatal gun accident. It happened every day.

But, instead of calling the police, Corbin retrieved the pistol from his classmate's gnarled grip, returned it to his pocket, and slipped out the front door.

NEWS OF Walt Shipman's bloody demise broke a week later, when Walt's daughter Eliza, unable to reach her father on the phone, had dropped in on him to see what was up.

"Corbin," Martha asked, "isn't that your friend? The one you introduced me to at your class reunion?"

The TV screen displayed a photo of Walt smiling into the camera, not a care in the world. Yes, that was how Walt had looked on that memorable day when the .38 Special had blown his brains all over his ceiling.

"No," Corbin said simply. "I don't think so."

"But his name was Shipman. I remember distinctly." Martha was not a woman who missed much.

Corbin studied the photo before it left the screen and was replaced by a wafer-thin, blonde anchorwoman. "Police found open beer bottles near the body, but no weapon. They say it didn't appear to be a burglary, as nothing was missing. Police are investigating it as a homicide. So far, no suspects have been identified."

"Maybe you're right, Martha," Corbin conceded. "Maybe that is the fellow from the reunion." He tried to sound nonchalant, but a tremor sneaked into his voice. He worried the police would find his fingerprints on the Mooseheads, though he didn't think his prints were on file anywhere. Yet.

Martha gave him a curious look, which Corbin pretended not to notice. But she didn't know anything. For all she knew, Corbin had last seen Walt Shipman at the reunion nine years ago. As far as where Corbin was on the day Walt joined the angels, well, he was shooting pool at Two Stooges, of course.

"Are you going to his funeral?" Martha asked.

"I don't think so." Walt made a face. "Our friendship was long ago, and you know I can't stand being around dead people."

But he'd already been around this particular dead person at the very moment of extinction. He'd witnessed the explosion of lead through flesh, had seen the eyes in Walt's hollowed-out head roll and go blank, had watched him tumble lifeless to the floor. Corbin knew he should've been shocked by the sight, even traumatized by it. But he wasn't.

He *wasn't*.

Instead, at the time, all he'd thought about was wrestling his .38 Special from old Walt's lifeless claw. When Corbin had fled the house, he'd walked casually to his car, as if unperturbed, glancing around to make sure no nosey neighbors were looking on, and, as he pulled out into traffic, he'd been careful not to make eye contact with any fellow drivers on St. Claire Avenue.

He'd driven around St. Paul for an hour or so, stopping for coffee at the Day By Day Cafe on West Seventh Street, chatting up the waitresses, killing time.

He'd arrived back home just as Martha was preparing dinner. He'd half-listened to her going on about some blight that had gotten into the roots of her radishes

Then, after dinner and viewing a rerun of *The F.B.I.*, they'd called it a night.

Once he was safely tucked into his bed with a snoozing Martha beside him, he'd stared at the ceiling, amazed by the events of the day and by how well he'd handled them.

He was, by his reckoning, one cool customer.

CORBIN VENTURED into Two Stooges, feeling full of himself. Since purchasing an Alien Gear ShapeShift ankle holster, he'd taken to bringing the .38 Special with him everywhere, whenever possible. This meant exclusively wearing full-length pants, even on the hottest days. Martha found strange his sudden avoidance of shorts—especially when it came to the cargo shorts, which had all the pockets he'd always so delighted in. But sweltering knees were a small price to pay for the reassuring touch of the neoprene holster and the confidence he gained walking about in a dangerous world with instant death at his very fingertips.

He found Fast Benny at his usual table.

"Corbin," Fast Benny said, looking up from his shot.

"How's it going, Benny?"

"Not too good, I'm sorry to report."

"What's the problem?"

Thwack. The cue ball blasted the blue-striped ten ball into a corner pocket. "A cousin of mine was found dead in his apartment a few days ago. Actually, he was my second cousin. Mikey was his name. A good kid who ran with a rough crowd."

"Sorry to hear that, Benny. What happened to him?"

"What else? Gunshot between the eyes. Twenty-two years old. Must've been dead for a week. The neighbors in his apartment building complained about the smell. Our friends in the *po*-lice department said they found crystal-meth residue on the body. Guns and drugs, the bane of our existence."

"That's too bad."

Fast Benny paused in his pool shooting. "I was at that boy's baptism. At his first communion. At his high-school graduation. I never thought he'd become president or anything, but I thought he had good potential for the business world. Level-headed but funny at the same time, you know? Didn't let anything get him down. Just got mixed up with the wrong people. Poor Mikey."

He bowed to the felt with his stick.

Corbin saddened a bit, but the weight of the pistol at his ankle reassured him that he would not end up like Mikey. Just the same, he needed to practice his quick draw.

He let a moment pass, then changed the subject: "You going to the tournament in Burnsville?"

"Nah. I don't need to prove my chops to a bunch of suburban chicken necks."

"Top prize is three-hundred dollars in each division."

"You go for it. Let me know how it turns out."

Fast Benny never asked Corbin what he did with the gun he'd found, and Corbin never brought it up. That's the way it was with Benny, one of the things Corbin admired about him. He always knew when to mind his own business.

SHOOTERS BILLIARD CLUB and Cafe in Burnsville features sixty-two tables, mostly Brunswick Gold Crown and Diamond professionals in assorted sizes. Competitions were strictly on the nine-footers. The food was standard burgers and pizzas, but Corbin didn't come clear to Burnsville for the cuisine.

Corbin came for the pool.

He liked to think of himself as an ace pool shooter, but the truth was he tended to be streaky. Now and then he'd catch that magic edge that sent him into do-no-wrong territory. Then he shot like Efren Manalang Reyes, the greatest pool player of all time. Generally, though, Corbin was just a little better than average. He lost about seventy percent of the time to skilled players like Fast Benny.

But tournaments took place in a rarefied atmosphere where fear and adrenaline got the blood in your temples pumping, and your concentration became either hobnail-sharp or blurry as an eyeful of sweat.

That Saturday at the Shooters tournament, Corbin shot streaky as ever, making a cross-table, two-bank shot one minute and missing on a side-pocket duck the next. He squeaked his way through the first round of Class B, but not the second. That one he lost to a beefy farm kid from Brooten who bore more than a passing resemblance to Minnesota Fats. Needless to say, Corbin was out his thirty-dollar entry fee. But now he could relax and watch the action.

It fascinated Corbin how different contestants chose different shots, playing to their strengths. A power shooter needed to control his English just right, or the cue ball could end up anywhere on the table, maybe even knocking in an opponent's ball. A finesse player could edge his way into a crowd of balls and kiss the right one into a pocket while leaving himself with a decent rail shot. A bank shooter could leave a duck for later, instead ricocheting off the side bumper first for a ball all the way across the table. And good angle shooters combined an eye for geometry with a mastery of backspin.

Of course, players could lean into any of these styles if the need arose, but most had a definite preference.

Night had fallen by the time Corbin fired up the Patriot for the long drive home. His mind soon drifted from eight-ball to the .38 Special tugging at his ankle.

He'd become proficient at the quick draw. Hours of late-night practicing had paid off. While Martha snoozed peacefully in bed, he was in the den playing with his pistol. He'd never actually fired it, but he'd seen the damage it was capable of thanks to Walt Shipman's clumsiness. He imagined what it would be like to draw on some miscreant, pull the trigger, hear the bark of the handgun and see through the rising smoke as the bullet riveted between the villain's eyes, and his brains burst pureed from the back of his skull.

Sometimes Corbin stayed up until two in the morning, fantasizing. *Two in the morning.* He hadn't stayed up that late since his college days!

He wasn't more than five minutes away from Shooters Billiard Club before a white truck began tailgating him. The glare of its headlights had Corbin squinting. He rolled down his driver-side window and waved for the truck to pass him, but it stayed right on his tail, and the truck's operator laid on a powerful blast of the horn.

The passing lane was traffic-free. *What was it with this guy?*

Shielding his eyes from the relentless beams, Corbin dropped his speed, hoping that would goose the truck past him. Instead, the vehicle slowed right down with him, and began sliding from one side of the lane to the other. *Does he want me to pull over? Is that what this is all about?*

Now the truck driver hit the high beams, and Corbin could barely see the road.

He adjusted his rearview mirror, sending flooding light back at the truck.

I don't know what your game is, mister, but I'm not pulling over.

The high beams switched off, and the white truck dropped back a few feet.

Road signs ahead announced Corbin's exit. The truck driver would probably leave him alone once he was on the highway. Maybe move on to bother somebody else. Maybe go home to sleep it off.

In a wild squeal of tires, the truck careened past him in the passing lane. The hurtling metal was a white blur, but Corbin could make out the truck's dented body and a scowling, bearded ruffian eyeing him furiously from the passenger window.

There were two of them.

The truck swerved directly in front of him, and the driver pumped the brakes.

Corbin reached down for the .38 and swapped it to his left hand. Maybe he could shoot low and take out one of their tires.

The shiny blue metal buzzed in his hand.

The truck driver pumped the brakes again, slowing to a crawl.

Maybe Corbin could just shoot into the night air. Perhaps that would be enough to chase off these lowlifes.

He raised the gun, lowered it, raised it again. He didn't remember pulling the trigger.

In an instant, the truck's rear window blew in, and Corbin watched, mesmerized, as the vehicle drifted from the road, began to wobble, and fell over on its side with a thunderous crash.

He sped past the fallen truck, slipping the .38 Special back into his ShapeShift ankle holster, and pulled onto Highway 494, headed north.

THAT NIGHT, Corbin left the .38 Special and the holster under the front seat of the Patriot. It still smelled of gun smoke, and he didn't want to take a chance of alerting Martha to anything suspicious.

Walking from the garage, he was startled by the slam of a screen door.

"You bastard! You can't treat people this way." Bunny's voice.

Corbin stopped in his tracks. The ruckus was coming from Tanoh's side door, out of sight on the far side of the neighbor's home. He listened keenly.

"Princess, please." The door rattled open. "You know you mean everything to me."

"Fuck you, Tanoh. My mother was right. You're a pig."

"Don't be this way, Bunny."

"I saw the way you looked at her. I'm not blind."

"Princess, it's just a TV show. Come back inside. We'll watch something else."

There was a pouting stubbornness to Bunny's voice. "You'd rather be with *her* than me. Admit it."

Corbin had heard enough. He stepped away.

The lights were still on in his living room. Martha, on the couch, sipped tea from a floral teacup. "What's all that noise about?" she asked without any real concern.

"Nothing. Bickering. Tanoh and Bunny. You know how those two can be."

Martha nodded. "How did you do in the tournament?"

"Knocked out in the second round by a kid from Brooten who didn't look old enough to shave." He sat beside her and looked up at the television program Martha had on.

"What are we watching?" he asked.

Later, he lay awake in bed listening to Martha's soft snores. He stared at the ceiling, reimagining the night's events: the blinding lights, the squeal of the tires, the roar of the pistol, the explosion of glass. The dented white truck tilting from its wheels and crashing to its side. He should have blared his horn at them, just as they'd blasted theirs at him. That's the sort of thing private eyes do on television shows to tie a scene up neatly. It's the sort of thing spies did, rogue cops, other dark, vengeful characters with guns. *How cool would that have been?*

Corbin drifted to sleep with this imagery whirling in his brain. He should have felt saddened, he knew. Saddened by the prospect of having injured or possibly even killed one of the back-road ruffians. But, instead, invigoration coursed through his body, bringing a tingle to his temples and—*surprise!*—to his midsection a rare nocturnal erection. He was now, after all, a man of action (even if he hadn't purposely aimed and fired the weapon). For the first time, the unleashed power of the cold steel had bellowed in his hand.

And he was its master.

He dreamt of a crowd gathered in front of a store. When he pushed through the gawkers, there was a lizard in the display window staring him. A tremendous yellow-spotted night lizard who left a trail of slime on the window's edge. The lizard's tongue snaked in and out.

Looking closer, Corbin could see the lizard's eyes weren't really eyes at all but collected bits of colored mirror that reflected a multitude of Corbin's images back at him. But there was something false about the reflections. Corbin couldn't quite put his finger on what it was.

When he awoke, Martha was already out of bed. The bedroom door stood open, and from the kitchen came the metallic pop of the toaster while a TV-commercial pitchman pedaled insurance in the living room. The smell of fresh coffee flared his nostrils.

The morning local news had the story about the truck in Burnsville with the shot-out window. Neither the driver nor the passenger was killed in the incident, but the bullet had grazed the driver, and both men were hospitalized with injuries suffered in the crash. Corbin supposed he should feel good about not killing anyone, but his actual reaction was more ambivalent.

"Do you know if the Twins play today?" he asked his wife.

He puttered around the house: sorted his tools, took out the trash, fixed that drawer in the kitchen that was always sticking. He tried getting into a spy novel, but not even Ian Fleming could hold his interest today.

He kept thinking about the pistol.

The .38 Special was more than the sum of its parts, more than its latches and levers and firing pin. More than its trigger and hammer and grip. It was, for Corbin, as majestic as justice and liberty and self-determination. Something almost to be worshiped. Not in a blasphemous sort of way, but as a holy object nonetheless, like a sacred relic.

When it affixed itself to him, it was a divine appendage, one that gave him power and a feeling of invincibility. It'd been many years since he had felt that way. In those intervening years, the working class had dissolved all around him, and the liberals had villainized the very captains of industry who had the means to rescue the country. Women were taking over the boardrooms. Black men were being elected president. Down was up and up was down.

Except when it came to guns.

Guns were the one constant. Guns were the equalizer. Why hadn't he seen this before? Cowboys on the range knew it. Soldiers in the foxhole knew it. Now he understood why Charlton Heston had vowed the only way he would give up his gun was if it were pried "from my cold dead hand." Increasingly, Corbin understood this way of thinking.

When he took the trash out to the bin in the garage, he retrieved the .38 and its holster, attached them to his ankle, and wore them under his pant leg for the rest of the day.

CORBIN BEGAN HAVING TROUBLE sleeping without his gun.

This started up almost immediately after his run-in with the white truck. At first, he pushed away the thought. It was silly, really. Sleeping with a gun. Where would he put it? Not under the pillow. He supposed he could stuff it under the mattress, but it seemed too big a risk. He might get caught, either putting it in or taking it out. Martha didn't miss much.

He could always come clean with her. Say he found the gun, and he thought it was a good idea to have one around the house. To ward off burglars or, God forbid, serial killers. It was becoming a dangerous world for old folks. But he doubted she'd buy it. He could hear her now: "Corbin, you're more likely to blow off your own head than any burglar's."

He tried to ignore it, but the pain of being separated from the gun at night grew worse and worse.

He *needed* to have it near. Not just for protection but for the overall sense of security it brought. A man of action *needed* his gat, his shooting iron, his heater. Remove it, and a dull ache took its place.

When unattached, the .38 had become something of a phantom limb.

GRADUALLY, CORBIN'S NIGHTS without his gun became torture. He tossed and turned, bunched his pillow, pulled the covers up over his face; nothing helped much. He managed only snippets of sleep, and strange dreams haunted these.

One night he dreamt he and Walt Shipman were in the playground at the old Robbinsdale High School building. They were boys again, twirling either end of a jump rope. Walt wore his Robbinsdale Robins football jersey and a cunning grin. The wind ruffled Walt's shaggy umber hair.

In the jumper's spot, a wizened old nun with a gull-winged habit skipped as Corbin and Walt chanted, "Bang, bang, shoot, shoot, blood on his zoot suit, don't try to be cute, time to come clean."

The nun, in stark black and white with an ivory cord tied around her waist, and a tremendous oaken cross jostling on her breasts with every leap, held out a blue-steel wheel gun in the classic pose of a duelist. Clopping up and down on the playground tar in her orthopedic shoes, she faced Corbin, her eyes bright with an uncanny glee, as if she and he shared a secret. She joined the boys in their chanting: "Bang, bang, shoot, shoot." Spittle flew from her pruney lips.

When he looked back at Walt, the top of Walt's head was blown open, and torrents of blood ran down his face, dripping from his chin.

"Bang, bang, shoot, shoot...."

Corbin awoke from this nightmare to sweaty pillowcases and sheets, watery-eyed and giddy with terror.

"Are you feeling alright, Corbin?" Martha would ask him at breakfast. "You look as if you haven't slept in a week."

"I'm fine, Martha. Guess I haven't been sleeping very well lately. Too wound up for some reason."

"You let politics get to you. Those ridiculous programs with those people ranting all the time about this and that. It's bad for your blood pressure; now it's keeping you awake at night." She patted his hand. "Life isn't so bad, Corbin. You know that."

Life is only bad when I don't have my gun with me, he wanted to say.

But he said nothing.

He began taking catnaps in the afternoon. They kept him from nodding off in front of the TV or—God forbid!—behind the wheel of his Patriot. These midday snoozes helped him stay awake but not really alert. Lethargy became his constant companion.

One night, he wore just the holster, not the gun, on his ankle under his pajamas. Perhaps, he reasoned, the snug pull of the neoprene straps would be enough to smooth away the rough edges of his insomnia. But the holster without the .38 Special was useless. It throbbed on his lower leg all night, demanding to be filled.

Finally, he could take it no more. He decided to wear the revolver in bed. Just one night, so he could get some rest. He waited till Martha was fast asleep, then slipped off to his den and strapped on the pistol.

He crawled back under the covers and fell fast asleep, contented as a babe full of mother's milk.

"You're looking better today, Corbin," Martha noted at the next morning's breakfast.

He yawned, stretched, and swiveled his neck. "Feeling better, too. Last night, I slept like the dead."

They ate flapjacks with syrup in front of the tube. The local morning news show featured the skinny blonde anchorwoman yakking with a weatherman about what a beautiful day it was going to be. The meteorologist, who came to the station from Seattle, voiced concern about a heat wave Washington had suffered under for the past week.

"I suppose he's going to blame fossil fuels for his state's warm spell," Corbin said. "These environmentalist wackos will have us all driving around in two-seater, wind-up cars before you know it. Half the horsepower for double the price. You see if I'm wrong."

Martha shook her head. "I'm just happy you're feeling yourself again, Corbin."

The coffeemaker dinged, and she went out to the kitchen to fetch them mugs of joe.

Corbin's good mood broke suddenly when the blonde newscaster turned to the headlines. On the screen flashed a photo of two teenage girls with stringy hair, one with a nose ring and the other with a small cut over one eye. He recognized them at once. *The girls who left the gun in my trash!* The gun that was even then strapped to his ankle.

"Brooklyn Center police have arrested two young women in connection with a fatal shooting in New Hope last month," the anchorwoman said. "Nineteen-year-old Brandi Castellanos of Milwaukee, Wisconsin, and eighteen-year-old Anna Lee Bronski of St. Paul have been charged with second-degree murder in the death of New Hope resident Michael Santiago. The two women were identified from security-camera footage and from an eyewitness who saw the women leaving Santiago's apartment on the night of the slaying. Police say the crime appears to be drug-related."

Michael Santiago? Was that Mikey, Fast Benny's cousin? He said his cousin had been shot dead. Said drugs were involved.

Corbin shuddered from a coldness deep at his center. Was he wearing on his ankle the actual gun used to kill his friend's relative?

Martha entered the living room with two steaming mugs. She eyed him quizzically. "Corbin, are you alright? You look like you've seen a ghost."

He smiled weakly, trying to shake off his stunned reaction. "Just a little gas, I think."

But his mind was racing. *What if the girls told the police where they dumped the gun? Should I expect a knock on the front door?*

Now was the time to get rid of the .38. That gun directly tied him to a murder, a fatal accident, and a random shooting. He wasn't sure he could explain all that to the cops should they come around.

After breakfast, he wiped the blue-steel revolver and the holster clean of fingerprints, put them in a plastic Target bag, and carried them out to the garage. He was about to deposit the bag in his trash receptacle when it occurred to him that the garbage wouldn't be collected for two more days. That gave the police two days to come calling for the gun.

There must be someplace else to take it.

Wait a minute. What if Corbin sneaked it into a neighbor's garbage bin? That could work. If the police came calling, Corbin could deny any knowledge of the gun. Martha would deliver her usual diatribe on the dangers of keeping guns in the house. *Just a couple of law-abiding senior citizens here, officer. If the girls left the weapon in my trash, it's long gone to the garbage dump by now, but feel free to search the house, if you want.*

He stuffed the bag back into his waistband, entered the code that closed the garage door, and stood for a moment, staring into his neighbor Tanoh Ridley's backyard. Tanoh kept his garbage receptacles near the back steps where Bunny smoked her cigarettes.

Corbin scratched his chin. That night, once again, he would be a man of action.

He would take the gun over to Tanoh's and be rid of it once and for all.

THE DAY DRAGGED ON tediously. Corbin watched some television with Martha but, his mind engaged elsewhere, failed to comprehend what the programs were about.

He'd get up, walk to the kitchen, stare out the back window at the copse of greenery that was his yard, return to the living room, watch TV for a while more, retreat to his den.

The thought of getting rid of the handgun troubled him greatly. It took all his willpower to not play with the pistol one last time, to feel the warmth and soft buzz of it in his grip. But he was afraid if he took it from the Target bag and strapped it to his ankle, the gun would move beyond his ability to part with it.

He wasn't just getting rid of the gun but, in a very real way, a piece of himself.

Corbin picked at his lunch, picked at his dinner. He half-listened to Martha droning on about his cousin Darlene's progress, now that she was off the ventilator; about how exciting it was that St. Alfonzo was raffling off some Japanese hybrid hunk of junk for the Fourth of July; about how she was so happy to see her tiger lilies blossoming the most lovely shade of orange in the garden. Martha's recurring theme was, as usual, that life wasn't so bad; that the world was not going to hell in a handbasket, after all.

But Corbin was unconvinced.

When night fell at last, and Martha was in the peaceful clutches of la-la land, he slipped from their bed, entered his den, grabbed the bag with the gun, and whisked off with it under his pajama top.

In his slippers under a waxing crescent moon, he lifted the latch on his neighbor's side gate and stepped into Tanoh's backyard. *One last adventure*, he told himself.

In Tanoh's house, all was dark and quiet. Slowly and carefully, like an antelope sneaking past a sleeping lion, Corbin made his way to the chocolate-brown garbage receptacle and opened its lid. He looked from left to right, making sure there were no eyes on him.

Goodbye, midnight quick-draw practices. Goodbye, bark of flame and cough of smoke. Goodbye, Corbin Grimwood, man of action. He would never again feel the reassuring caress of the pistol's grip panels on his naked palm.

With a sigh, he leaned into the trash bin and wedged the weighty bag into a corner, behind a twist-tied sack that gave off the sickly-sweet smell of rotten apples. He closed the lid.

Mission accomplished.

THE NEXT TWO days were the longest of Corbin's long life. Every perceived noise from next door brought dread pulsing to his chest and had him stealing a peek to see if Tanoh or Bunny were outside, making use of their trash receptacle. He pictured somber Tanoh opening the lid with a sack of refuse in his hand, then suddenly pausing to peer inside. In that moment, perhaps he would look up and catch Corbin spying on him, and put two and two together.

But that never happened.

If Tanoh or Bunny discovered the Target bag hidden in their trash, Corbin failed to observe the incident. No searing glances of suspicion were directed his way. No police pounded at the Grimwood door. Overall, the days passed uneventfully.

Martha worked in her garden and he watched folks on television who were angry with the government. During those two days, he slept poorly while Martha, as usual, slept like a log.

The garbage haulers came and went on Wednesday. He watched from his bathroom window as the robotic arms of the truck dumped the contents of Tanoh Ridley's receptacle into the hungry maw of its rear. He hoped to catch a blur of white plastic amid the plummeting waste, and maybe he did, but he couldn't be sure. It happened so fast.

Local newscasts repeated the facts about the two girls being held in the murder of Mikey Santiago. A bail hearing was set, pleas were entered, lawyers appointed. The facts were just rehashes of what had already been reported.

Relatives and friends threw Mikey a modest funeral at Gethsemane Cemetery on 42nd Avenue North.

Fast Benny was a no-show for the ceremony, Corbin later learned. "I'm not a funeral-goer," Benny revealed to him under a table lamp at Two Stooges. "I remember people in my own way."

Soon, the woeful tale of Mikey Santiago, Brandi Castellanos and Anna Lee Bronski disappeared from the airwaves, and from the public consciousness. Guns and drugs: just another in a series of endless tragedies.

Corbin heard something about a plea deal involving the girls, but what difference did it make? Mikey wasn't coming back, and locking up a couple of teenagers for eternity seemed hollow justice. What would Tucker Carlson say about all this? Fry 'em, probably.

The world had, indeed, gone to hell in a handbasket.

But things were about to get a whole lot more hellish.

WEEKS LATER, CORBIN WAS FADING INTO an uneasy sleep when a hand on his shoulder shook him. "Corbin, did you hear that?" Martha, one of the soundest sleepers he'd ever known, was sitting up in bed, fully awake, with the bedside light turned on. Her face was so pale it might've been carved from soap. "It sounded like a woman screaming, from outside."

Corbin yawned. "Probably Tanoh and Bunny going at it again."

He listened, eyes tight in anticipation. He didn't have to wait long.

"... Kill you ... bastard ... motherf— ...." It was Bunny's voice alright, coming from next door, piercing the night and the outer walls of Corbin's house, echoing through his living room, down the hall, and all the way into his bedroom. Bunny's voice, saturated and dripping with rage.

"... Tired of it ... live like this...." Tanoh shouted. "This time you've gone too far!"

"Should I call the police?" Martha asked, the register of her utterance higher than usual.

Corbin stepped into his slippers. "Let's take a look first. See how bad it is. Maybe I can get them to calm down."

He hurried to his front door, Martha in tow.

The door swung open on a surreal scene. Tanoh, lit by the quarter moon and the glow of light escaping through his front window, scrambled across his weedy yard, almost—it seemed to Corbin—like some stop-motion character formed from clay. Behind him, in a gossamer nightgown, the wind flaring back her long black hair, stood Bunny aiming down the barrel of a blue-steel handgun.

The weapon's familiar roar split the night, cleaving it two. The bullet exploded through Tanoh's shoulder, sending shreds of muscle and blood flying. He whirled at the impact, clutching his mangled scapula. He tried to say something, but the words caught in his throat.

Bunny fired again, and Tanoh buckled at his waist like a beaten rug on a laundry line. Having exited Tanoh, the bullet whizzed past

Corbin's ear, nearly grazing him. Tanoh tumbled to the shaggy lawn amid the cockleburs, gushing blood that was black in the moonlight.

In a daze, Bunny pointed the gun at Corbin and pulled the trigger. The hammer struck on a spent cartridge. *Click-click-click-click-click.* She ran through every chamber.

Of course. There were no live rounds left.

One had claimed Mikey Santiago, one had taken Walt Shipman, one had caused the truck to crash, and the final two now threatened to wrench the life from Tanoh Ridley.

Corbin held up his hands. "Put down the gun, Bunny. It's over."

But it wasn't over.

Behind him, Martha slumped to the ground.

Turning in horror, Corbin stared down into her vacant eyes; her slack, plump face; her gaping mouth. Then, weighty as a load of lumber, despair dropped him, at last, to his knees.

By the time the police arrived, Bunny had fled. Corbin was still kneeling, and Mrs. Chan from across the street—whom he hardly knew—was holding him by the head, rocking him and asking him if he was alright. He tried to answer her, but his words came out in tears. He cried, not in the dignified manner that men were supposed to cry in, but like a lunatic whose whole world had imploded. He cried ugly, shuddering, snot running from his nose.

This was the last thing he remembered from that night. Being rocked like a baby by Mrs. Chan in her housecoat and fluffy slippers as sirens screamed and his vision became a blurred field of sweeping red and blue lights.

The Keeper of Cat's Back Ridge

"The livid eyes of the monster fastened on the form of the herdsman, even amidst the thick darkness of the pine. It paused, it glared upon him; its jaws opened, and a low deep sound, as of gathering thunder, seemed to the son of Osslah as the knell of a dreadful grave."
— Edward Bulwer-Lytton, "The Fallen Star"

Wash Greavor awoke stiff and disoriented. Empty cans of Schmidt beer littered the floor of the cab of his 2000 Chevy Silverado 1500. Beside him, Billy Griggs and Matt Dribbin snored, still out of it.

Billy's head rested on Wash's shoulder, and drool from Billy's mouth ran down the sleeve of Wash's flannel shirt. With a rough shrug, he flipped Billy's head over to Matt's shoulder. Matt was fogging the passenger-side window with his wood-sawing serenade.

Wash squinted past his windshield into early-morning daylight that blazed through the leaves of a Norway pine.

Oh, yeah. Now he remembered why they were parked in the middle of nowhere.

He checked his cell phone for reception: no bars. Figures.

"Where the hell are we?" Billy asked, opening just one eye.

"Buena Vista State Forest, I'm pretty sure," Wash said.

"Hey, Matt! Wake up, will you?" Billy jostled his sleeping comrade.

Matt was visiting from Gary, South Dakota, and they'd decided to take a ride, drink some beers and do some four-wheeling on Puposky's old logging trails. Billy and Wash hadn't seen Matt for two years, and they figured they were two years overdue for a good time.

The reason they hadn't gathered in so long was partly due to the Covid-19 pandemic that had shut down unnecessary travel since the previous March, but it also had to do with all the sadness and grief surrounding the death of Matt's dad. Matt needed time to heal, and they didn't know what to say to him anyway, so they'd given him space. *But, really, how could you ever recover from a thing like that?*

"Matt!" Billy thundered.

They were all in their mid-twenties, country boys. Wash and Billy were from the Northwoods haven of Puposky, Minnesota, and now worked at the Home Depot in Bemidji. Matt was from Maitland, South Dakota, originally, but now lived in Gary. Three graduates of Bemidji Technical College. When the story about Matt's dad broke, *The Pioneer* ran Matt's Bemidji Tech graduation picture on the front page.

Matt still looked like his photo, maybe a little hollower around the cheeks and eyes. He was easily the smallest of the three at a little over five feet, a rangy dude with already thinning hair and a wisp of a mustache. He wore a T-shirt that read MINNESOTA STATE BIRD and had a giant mosquito on it. He blinked his watery eyes, looking offended.

Then he stretched out his lanky arms, yawned, and farted.

"Jesus, Matt," Wash said. He couldn't get the cab door open fast enough.

The first order of business was draining their lizards. The three of them lined up like they were giving a twenty-one-gun salute and whizzed into the thick grass.

"Got anything to eat?" That was Billy, hulking and bearded and always thinking about food.

It felt good to have the three amigos together again, even if Wash wasn't quite sure what they were going to do next about being stuck deep in the woods.

"Might be some chips left in the bag," Matt said as if he doubted it.

They stepped over to the truck and inspected the damage. The rear tire was flat, and the wheel hung useless over a two-foot hole. Last night, they'd just come out of a dry creek bed and were inching over the scraggy crest of a hill when the wheel started spinning. Wash had gunned it, hoping he could generate enough momentum to get the Chevy unstuck, but, of course, that didn't work. The thing to do at that point would have been to shovel dirt into the hole, pack earth up under the wheel and try to gain some traction that way, but he was drunk and lazy and, instead, he'd just laid on the gas.

Boom! The tire blew like a gunshot. And, you guessed it, he hadn't thought to bring along a spare tire.

"Don't suppose you have a winch?" Matt said.

"Do you *see* a winch?" Wash asked. "Besides, a winch wouldn't do us any good with a flat tire. And don't even ask me about a spare."

Matt didn't.

Billy opened the cab and found the party pack of Old Dutch Rip-l potato chips. He dumped the crumbs into his hand and stared at them with his soulful gray eyes. Billy, who wore a full black beard to cover up a skin condition he didn't like to talk about, was big enough to suit up as defensive end for the Vikings. He wolfed down the crumbs, crumpled up the bag, and tossed it back in the cab, then slammed the door.

Matt looked around, hands on his hips. "Wash, you've been out in these woods before. Anything look familiar?"

"Not really. You see anything, Billy?"

Billy wiped chip crumbs from his beard as he scanned the horizon. He shook his head. "I'd say, in my expert opinion, we are good and lost."

"Well, boys," Wash said, "looks like we're going to have to hoof it."

Billy nodded. "Like Uncle Buster says, 'It's time for our boot heels to be a-wandering.'"

"Which way?" Matt asked.

"What do you say, Billy?"

"I say I'm following you. Pick a direction."

Wash scratched his chin. "It seems like we traveled too far to turn back. Let's follow this logging trail and see where it goes. It must've led somewhere at some time. Maybe we'll get lucky and run into a highway."

"Or a bear," Matt said grimly.

"Or a bear," Wash agreed.

The rutted trail, overgrown with grass, wild oats, and lamb's-quarters, coursed down between red oaks and cedars into a valley, and then ambled up again.

Billy had snapped an oak branch along the way to use as a walking stick. "When we get back to a town, let's get some breakfast. A nice steamy plate of pancakes sounds good to me. With blueberry syrup, if they've got it."

"Sorry our reunion wound up this way," Wash said.

Matt scratched his skinny neck. "You should've bought a Ford."

"Ha, ha. Very funny. You're a regular comedian."

But Wash was feeling sweet-tempered. He liked being ribbed by his old friends, especially by Matt. A smile looked particularly agreeable on Matt after all he'd been through.

Matt's had been an unfortunate case. Two summers ago, his father, Ben, a realtor in Maitland, had traveled to Indianapolis for a trade convention. On June 21st, Ben had left the convention center in the company of a mystery man. Several days later, Ben's body was discovered in a wooded area near White Lick Creek in Plainfield, Indiana, dismembered and partially consumed. He'd fallen victim to the crazed cannibal killer known as the Midwest Butcher.

And if that wasn't bad enough, the Butcher had sent a letter to Matt's mother, with grisly details of her husband's slaying, and promised, if he was ever in Maitland, to pay a visit on her and her children.

Mrs. Dribbin and Matt's younger sisters, Georgann and Lorilee, had moved to Sioux Falls after that. Matt moved to Gary, where he made a living fixing farm machinery and truck engines and doing some auto bodywork.

Wash and Billy got the feeling that Matt was about talked out when it came to his dad's death and the Midwest Butcher and all that, so they'd just let those subjects drop.

They walked about a mile, soaking in the grassy smells of summer, the sound of whistling birds, the sight of trees as far as the eye could see. They spotted a gray fox and a rabbit, and, possibly, a shrew, though it was hard to tell if that's what it was.

"I've got to admit," Wash said, "those pancakes are starting to sound pretty good."

Another mile and they came to a clearing and a weathered wood house half fallen over with rot. The windows had long ago busted out, and most of the roof was gone. They looked inside at piles of boards and rusted furnishings, partially covered in dirt and rocks.

"Hey, look, there's an old coffee pot." Billy pointed with his walking stick.

"Maybe there's a pump around back where we could get some water," Wash suggested.

They stepped past the leaning house to the rear, and, sure enough, a rusty pump handle budded from the ground. Wash worked it a few times, and water gushed out, reddish at first, then so clear as to seem unnatural. He sampled a handful. It was icy cold with only a hint of iron taste.

They took turns pumping and drinking.

Matt wandered over to the back area, a grassy meadow, and shielded his eyes from the sun. "You guys ever see anything like this before?"

A furrow thick as a man's thigh cut through the tall grass to a far line of birch trees in the distance. It looked well-worn like something had passed over it in both directions, again and again.

"Looks like somebody dragged something through here," Matt said.

"Like what?" Billy said. "A bowling ball?"

They followed the groove across the meadow and into the dense shade of the trees beyond. The channel wound through places so tight they could barely squeeze between the papery bark of the birches. Then it emerged in a clearing with maybe two dozen grave markers, some stone, but mostly wood.

Before the graveyard stood a weathered wooden sign with burnt-in letters.

Wash touched the sign as he read it: CAT'S BACK RIDGE.

"What do you think it means?" Matt asked.

Billy pointed with his stick past the grave markers to a crystalline rock formation in the distance that looked roughly like the back of a tailless cat. The furrow skirted the edge of the old cemetery before disappearing in a wedge of shadow at the rock's foundation.

They walked among the markers, reading names and dates where they could. Most of the carvings were worn smooth by centuries of wind erosion, rain, and snow. They could make out a few names: Holly Lindorm, Amos Lindorm, and Lars (last name illegible). The dates were all a hundred years ago or more.

"You don't think some kind of animal made that rut?" Wash said.

"Like what?" Billy said. "A snake?"

Matt played with his wispy mustache. "It would be a hell of a big one. Like a python or boa constrictor. There's nothing like that in Minnesota."

"Let's take a closer look," Billy said.

They followed the trail of the groove cautiously. As they drew nearer, they could see the crevice into which it led. Keeping back from that area, they checked out the type of rock that made up Cat's Back Ridge.

"What is this?" Matt asked. "Granite?"

Billy studied it where a chunk of its surface had cleaved away. Large grains of black and gray and salmon-colored minerals swirled in it. "That's not granite. I've seen this before. My Uncle Buster is a rock hound, and he has some of this on display in his living room. Gneiss, he called it. Said it's one of the oldest rocks in the world. He found his in Redwood Falls, I think."

The other two examined it appreciatively.

"One of the oldest in the world, huh?" Matt said.

They were still studying the gneiss' swirls when Wash felt the hairs on his neck stand up. Someone or something was watching him. He turned and nearly fainted at what he saw. "Guys," he said weakly.

From out of the crevice at the base of the rock was what they wanted to say was a snake, but it looked more like a dragon. The creature had a massive snout, flat and square, and two eyes that bugged out black and yellow from below a beetling brow. The eyes had what could only be described as a malignant quality: fierce and sly, and sparkly, like the beast was amused by the sight of them.

"Jesus," Wash said.

Billy hugged his branch to his chest. "Holy shit. What the hell *is* that?"

Matt just stared, his face drained of color, his jaw hanging open.

The snake-thing was black and scaly, with hair like a horse's mane on its throat and a piss-yellow belly. From between its closed lips fluttered a black, split tongue. It slinked from its hole, never once taking its bug eyes off the three young men. It slinked, and it slinked, the length of it by the time it had finally fully exited the rock was nearly twenty feet. Its great bulk curled and contracted effortlessly behind it in the grass. It brought with it a great stench.

Other smaller snakes—baby snakes—followed it from the hole. There must have been a dozen of these, fanning out around Mama Snake but not straying too far.

"Okay, we're just going to back away now, slowly," Wash advised.

"What the *hell* is that?" Billy said.

"Nice and slow," Wash said. "We don't want to spook this thing, whatever it is."

Wash and Billy took a cautious step back, but Matt just froze.

The snake lifted on its tail, rising six feet off the ground, looking ready to strike.

"Matt, come *on*!" Wash urged as he and Billy took another step back. But Matt wasn't moving an inch.

The serpent opened its mouth, displaying long and pointy ivory teeth. It hissed, then it huffed and brayed at them, its black-and-yellow bug eyes now rolling crazily in its head.

Wash leaned forward and tugged at Matt, trying to snap him out of his stupor. "Let's go, man." But Matt didn't budge.

The snake edged forward, head still six feet off the ground, eyes rolling, teeth bared, barking like a burro. Even though it was still a good six yards away, Wash could smell it, gamey like a dog's coat after being rained on, but times ten as strong.

Wash pulled on Matt's arm, but Matt pulled back. "Come on," Wash pleaded to no avail.

The serpent moved on them threateningly, closing the gap by more than a yard in a single burst. The great spiky teeth flashed. The little snakes followed Mama.

Wash and Billy struggled to keep from flat-out fleeing, moving backward, slowing, step by step, their bodies shaking with the effort. Matt still stood petrified, and there was nothing they could do for him.

In an instant, the serpent closed the gap by another yard, then another, looking more ferocious than seemed possible. Then the creature reared back and coughed a stream of venom at Matt that had him dancing and twirling and clawing at his face. He wailed and shrieked in a soul-wrenching outcry that would cause even the most pitiless to cringe.

As Matt fell to his knees, the serpent sprang at him.

Wash and Billy ran wildly through the forest for their lives.

THEY MATERIALIZED in the late afternoon on Highway 32 just south of Nebish, walking along the side of the road like a couple of drunken zombies. Deputy Sheriff Wade McNeal spotted them in his cruiser at 4:37 p.m. and could tell right away that something was wrong.

The story they told didn't make much sense to the broad-shouldered deputy, but he could tell they'd had a fright and were worried about their friend who was still in the woods somewhere, possibly hurt. At least one of them, a bearded fellow holding a tree branch for a walking stick, looked to be in shock. He radioed for an ambulance, dug a couple of blankets out of his trunk, and had them sit in the cruiser's back seat until help arrived. The bearded guy hugged his stick for all he was worth.

Police and volunteers scoured the area, locating Wash Greavor's Chevy truck, full of empty beer cans, just past nightfall. They never did find any trace of Matt Dribbin, though they spent three days searching for him. They never found the old homestead, the ancient graveyard, or the gneiss rock formation either, not even with the help of expert trail guides.

One night, about a month later, Deputy Wade got to talking with an old-timer at a bar in Blackduck, and told him over a couple of

Grain Belts about the two guys and the tale they related about the house, the graveyard, and the giant snake.

The codger, a liver-spotted and rail-thin Swede, maybe ninety years old, in threadbare clothes and in need of a bath, listened carefully. He didn't seem surprised by Wade's story at all.

"My grandfather used to talk about snakes like that," the old guy said. "Farfar—that's what we called him—said in the old country these serpents, huge and quarrelsome, stood watch over graveyards and would attack anyone they found suspicious. He told me that one day he'd seen one with his own eyes." The codger shrugged. "He was a child back then, of course."

Wade had never heard this legend before. "Your grandfather said he saw one of these things in Sweden?"

"In Värend, that's where Farfar was from. It's a province in Småland. One day he was hiking in the woods with my great uncle when they came across this huge snake, lying dead in the path. He said the snake was longer than a train car, and it had these eyes that were big as saucers, bulging out of its head. Said it was black and had a chin beard, but no chin."

"Did he say anything else about it?"

"Hmmm." The old-timer scratched his cheek. "I remember he said that the dead snake smelled something awful. Said it smelled so bad, it made him ill."

The old Swede sipped his beer. "Tell you one thing, though. Farfar was scared to death of snakes after that."

Cutter

"'Here,' said the duke, 'ye have seen my vengeance, which is, like my blade, both sharp and ready.'"
—Robert Louis Stevenson, *The Black Arrow*

I t was almost 4 p.m. when Shelly Loomis awoke. The honeyed light of late afternoon lengthened the shadows of her room and gave it a surreal glow. She swung her feet from the twin bed to the cold tiles and sat for a moment, huddled, running a hand through her dark-brown hair.

Hers had been a restless night. In what little sleep she'd managed, a nightmare hounded her relentlessly. A nightmare about the real and imagined terrors of this past summer. *Just like every other night since then.*

With one finger, she lightly traced a white scar on her forearm.

Her room, which she'd kept fastidiously neat when K had stayed over, was now a hopeless mess. Clothing, papers, dog-eared books rifled from a shelf, and empty cola cans ran riot across the floor. Her dresser drawers were half out, and the jewelry box on top was gathering dust. Her open closet held mostly just naked wire hangers.

Pulling a blanket over her shoulders, she stood and picked her way to her window.

Outside, January had just laid down a fresh coat of snow. Not the dense kind that made good snowballs but the powdery kind that drifted in the breeze. A pair of squirrels, coupling at the root end of a birch trunk turned, suddenly alert, and ran off together, one still jostling along on the back of the other. In the distance, the Minnesota River glared at Shelly.

To one side of the yard squatted Uncle Moven's little house of horrors, vacant, of course, now that Uncle Morven was safely locked away. The snow rose nearly a quarter of the way up the door frame. A padlock, added by Shelly's dad after this summer's wickedness, gleamed from its hasp, dutifully sealing in Uncle Morven's dirty secrets.

She tugged on a T-shirt and blue jeans she collected from the floor and poked through a pile of clothes until she located her fuzzy pink socks. Slipping them on, she stepped out into the hallway.

Her clothes fit her more loosely than before, the waist of her jeans threatening to pass beyond her hips. That was one of the good things about grief: it tended to diminish your appetite. She figured she'd lost twenty pounds. The high-school boys would now ogle her lustfully, she supposed, if she ever went back to school.

"Is that you, Shelly?" Mom called from downstairs.

"No," she answered, "it's home invaders, come to steal your fortune."

"Haha. Very funny. Feeling any better?"

In the laundry room at the opposite end of the hallway, Mr. Frizzy, the cat, meowed.

Shelly followed the stairs down to the living room. "I'm still not sleeping very well."

Sandy Loomis stood in the kitchen, already dressed in the tan blouse and jeans that were the unofficial uniform of the Fetch and Go convenience store in Prior Lake, where she was the night manager. She still needed to apply her makeup and hot-curl her hair. "The pills aren't helping?"

"Maybe. A little."

"Still having bad dreams?"

Shelly nodded.

Mom blew steam from the coffee cup she clutched. "I hope you don't blame us, Shelly. Not too much, anyway. We feel just terrible about it. I do. Your father does, too. It's just one of those awful things that happen in life."

Shelly nodded. It wasn't their fault they had a dysfunctional family. They interacted in the only ways they knew how. If that dysfunction included agreeing to house the family child molester, well, that was just a judgment call that came back to bite them. They weren't blameless, but they might as well be.

"I stashed away a couple of those sugar buns you like," Mom said, raising her eyebrows. She fished two from far back on the cabinet's top shelf, where she kept the canned goods and held them up for Shelly to see.

Sugar buns. As if that made everything alright.

"Thanks, Mom." Taking the buns and a can of Coke from the refrigerator, Shelly headed back up the stairs to her bedroom. Mr. Frizzy followed her in and she shut the door.

SHE'D SEARCHED FOR NEARLY TWO HOURS, scouring the treelines and tall grass along the Minnesota River until the footpath began to peter out. Overhead, rainclouds, which had been gathering all morning, let loose a slow but steady downpour. Rounding a clump of birch trees at the water's edge, that's where she'd found Kelishea Taylor, her tawny-blonde friend, hair dangling over her face, her fragile body stick-thin in torn and grubby pajamas, looking up at her, lost and soulless.

Every time Shelly remembered that moment, she felt a stab of frosty numbness that worked at her bowels like the prowling steel of an icy dagger.

In her bedroom, on her bed, Shelly scooted her butt up from the mattress and dug into a pocket. There was only one way to stop this feeling.

Oh, K, I'm so sorry I ever let you stay here with this crazy family of mine. You were too pure, too generous, too high-minded for us— utterly unprepared for the Loomis brand of depravity. We took you in and infected you. How can you ever forgive me?

The moment the ambulance doors had closed on rain-soaked Kelishea in the front yard of the Loomis' rural Shakopee home, Shelly knew with certainty she would never see her friend again. Mom and Dad had offered clumsy comfort as the hospital wagon drove off, sirens wailing, but Shelly was having none of that.

She'd broken away from their embrace and, before anyone could stop her, ran toward the little house where Uncle Morven lived.

She'd flown through the open door.

Inside, his great bulk nearly filled a loveseat. His ratty jeans ended at mid-calf, and a filthy T-shirt stretched putrid over his swollen gut. Dear old Uncle Morven, the human scar: skin burnt and bunched and deepest red, from his hairless head to his horned and dirty toenails. Melty Man, she'd called him when she was a little kid. His ears scalded away, his nose little more than a flap of burnt hide—even his eyelids were ill-fitting and crooked—all reduced by a fiery explosion on some long-ago battlefield the world had all but forgotten.

Yet his true ugliness crouched within him in the dark shadows of his heart.

And beside him—in the roaming left hand over which he had no control.

A pair of deputies were grilling him when she burst in, and the surprised looks on their faces were almost comical.

"What the ..." one of them managed before she was on Uncle Morven, pummeling him with her balled fists.

"What did you do to her, you filthy bastard?" she screamed. "What did you do to my friend?"

The deputies peeled her from him, her arms and legs flailing wildly, tears of grief and hatred muddying her vision. Uncle Morven pushed out at her with a three-fingered hand.

"Let us take care of this," one of the deputies said, holding her at arm's length.

"He did this," she sobbed. "I know he did. Everyone knows he did."

She didn't remember being escorted out of the tiny house, barely remembered Dad carrying her up to her bedroom. She did recall wanting to see Kelishea in the hospital, begging Dad to take her there, but K's parents forbade it. After the *incident*, they forbade her ever to see Kelishea again.

Even though she stopped going to work at Valleyfair and, come September, had quit high school for good, updates on K's condition filtered back to her, through reports on TV news, on the radio, in the *Minneapolis Tribune*, and when those sources dried up, through Bruce, Shelly's pasty-faced little brother.

"She's still completely out of it," according to Bruce's latest report. "That's what all the kids are saying. She isn't talking. I don't think she's even going to the bathroom by herself. They've taken her to the Mayo Clinic, but they were no help. There's talk her parents might put her away for a while. In a nursing home. That's all I know."

A nursing home! K was barely seventeen years old.

Maybe I need to go to a nursing home, as well.

The silver jackknife she'd groped from the pocket of her jeans now rested in the palm of her hand. She lifted it lightly, as if estimating its weight.

The cutting had come to her naturally. It wasn't something she's heard about or planned to do. It just happened. One minute the blade was open, then came the slice, then the first bubble of blood. And all the tension in her body leaked out through that one little cut.

It didn't even hurt.

Suddenly, she was empowered—invulnerable in a trippy sort of way. Serenity washed over her as the warmth welled to the edges of each slight gash.

Sometimes just stroking her scars made her feel better.

SHELLY ENJOYED READING true-crime books. That is to say, she enjoyed reading them as much as she enjoyed anything anymore. Half the dog-eared paperbacks on her bedroom floor were about criminals and their exploits, their lives and loves, their victims and their deaths.

For her, these books were both an escape and a way—other than sleeping—to fill the dreary, monotonous hours of each day.

One tome, *The London Monster*, concerned a man named Renwick Williams, who, nearly a hundred years before Jack the Ripper, had stalked the streets of London randomly stabbing women.

According to witnesses, he crept up on them from behind while they unlocked their front doors, whispered lewd remarks into their ears, then brutally thrust a knife, a pin, or a needle into their bottoms. In all, from 1788 to 1790, more than fifty women reported being attacked by the madman, though some managed to flee before he could penetrate them.

His intent was not to kill them, merely to pierce them in their cushioned zones of intimacy and softness. But this he did often with savage fury, opening a wound on one victim nine inches long and four inches deep. In several cases, he dropped to one knee to get the leverage necessary for driving the steel deeper.

He had a special appetite for women in silk dresses.

When the authorities at last apprehended Williams, he was no one's idea of a depraved attacker. Instead, he turned out to be a handsome, thirty-five-year-old Welshman, highly skilled as a violinist and regarded as something of a ladies' man. His superior musicianship even landed him concert performances at Westminster Abbey and the Pantheon Theatre.

The courts, never before having faced a case quite like this one, were at a loss with what to charge Williams. Londoners were screaming for his blood, but he hadn't killed anyone. His true crime, beyond the attacks, was that he'd kept the city in a state of panic for two years, with women looking over their shoulders with dread every time they unlocked their doors. But lawmakers had never anticipated such an offense and had provided no redress.

Then there was the nature of the crime to consider. Williams appeared to be acting from some sexual compulsion, never before seen or imagined.

In the end, the court found him guilty on three counts of misdemeanor assault. He served only six years in prison. Williams professed his innocence even after serving his sentence, and some have questioned whether he actually was the London Monster.

But most criminals proclaim their innocence, don't they?

What fascinated her most about the London Monster and people like him was their cavalier willingness to repeatedly break the most fundamental of social compacts. *We're taught from birth, aren't we, not to harm our neighbor? Do unto others and all that. Even if no one teaches it to us, we pick it up by osmosis. We know it's wrong to do it, and that knowledge is enough to prevent us from doing wrong. Most people would cringe at the idea of stabbing another human being, even in self-defense.*

> 48

But others, apparently, so relished the thought, they felt the need to act on it.

Sometimes she wondered what it would be like to live like that. With no regard for kindness or empathy. Just mindlessly following an impulse wherever it leads.

EVERYONE KNEW UNCLE MORVEN had done something to Kelishea. Something so degrading, so horrible it robbed K of her will to live, turned her into a zombie. Shelly knew it. Her parents and Bruce knew it. All the neighbors knew it. Hell, all of Shakopee knew it, including the sheriff and the deputies.

But knowing wasn't proving, and there lay the stumbling block.

Uncle Morven denied doing anything. Denied seeing K that night. Denied even knowing who she was. A thorough search of his quarters uncovered no evidence to the contrary. As far as his past transgressions were concerned—whispered rumors about his relations with young children—all that was just innuendo. Formal charges had never been pressed against him. Besides, it was all so long ago.

The one person who could settle the matter beyond all reasonable doubt wasn't talking. Wasn't even acknowledging the outside world anymore. *Poor Kelishea.*

The county held him under suspicion as long as the law allowed. Then he went to a psychiatric facility in St. Paul for observation. Those people couldn't find anything wrong with him.

"So, they're letting him go," Dad said.

"Go?" Shelly asked. "Go where?"

They sat around the kitchen table: Mom, Shelly, Bruce, and Dad. It was a Saturday afternoon, and neither of Shelly's parents worked that day. Mom and she had just woken up, and they still had their sleep hair. Mom sipped her coffee, glum-faced, knowing what Dad was going to say.

In her heart of hearts, Shelly guessed they all knew.

"He's coming back here to live with us. No one likes it, but it's all we can do with him right now. Until we can figure out some other arrangement."

"Lock him up somewhere!" Shelly said. "Kelishea's parents are thinking of locking her up in some institution. It isn't right that he should be able to go on with his life as if nothing happened!"

"We can't just lock him up, Shelly. As far as the law is concerned, he hasn't done anything."

Frustration boiled up within her. She turned to her mother, "Mom, you can't allow this. If you do, I'm not sure I can take it."

Sandy Loomis looked from Shelly to Dad and back again. "Your father is right. But it's only temporary, I promise. We'll get him out of here as quick as we can."

Bruce stared blankly at the tabletop.

Shelly felt as if the bottom fell from under her. Lightheaded, she stood, leaned on the table for a minute, then awkwardly headed out of the kitchen to go to her room and run a blade down her forearm. To let the pressure out from beneath her skin.

As she crossed the living room, she thought, *I know what the London Monster would do.*

SINCE THIS SUMMER, she'd become adept at handling the silver jackknife. She'd twirl it in her fingers, toss it from hand to hand, play mumbly-peg with it on the linoleum tiles of her bedroom floor. In a daze, she sometimes watched the flashing metal for ten minutes or more, sometimes even as the blood welled on a fresh cut.

She'd found the knife while working at the High Roller roller coaster, Valleyfair's premier attraction. At the end of every day, ride operators scanned their areas for customers' belongings. A wallet, keys, or a pair of eyeglasses, these were the sorts of things people dropped from amusement rides. If an item looked important, the employee turned it in at the lost-and-found desk. Usually. Unless it was something really special.

Like the jackknife. She knew at once she would keep the jackknife for herself.

Opened, the knife featured two blades, a two-and-a-half-inch spear blade, and a one-and-five-eighths pen blade, both stamped "Tru-Sharp Surgical Steel." Brown wood (possibly sycamore) inlaid the handle. The bolsters looked to be polished nickel. She always kept the knife cleaned and oiled so the blades folded out smoothly.

She wondered whether knives like this existed in 1788.

Outside her window, she heard her father's Mustang pull into the drive. Heard car doors slam. Heard voices, though she couldn't make out the words—Dad and Uncle Morven, arguing about something. The sound of Uncle Morven's voice cast a shiver through her.

"Give it a week," Mom had told her. "By then, maybe we'll have it all figured out."

But after a month, it became clear to Shelly there wasn't going to be any figuring out. Uncle Morven—and his disability payments from Social Security—weren't going anywhere.

At least Dad kept the padlock locked on the outside of the little house. That was something. But even locked up outside in a separate space, Uncle Morven's presence fouled the air. She tried to keep his scent from entering the pores of her skin, but even wearing gloves and long sleeves and a hat with a makeshift veil couldn't protect her from being violated by the man's wicked essence. He had a way of worming into her regardless of how many locks and doors stood between them.

"YOU CAN'T KEEP going on like this, Shelly." Dad stood at the threshold of her bedroom.

January had yielded to February, and still the only things that seemed real were the haunting presence of Uncle Morven and the slice of her silver jackknife. Beneath her covers, she silently opened the knife and ran a thumb lightly along the edge of the blade.

"I'm not going back to school," she said. "I won't be a freak show for them to point at and talk about."

He sighed. "That's fine. But you can't live bottled up in this house. You have to get out into the real world. Your whole life is ahead of you."

"Whatever that means," she said softly.

He winced. "How would you feel about talking to someone?"

"We're talking, aren't we?"

"You know what I mean. With a counselor. About what's holding you back."

"You want me to talk to a shrink?"

"If it helps, why not?" He shrugged. "Think about it."

She pressed her thumb against the sharpness of the blade with enough pressure to cut the top layer of skin but not deep enough to draw blood. *A shrink could make a living off the Loomis family,* she thought.

In the end, she agreed. She had to do something, right?

Her mother had a church friend, Mrs. Larsen from Faith of the Covenant in Hopkins, whose daughter studied psychology at the University of Minnesota. Fanny Larsen wasn't a full-fledged doctor, but she was knowledgeable in the workings of the human mind and would probably have some helpful advice, Mom said.

Fanny dropped by the Loomis house the following weekend.

"Shelly?" She stepped into Shelly's messy room, attired semi-formally in a black dress, black cloth coat, and nylons. A butterfly barrette pinned a sweep of coffee-colored hair off her forehead, and black-framed eyeglasses gave her gaunt face an intelligent look. She clutched a black purse.

She walked through clothing and pop cans with a hand extended. "I'm Fanny," she said.

Shelly stood from her bed and shook Fanny's hand. Then they both sat down on the bed.

"I heard about your friend," Fanny said. "How is she?"

"I haven't heard from her. That's her parents' doing. But she's supposedly in a nursing home, getting treatment."

"And they still haven't figured out what happened to her?"

"We have our suspicions, but nothing we can prove."

"And what about you? I hear you dropped out of school over all this."

"School's not for everybody."

"I agree," Fanny said. "But the reason you dropped out was because of what happened to your friend?"

"Her name's Kelishea."

"You dropped out because of what happened to Kelishea?"

"Yes."

"You think your uncle did something to her?"

"Yes."

"And you blame yourself for bringing her here?"

"She needed a place to stay. Her family was going to Wisconsin on vacation for two weeks and they didn't want her staying by herself while they were gone. If she couldn't find someplace to go, she would have had to quit her job. We worked for the summer at Valleyfair, running rides. Anyway, I told her she could stay here." Shelly paused. "If I'd kept my big mouth shut, she'd still be okay, we'd still be friends; none of this would have happened."

Fanny looked at her for a long time without blinking. Then she said, "It's been, what, six months since this happened?"

"I guess."

"And, during that time, what have you done?"

"Nothing. Read, listened to music. Just trying to figure things out."

"Any progress on that front?"

"Not really."

Fanny told her that sometimes the mind gets caught up in patterns of thought that just go around and around. That sometimes we need to take some kind of action to derail that circular pattern and allow ourselves to get headed down a new path.

"Go for a walk," Fanny suggested. "Take a drive to the library. Have lunch with a friend. Don't just lie in bed all day and believe things will magically get better. Take action. Do something to force yourself out of this routine. That's the next step in your recovery from grief."

Take action.

Yes. Shelly felt this advice was spot on. *Take action. Do something.*

KELISHEA TAYLOR DIED the next day at Golden Dawn Group Home in St. Paul. She overdosed on one of the psychotropic drugs they were feeding her. Nurses suspected she'd hoarded her pills until she'd collected enough for a lethal dose. Word of her death made the WCCO-TV six o'clock newscast.

Shelly stood behind her brother Bruce in front of the TV, trying to understand what she was hearing. Numbness crept through her, and, for a moment, she thought she was going to faint. Mom came out to join them.

"The seventeen-year-old Shakopee native was found wandering along the Minnesota River in a traumatized state in July of this year," anchorman Dave Moore rasped from the screen. "She never recovered, and authorities are at a loss in determining what caused her condition, though foul play hasn't been ruled out. Funeral services are set for this Saturday at St. Alfonzo's Catholic Church in New Hope."

Bruce, who was sitting on the floor, looked up and searched Shelly's face for some reaction.

Dad, arriving home from work, rushed through the front door at that very moment. "I heard the news on the radio," he said, halting uncertainly just inside the living room. He held a six-pack of Schmidt beer. "How are you guys doing?"

"Not good," Shelly said. Bruce just stared. Mom gave a helpless gesture.

Setting the cans down on an end table, he stepped toward his kids in long strides and, crouching, gathered each in an arm and pulled them to his oily work shirt. "I'm so sorry. I'm so sorry. I'm so sorry."

Bruce returned the hug, but Shelly just stood there.

Mom stayed home from work that night. The Fetch and Go would have to get along without her. They debated whether to attend the funeral but, in the end, decided against it.

"Should we at least send flowers?" Mom asked. Shelly said nothing, opting instead to head upstairs.

Shelly entered her room and closed the door.

She was dead. Kelishea was dead.

Shelly felt deadness growing inside her.

She remembered the first day Kelishea had come to her room. She'd walked to the window, looked out, and asked, "What's with the little house?"

"That's where we keep the devil," she should have said.

Sitting, she turned on her bedside lamp, tugged one jeans leg to her knee, then pulled the silver jackknife from her pocket and began cutting. She traced an existing scar over her anklebone with the edge of the Tru-Sharp surgical steel blade. Her skin reopened, and fresh blood bubbled up. She drew another red line above the first, then another. Three stripes of crimson gleamed up at her.

Take action, Fanny had said. But she hadn't meant this kind of action.

Shelly stretched out on the mattress and softly cried herself to sleep.

WHEN SHE AWOKE, the light was off. At first, Shelly thought Mom had turned it off, but when she tried turning it back on, it just clicked. The bulb was burnt out. She sat up, feeling cold, and remembered Kelishea was gone.

Gone where? To a better place, people were always saying. But they didn't know. Not really. They just said what they wanted to believe.

She wondered what time it was. *Late, for sure.* She rubbed the dried blood on her ankle for a while, then fished around in the dark for her sneakers, pulled them one at a time over her cold feet. Rubbing her arms, she made her way through the hall, down the stairs, and into the living room.

She expected to find Mom on the couch, but she wasn't there. She and Dad must have gone to bed together, something of a rarity given they worked opposing hours, Dad days at the St. Paul Civic Center and Mom nights at the Fetch and Go. She looked down the corridor to their room and saw the light was out.

Her coat was on the railing where she'd left it months ago. She pulled it on and, zipping it up, stepped out onto the porch and into the crisp night air. A polymer porch swing suspended from rusty chains creaked back and forth in the slight breeze. Ahead, the road stretched still and quiet in pools of blackness. Beyond it, the barn and silhouetted outbuildings of Cabe Reynolds' dairy farm also lay still. Even the cows were asleep.

She walked through the snowy crunch of the front yard, around to the left.

On a hand wedged into a pocket for warmth, the cool steel of the jackknife kissed her fingertips.

Toward the back, in the glow of a quarter moon, the dark little house called to her. As she approached, her breath fogged and swirled in the night. Although she still heard the gnash of crusted snow beneath her, she seemed to be floating, half out of her body, toward a rendezvous that now seemed inevitable.

The padlock on the door gleamed weighty and vivid. There would be no forcing it. Instead, opening the one-and-five-eighths pen blade of her jackknife, she attacked the screws that held the hasp to the wood. The task was more difficult than she imagined, her father having used one-inch screws and tightening them past flush with his electric screwdriver. When the first one groaned free and fell to the ground, she noticed a knuckle on her frozen hand dripped blood, but she felt no pain. Nothing. She set to work on the next screw.

Inside, Uncle Morven moved. Maybe in his sleep, maybe out of an awareness that a specter of judgment day was clawing its way toward him.

When the second screw twisted free, she wiggled the hasp, raising the remaining screws from the wood to where she could quickly dispatch them with her blade.

She turned the door handle and pushed.

A microburst of trapped air rushed out at her. It was as if Uncle Morven's presence was a tad too much for the tiny house to hold.

Inside, in the shadowy gloom, she could hear him breathing. She blinked her eyes, helping them adjust to the dark. Gradually, his vast shape took form on the loveseat, his animated left hand disappearing in a scoop of shadow.

"I've been expecting you," he said.

The enclosed darkness of the little house magnified her sense of floating, of becoming ethereal. Shelly clutched the handle of her knife in a death grip, the tactile sensation of the inlaid wood her sole anchor to reality.

"What did you do to her?" she whispered.

Uncle Morven sighed. "There are hard lessons to be learned. About the human condition. About the black abyss that swallows us all from the inside out. About the tomb in the heart of the garden."

"Make sense."

"In '44, on the banks of the bloody Rapido, the Thirty-Fourth Infantry tried to capture that holiest of shrines: the abbey of Monte Cassino. The tottering ground opened in chasms as artillery thundered. From overhead came the steady whine of the bombers dropping their incendiary payloads. Crawling through the smoke and ashes, through the twisted, gray ruins and the screams of soldiers in this most distant part of the world, you cannot bring your eyes to fathom the terrible sights you behold."

There came into the room a dim flow of sparkling amethyst, whirling slowly in a blackness it brought with it, smelling of limitless space, tasting of starless infinity.

His left hand crept out into the faint light, cautiously.

"As is the case in most fields of battle, soldiers were not the only casualties. The cursed ground gave up bodies young and old, and the air grew heavy with the perfume of corrupted flesh."

The eddying stream of amethyst circled over the hulking devil, limning the scarred surface of his face and massive chest. "I remember, in particular, a young girl staring up at me, her head broken in, the contents of her skull leaking out. She could easily have been you or one of your friends. Where are your tears for her?"

The hand became restless, roaming the loveseat's cushion. Uncle Morven appeared to pay it no mind.

Shelly fought a waning of concentration. She returned to her initial question, finding some footing in repetition. "What did you do to her? What did you do to Kelishea?"

"I like to think it was the bombing of the abbey that injured me. Is that hoping for too great an irony? That the shards and flames resulting from the blasphemous pummeling of that sacred shrine are what reduced me to my present state of monstrosity? Alas, it is my lasting legacy. When the abyss swallowed me from the inside out, it emptied all the goodness from me. It left me a soulless defiler."

The hand climbed to his massive thigh and out to his knee. It stretched two fingers, like antennae, toward her, taking its reading of her.

"Did you touch her?"

"Don't you see, Shelly? By and large, the things we value are useless. Illusory. We hope to triumph over evil, but evil is not conquerable. It is as much within us as without us. It's not a function of our brains. It's not contained in anyone's head. It's an entity all its own, and it has been since the beginning of time. Why not embrace it?

It is the font from which all of life and all of death flow, to some degree.

"Did I touch your friend? The answer is we touched each other. She brought purity, and I brought experience. Yin and yang, you see? I didn't force anything on her. I merely opened her to new possibilities."

"She's killed herself, you know."

He smiled, the glow of his teeth startling white in the light of the amethyst stream. "That was her choice. It's a choice we all have, every one of us. If we're so offended by sentient existence, if we're so eager to reject it that we are willing to rob ourselves of the only reality we will ever know, then so be it. The question is, what choice will you make, Shelly?"

She surged toward him in the pale light of the amethyst swirl, weightless and determined, the two-and-a-half-inch spear blade of her jackknife thrusting toward him. The wandering hand groped out at her, at first defensively, then touching her skin through the fabric of her clothes, as if she were some bare and nubile maiden. The throbbing fingers caused her breath to catch, even as she plunged through the great folds of his flesh, her blade releasing the bottled stench from his wretched bowels.

With his other hand—the three-fingered one—he tried pushing at her shoulder, but she could feel the strength rapidly leaving him.

His misshapen eyelids squeezed closed, and his arms dropped as she stabbed at him long after he had heaved his final exhalation. The haunted hand lay dead and upturned like a spider. The amethyst swirl died away, and a calming tide replaced it.

The tide carried her out the door of the cavernous little house and across the snowy yard. On the horizon, beyond Cabe Reynolds' rustic dairy farm, the first hints of daybreak bloomed. Overhead, the diamond stars and the quarter-moon in their fields of endless space were beginning to fade. A freshness came to the chilly air.

The breeze still rocked the skeletal porch swing as the front door of the Loomis house opened like a gateway to another dimension.

Inside, her father was in the kitchen, making coffee.

"Shelly?" he said, surprised to see her in the pallid cast of the kitchen light.

"The bastard is dead," she said, dropping to the living-room floor her blood-dripping knife.

She no longer needed it.

Her cutting days were over.

The Transmutation of Rhoda Beekman

"Strange is the passion that makes a world in itself, that individualizes the One amidst the Multitude; that, through all the changes of my solemn life, yet survives, though ambition and hate and anger are dead; the one solitary angel, hovering over a universe of tombs on its two tremulous and human wings,—Hope and Fear!"
— Edward Bulwer-Lytton, *Zanoni*

T he first time Rhoda Beekman died, her twisted body shuddered on the pavement where she lay, her chest gave a final heave, and she felt the spirit leave her like a clump of seeds scooped from a Halloween pumpkin. She passed through into the summer night, expecting to see a tunnel of white light and the approach of dead relatives coming to greet her. That was what she'd always heard it was like to die.

Or, how did that song go? The one with the hypnotic guitar intro. *"Don't Fear the Reaper."*

Truth was, at that moment, she didn't fear anything. Didn't *feel* anything really, just the golden passivity that comes from surrendering every fiber of your being to the inevitable. Whatever lay before her was now out of her control. She hovered over her body in the blazing blue-and-red-and-amber emergency lights of the two police cars and the ambulance.

A medical technician knelt beside her prone figure. "Stay with me, honey," she said to Rhoda. "Stay with me." She fought to keep her voice level, but her motions were hurried and clipped. One hand touched Rhoda's neck, fingers searching.

"I'm not finding a pulse," she said.

Another tech scurried over with a yellow plastic defibrillator kit, popped it open, and handed over the paddles.

A silver scrape scarred the bumper and grill of the red Peterbilt cab where her Volkswagen had struck it head-on. The burst glass of the semi's windshield glittered on the engine's hood and on the blacktop. Having pitched through the window, the still and bloody body of the driver lay sprawled on the hood. A cop stood nearby, but no one attended to the driver.

Her own vehicle, a '04 V-dub, rested on its side, so crumpled and distorted it looked like accordioned tin. The impact had shattered her windows, as well.

"Hey, you!"

Someone called to her from near the truck. At first, she thought it was the cop, but it wasn't him. Next to the cop, a dark shape swirled: a murky shadow, lacking substance or form.

"Hey!" the shadow said again. "Are you the bitch who killed us?" the voice croaked out at her angrily.

"The what?" *Killed us? What did he mean, killed us?*

"That's her. That's the one." A woman's reedy voice. Rhoda couldn't see from where that voice came. The other side of the truck, maybe.

"Clear!"

Rhoda's body recoiled from the defibrillator jolt, but her spirit felt nothing.

The technician now pushed hard in the center of the prone figure's chest. Again. Again. Then the tech listened for breathing.

Rhoda knew she wasn't breathing since she was still outside her body.

Two shadows swooped toward her in the night. Within these shadows, she caught a glimpse of smoky, vindictive features.

"Clear!"

This second jolt rocked her. It exploded in her chest.

She was back in her body, and agony raged through her every fiber, flooding her eyes with tears. Her hair and the side of her face were slick and gritty. Blood stained her T-shirt and jeans.

She squinted up at the tech.

"Take it easy, hon. We're going to give you something for the pain."

Before Rhoda could respond, she vanished into blackness.

THE SECOND TIME Rhoda died, it was on the operating table. This was during her third, or was it, fourth operation. (It's easy to lose count when you're in a coma.) Through the anesthetic haze, the surgeons and nurses worked on her sheeted form as eternity once again tugged her from her shell.

A monitor squealed.

"Doctor, we're losing her."

From overhead, she watched the medical staff scramble to revive her.

"Hey, what're you doing?" That voice again. The woman from the accident site.

"You ain't going nowhere, Sweet Cheeks." The harsh voice of the man.

They had somehow followed her. *But why? Do they want something from me? What could anyone want from a dying woman?*

They assembled in the air quite near her, their smoky faces leering. She cringed at the touch of their shadowy essence.

"Why are you here?"

"Why are we here?" the woman's voice said. "Where else are we gonna go?"

The ceiling of the operating room resounded with the flat laughter of these two presences.

Then she was pulled back inside her body, sinking into the numbing ripple of the anesthesia; into the velvety clamp of her deep, deep slumber. As the last traces of awareness slipped away, she had an uneasy feeling that someone else was in her body with her.

"I DON'T KNOW IF YOU CAN hear me, Rhoda, but you'd better not be faking it," Mindy said. "You have Mother and Father worried to death." Mindy had taken to calling Mom and Dad Mother and Father ever since she started dating Trevor Bates, thinking it made her sound more sophisticated. "Okay, maybe I'm a little worried, too. But if you can hear me, I'm begging you: snap out of it. We all have better things to do than hang out in a hospital all day waiting for you to come to your senses."

Mindy gave her time to respond. When Rhoda didn't, Mindy snatched an emery board from her purse and began contouring her long, carmine fingernails.

"Anyway, you should have seen the mess at Lydia Bassett's house. Looked like the Hell's Angels threw a party in there. I had to call Mother to help me clean it up. Then Lydia's dog started growling at us, so I called Trevor to come out, too, to protect us from the dog. Then the three of us ended up working until almost midnight trying to get that place in shape. I'm not sure what went on over there but remind me not to ask you for any more favors."

That's how it started. Mindy had asked her to go to Lydia's country house, to water the plants and feed the dog because Lydia was in Hawaii. *At a wedding?* Mindy and Trevor had a date that afternoon, and wouldn't Rhoda "please be a peach" and help her out? Only Toby—that was the dog—had gone on a rampage, tearing up the furniture and crapping on the floor, and when Rhoda got there, Toby bit her. Then he chased her into the kitchen, and she only managed to escape his snarling jaws by knocking over the kitchen table and setting it across the doorway.

Trapped in the kitchen, Rhoda pried open a nailed-shut door only to find it afforded no exit. As the hours passed, she began raiding the refrigerator for something to eat. That's when she'd come across the bowl of hardboiled eggs.

"... I thought for sure Trevor was going to ask me to marry him. That's the only reason I wanted you to go out to Lydia's that day. But he didn't. I'm still waiting. All I want is a ring. We don't have to get married *tomorrow.* Anyway, I think he's going to ask me pretty soon."

Trevor sold cars at a dealership in Rogers. He had boyish good looks with a spot of gray at the temples and the confidence that comes with having been a high-school basketball star. He was still something of a legend at Cooper High. *Go, Hawks!* Everyone thought he'd end up in the NBA, but he tore a ligament in his knee after a year at Mankato State University, which had ended his playing days for good.

Meanwhile, last summer, Trevor's sister, Pamela, had been a victim of the serial killer known as the Midwest Butcher. She was killed in an Illinois border town, and the Butcher, well, he was still in the wind.

Then, on Christmas Eve, his mom died. All the kids in the neighborhood loved Mrs. Bates. She was everyone's second mother.

It seemed Trevor's life just lurched from one disaster to another.

Now, he had Mindy on his hands. *What a lucky guy.*

Once again, Rhoda slipped into unconsciousness.

When she came to, her eyes were already open, and she was speaking—in the middle of a sentence, in fact—and she listened to her words as if they were coming from someone else. "... And I think I surprised the nurse when I asked her for a glass of water. But my throat was so dry, it was the first thing I thought to say."

Mom held her hand, smiling. "Oh, Rhoda, you had us so worried."

Over Mom's shoulder, Dad nodded, teary-eyed.

Rhoda cleared her throat and, with some minor effort, wrestled back control over her voice. "How long have I been out?" she asked weakly.

"Like we said, a little more than three weeks," Dad replied.

"How bad is it?"

Dad glanced at Mom uncertainly.

"Why don't we get a doctor to answer your questions," Mom said.

Yes, a doctor.

But already, she was slipping away from them again, darkness swarming to her as she drifted downward toward the core of her being. Normally, this was where she would give herself over to the soft lull of slumber, but something kept her from plunging all the way down: an awareness that something just wasn't right.

She sensed a malignant presence that did not belong.

Then, in this intimate place of solitude, this netherworld between wakefulness and sleep, the malignant presence suddenly reached out and groped her with greedy hands. It shoved her roughly. A sharp elbow caught her from behind, and she gasped. Blows rained down on her, and all she could do was cower and beg for mercy. Until sweet oblivion, at last, claimed her.

SHE DREAMT she was behind the wheel of the Peterbilt semi, cruising down Highway 94 at a little over seventy miles per hour. The radio was playing a Tom Petty song she'd never heard before. Something about living like a refugee. Her neck was bobbing to it, keeping time. She looked over at Vera, hair greasy and the collar of her blouse smudged and sweaty from three days of living on the road. Her clothes loosely draped her near-anorexic frame, and her pupils loomed large and glassy. She puffed on a Marlboro.

"Want me to take over for a while, Leonard?" Vera asked, grinding her teeth.

Rhoda licked her lips. "Naw, I'm good, Dollface," Rhoda replied in a familiar gruff voice. "I'll let you know when I need a break."

Something was coursing in her blood, electrifying her, making her feel invincible. Her heartbeat and breathing raced. On the steering wheel, her hands were grubby and damp, the fingernails untrimmed and dirty. Tufts of hair grew from her knuckles.

"How far we going tonight?" Vera asked.

"I figure all the way to Fargo." Rhoda tossed back half a can of Coke. Her mouth still felt coated in sawdust.

"When we get to Seattle, let's go to that chewing-gum wall," Vera said.

"Again?"

"You know I love that place."

"I got a better idea," Rhoda said. "Let's take a boat ride to Vancouver. Get us some Cuervo and a couple of thick steaks. The last time—"

"Leonard, look out!" Vera grabbed for the dashboard.

The Volkswagen drifted across the centerline and came straight at them, flooding the truck's windshield in headlights.

Rhoda wrenched the wheel, but it was no good. The car rammed the truck's grill. Tires screamed, metal crunched, glass shattered. The impact sent her airborne. Vera, too, though Dollface became little more than a blur of movement in the rush of the moment. The skin ripped off Rhoda's cheek as she flopped out onto the hot hood of the engine. The bones of her face and ribs collapsed; her legs smashed to bits.

The last thing she saw was herself, Rhoda Beekman, slumped in a pool of blood on the pavement surface just ahead, looking like a broken toy.

THE DOCTOR READ FROM A CLIPBOARD as he checked off her list of ailments: "A lacerated kidney. Broken collarbone, broken pelvis. Cracked ribs. Whiplash in the soft tissue of the neck. That's why you have the neck brace. Compound fracture of your left wrist. A serious break on your left foot that required the removal of the little toe. A tear in the meniscus of the right knee. Torn cartilage in the left knee. A torn ligament in your back. Facial injuries and scarring that will need surgical correction, I would think. Road rash on your backside and shoulders. A dislocated disk. Bruising and sprains, pretty much everywhere on your body."

"Otherwise, I'm in perfect shape?" Rhoda said weakly.

The doctor returned the pen to his pocket. "You're a very fortunate young lady. You had a head-on collision with a semi-truck in a tiny vehicle and lived to tell of it."

It hurt too much to nod, so she crinkled her eyes in acknowledgment.

"We'll start you on physical therapy as soon as you're up and about. In the meantime, get plenty of rest. We'll keep an eye on you for a few days, at least."

The physician started to leave, then something else occurred to him. "I almost forgot. You also have a fairly deep dog bite on your right calf. Apparently, the dog has had all of his shots, so you won't need to undergo the rabies procedure."

Toby. She remembered how the terrier's black lips had curled back as he buried his teeth in her calf. She'd had to wrap her legs with magazines and duct tape to get past him.

"Thanks, doc."

"The police will want a statement. They'll probably swing by later today or tomorrow. The two people in the truck died. They were high on amphetamines and had a trailer full of untaxed cigarettes."

He raised an eyebrow.

She wondered if she was in trouble with the law for her part in the accident.

"Thanks, doc. For everything."

Rhoda wanted to ask him if they'd found any chemicals in her system from eating those damn eggs, but she didn't. No sense complicating things. Whatever it was that had taken over her senses must have been some substance they didn't test for. Maybe something they'd never even heard of.

RHODA KEPT COMING back to those eggs. If only she hadn't eaten them. They'd looked okay. Though, to be honest, there'd been something about their shape and size that made her think they weren't regular chicken eggs. Maybe goose eggs. Or some kind of lizard eggs. Whatever they were, someone had put them in the fridge to keep them from spoiling. *That must have meant they were edible, right?*

She'd sniffed them, and they'd smelled alright. The outside was rubbery, as you'd expected hardboiled eggs to be, and there were pastel tracings on them like Easter eggs get when the colorful dyes leak through cracks in the shells. Were these eggs leftovers from Easter? No way. That would've made them over two months old.

She'd pinched off some of the spongy white flesh from one of the eggs and held it to her tongue. She'd pinched off some more and chewed slowly. It had tasted like a hardboiled egg. It tasted just fine.

She'd eaten the white from three of the eggs and felt better. The yolks, however, she hadn't been so sure about. But if the whites were okay, surely the yolks were, as well. She'd sniffed the yolks and nothing in their smell was out of the ordinary. And she'd been awfully hungry.

Oh, well. In for a penny, in for a pound.

In what could only be described as a leap of faith, she'd popped all three of the yellow balls of yolk into her mouth and bit down.

Instantly, she'd regretted this.

The egg yolks had made crunching noises and her mouth had flooded with burning, repugnant-tasting liquid. Before she could spit it out in the sink, the fluid soaked into all the membranes of her tongue, mouth, and throat. The burning turned numb, and the numbness leeched into her lips and the back of her throat, saturated her glands, and foamed in her nasal passages. Her head had felt as if someone had smacked her with a shovel.

Biting into those egg yolks was the biggest mistake of her life.

Hallucinations came at once in droves. Just like that, Rhoda was Alice in Wonderland, clenched by a madness that made a disappearing Cheshire Cat and a heartless Queen of Hearts look tame.

She didn't even remember climbing into her sunflower-yellow V-dub and zipping down the country road to Highway 94.

"There was no one else in your vehicle?" the cop asked, looking bored.

"Just me."

She didn't tell the policeman sitting in the chair beside her bed about the eggs. Just said that she was tired on the night of the accident and wasn't sure whether she'd crossed the dividing line or if the truck had.

"You crossed that line, you stupid bitch. You know you crossed it."

Rhoda looked up keenly at the cop, but he was busy taking notes. It hadn't been he who said it. And there was no one else in the hospital room.

Leonard again. Of course, it was. *Will you just leave me alone?*

The cop shut his notepad and turned disinterested eyes her way. "It looks like you might have been the one who crossed the line, but it's been ruled inconclusive, given the state of the crash scene. The driver of the truck was Leonard Mauler. The passenger was his wife, Vera. Toxicology showed they were both sailing pretty high on meth. Their cargo was contraband cigarettes headed for the West Coast. The Maulers were well-known to law enforcement in the SeaTac area. They weren't nice people."

"So, what happens now?"

The officer stood. "I doubt you'll be hearing from us again. Concentrate on getting well." He lifted his chin at her. "Take care, Miss Beekman."

The cop left, and she was alone in the room with Leonard and Vera inside her.

Why don't you go to heaven or wherever it is dead people go?

"Heaven. That's a rich one. What do you think, Dollface? Think St. Peter would let us in the pearly gates?"

"Heaven sounds like a snore fest to me," Vera said. "I like it just fine right here."

"Me, too. Looks like it's unanimous, Sweet Cheeks. Enjoy feeling in charge of yourself. Once we figure out how to work you, we'll gladly take over the controls of the Rhodamobile."

Rhoda shuddered at the thought of these lowlifes taking over her body.

But is that even possible?

Maybe. Maybe not. Who knows what the rules are in the afterlife?

NOW SHE WAS AFRAID to fall asleep, even though her body needed sleep to heal. The problem was that in her dreams, the Maulers had unfettered access to her essence, and, given their sadistic temperament, these meetings grew increasingly brutal. Sometimes they attacked in tandem, sometimes they took turns. They laid siege to her, crushing and mangling her, taking their indecent pleasures with her. Leaving her spent and aching, if only psychically.

Then there was the problem of her newfound passengers attempting to commandeer her body while she was unconscious. She'd already woken once to Leonard conversing with her parents. And, on another occasion, she awoke from a nap to hear Vera asking a day nurse for a cigarette.

"I don't smoke," the nurse replied.

It was three weeks before Rhoda could, with aid of a walker, limp her rickety, badly damaged torso up and down the hospital halls. Then the doctors decided to move her to a rehabilitation center.

The facility, located in St. Louis Park, was a combination nursing home and rehab center that included single-room suites, an onsite nurse, carpeted corridors, a visiting area, and the dreaded workout room where the staff put her through grueling paces of exercises designed to strengthen and heal her injured limbs. Adding to her difficulties, was the presence of Leonard and Vera, who often jabbered unending inanities in her head while she was trying to concentrate.

"When we get out of here, Dollface, we're going to have to make up for lost time."

"You got that right, Leonard. We're overdue for painting the town red."

"Being in the body of a woman now, that opens us to some interesting possibilities, if you get my drift."

Don't get too comfortable in here, you deviants. I'm getting rid of you as soon as I can figure out how.

"We're not going anywhere, Sweet Cheeks," Leonard growled. "We're here for the duration. I guess you could call us the shit you can't scrape from your heel."

THE BESPECTACLED PRIEST popped his head into Rhoda's room one afternoon. "How's everything in here?" he asked pleasantly. "They treating you alright?"

The black of his cassock made his pale face look all the whiter, and it was only his piercing blue eyes that saved him from appearing ghostlike. She guessed he was maybe sixty years old.

"Yes, I'm fine." Rhoda looked up from a *People* magazine article about Brad Pitt's latest movie. "Thanks for asking."

He nodded and was about to leave when a thought occurred to her. "Reverend, do you have a minute?"

"I always have time for a friendly visit," he said, entering the room and stepping to her bedside. "I'm John Lipman from St. Alfonzo's." He extended a hand.

She shook it gingerly. "I'm Rhoda Beekman. I'm here rehabbing from a car accident."

He pulled up a chair and sat down.

"Reverend, I'm not Catholic. Does that matter?"

"It doesn't matter to me." He folded his hands and tilted his head to one side.

"What I mean is ... can I ask you for some spiritual advice?"

"Of course."

"It's going to sound a little weird."

"A little weird is right in my wheelhouse."

"I'll bet it is, you old letch," Leonard said in her head.

"It's just that, ever since my accident, I've been hearing voices."

Father Lipman frowned. "Voices?"

She glanced uneasily at the open door. "Yes. I know it sounds like I'm going crazy, but I hear the voices of the people from the other vehicle in the accident. The ones who were killed."

He rested his chin on his fist and eyed her intently. "Go on."

It poured out of her in a gush: the whole story. From the morning she'd left her apartment, to the odd adventure in Lydia Bassett's home in Rogers, to the crash and the hospital and her current situation in the rehab center. He listened to the whole thing without asking a single question.

He let her get it all out, his eyes occasionally narrowing behind his rimless glasses, waiting until she'd finished before clearing his throat and saying, "That's quite a story."

He steepled his fingers and brought them to his lips, thoughtfully. "I'm only a priest, Rhoda, not a doctor. However, it's clear you've been through an ordeal that would leave anyone traumatized, and that kind of anxiety often causes severe reactions."

"But these voices—"

He held up a hand to calm her. "I'm not saying the voices aren't real. I believe everything you've told me. I believe this is how you see things. At the same time, I think you would benefit from speaking with a counselor. Under the circumstances, I'm not sure my advice would be of much help to you. But I'll give it to you anyway."

He removed the eyeglasses and gestured with them.

"The voices you're hearing may be spiritual. Perhaps they speak to you from beyond the grave. It's happened before, based on the teachings of the church. Maybe the souls of these people who died have sought refuge inside you somehow, in an effort to cheat the afterlife. Possessed you, if you will. If that's the case, perhaps they will eventually see the folly of their ways and leave of their own accord."

"But what if they don't leave?"

He slid the glasses back onto his nose. "I think they will, given time."

"But what if they have other plans?"

"What sort of plans?"

She looked straight into his piercing eyes. "What if they plan to take control of my body? Overpowering me, so to speak."

He stared back at her in silence. He no longer had any advice.

THREE MONTHS LATER, she returned to her apartment. This was after a hellish week at her parents' home. It wasn't their fault things got so uncomfortable; they just didn't know how to handle their now semi-invalid daughter. They either hovered over her, making her nervous, or they continuously brought her things she didn't require. Half-full water glasses and plates of windmill cookies collected at her bedside.

Mindy brought friends over to gawk at her sister as if she were a sideshow freak. Well, in all honesty, the accident had left her looking like some character from an old Lon Chaney film. The first time she saw herself in a mirror, she'd winced in horror. She planned on getting that fixed but doubted she'd ever return to her former pretty-in-a-down-home-sort-of-way self. In any event, the visitors weren't able to cheer her up. And, even with her pain meds, the constant torture in her joints and muscles made her irritable and argumentative.

Adding to the circus of torment, her phantom lodgers, Leonard and Vera, could always be counted on to bicker, taunt, threaten and otherwise assail her. Day after day of their constant diatribe drove her to the brink.

"Come on, Sweet Cheeks," Leonard said in his raspy voice. "When are we going to have a little fun around here?"

"Yeah," Vera added, "I could sure use a cigarette right now. Be a doll and buy us a pack."

"Hell, buy a carton. And, while you're at it, throw in a bottle of Cuervo Gold."

What do I have to do to get rid of you two?

"Whatever you do, don't give up on the pain pills," Leonard advised. "They're the only buzz we get around here."

"Yeah. Maybe we need a stronger dose."

"Or, like I said, a splash of tequila would hit the spot."

"We're just *dying* to go on a bender. Ain't that right, Leonard?"

"Now, you're talking, Dollface."

Before her accident, Rhoda had managed nights at Willow Creek Theater in Plymouth, and though they said she could have her job back when she was better, Rhoda worried she might never be well enough to return to work.

She still limped along stiff-legged. Most of the mobility had returned to her right arm but her left one only lifted so far, and there was a jerkiness to her movements that bordered on the spastic. Sometimes she had trouble focusing with her right eye, and her back nerves often lit up with searing pain.

Even on her best days, her endurance was spotty. She generally slept away the better part of afternoons, which, in turn, made her increasingly vulnerable to the Maulers and their wickedness. Besides harassing her pitilessly in her dreams, they exploited her unconsciousness to access the workings of her body, which they were getting ever better at controlling. More and more, she awoke to find herself upright in her apartment—at the kitchen table, at the door, even at the stove.

One day, when she was taking the garbage to the shoot down the hall near the elevator, Mrs. Higgins, the prim old librarian from the Maple Grove Library who lived next door to Rhoda in 14C, stopped her in the hall. Mrs. Higgins had a fondness for flowered dresses, and wore teardrop eyeglasses suspended from a slender chain around her neck,

"I see you're getting along much better today, dear," Mrs. Higgins said. "Yesterday, I thought you were going to stumble to the ground for sure."

"Yesterday?" Rhoda hadn't been outside her apartment yesterday.

"Yes. I was slightly taken aback when you didn't acknowledge my greeting, but then I realized you were probably just embarrassed to be seen lurching around in your condition."

A chill spread on the back of her neck.

During yesterday's nap, the Maulers must have commandeered her out the door, into the hall, and back inside again, without her noticing. *Had they done that before?*

What else had they been up to?

"My apologies, Mrs. Higgins. Since the accident, some days I don't know whether I'm coming or going."

"Of course, dear. Well, I wish you a speedy recovery and hope to see you soon at the library."

"Thanks, Mrs. Higgins."

Retreating with her sack of garbage, Rhoda weighed her thoughts carefully.

You two haven't been out of the apartment while I'm asleep, have you?

Laughter erupted inside her head.

"We may have taken a stroll or two," Vera said. "Nothing to worry about. We returned you in one piece, didn't we?"

Rhoda could only imagine what these two were capable of without supervision.

I don't want you doing that anymore. Do you understand?

"And if we disobey you," Leonard said, "what are you going to do? Spank us?"

A new round of laughter exploded within her.

THAT NIGHT, she sat on the living-room couch, picking at her mac and cheese, and coming to terms with what she was about to do. After lengthy phone conversations with mental-health officials during which she'd once again detailed the craziness in her brain and the feeling of utter hopelessness that had seized her, a doctor suggested she come in for an evaluation. He told her to come prepared to stay the night.

Setting aside the bowl, she gathered a shopping bag of overnight essentials and, with her walker, shuffled clumsily down the hall for the elevator. Her Uber driver was scheduled to arrive in twenty minutes. In her condition, it might take her that long to get out to the front door. She wasn't taking any chances.

"Oh, come on, Sweet Cheeks, you're not going to let some shrink cart you off to the loony bin, are you?"

I don't owe you an explanation, Leonard.

"What if we promise to only take control of your body when you're awake?"

I don't want you controlling my body anymore, Vera. If the doctors can't get rid of you, then I'll just have to commit myself. Become institutionalized, until I get better.

"What about us?" Leonard asked. "If the doctors succeed in getting rid of us, where do we go?"

Anywhere but here, Leonard. Anywhere but here.

Grimly, she set one leg awkwardly in front of the other, but her steps grew more difficult. The Maulers were fighting her. She felt their resistance, and their concern. They feared her plan just might work.

They pleaded with her.

"If you could find us another accident scene," Leonard suggested, "maybe we could slip into someone else."

"Or take us to a hospital. We can probably find ourselves a new home somewhere in there."

Rhoda shut them out. She wouldn't wish these two on anyone else.

As the Maulers chattered increasingly bizarre suggestions and redoubled their efforts to slow her progress, she came to the elevator and her heart dropped. Someone had taped up a handwritten sign that read, OUT OF ORDER.

"You see, Rhoda?" Vera said. "It's an omen from the gods. You're stuck with us."

Anger seethed up within her. She took one determined step toward the stairwell door.

"Don't be ridiculous, Sweet Cheeks. You can't make it down two flights of stairs in your condition. You don't have the strength."

She took another step and another and yanked open the door. Twenty minutes. That's how long she had to get down those stairs with her shopping bag. She shambled through the door to the landing and looked down. Two flights had never looked so lengthy.

Rhoda gripped the railing with her right hand, shifted her walker and the paper bag to the other hand, and raised a wobbly left foot over the first step. Her foot settled on smooth linoleum and, though the action triggered a flare in her ankle, her footing remained solid. Leaning forward, she brought her right foot down. The Maulers jolted her still-mending pelvis backward, nearly sending her tumbling. This was a warning.

Gasping in pain, she clutched the banister for dear life.

Righting herself, she paused, a trickle of sweat stinging her good left eye. She squeezed the eye shut and motioned with her head to shake the salty wetness from her brow. The effort of moving down the hallway, into the stairwell, and down the first two steps had turned her hair into a cap of dripping perspiration. She breathed deeply, the view down from her unreliable right eye became unfocused.

Her whole body trembled. The Maulers weren't giving up their battle, and her injured muscles barely heeded her commands. Treading into blurry exhaustion, her left foot sought another step, but failed to find purchase.

The bag and the walker flew from her left hand, the railing slid from her right, and a sensation not unlike the pitching of a Valleyfair roller coaster took possession of her.

The third time Rhoda Beekman died was, as the saying goes, the charm.

She abandoned her body once and for all as it plummeted to the second-floor landing, whipped past to the final set of stairs, then noisily tossed to the main floor, where it collapsed in tragic disarray. With the body, she shed at once the pain and frustration that had haunted her since the crash.

As the blood spread beneath her crumpled form, the spirit of Rhoda Beekman ascended, slowly moving farther and farther away from her corpse.

Then, as her spirit edged toward the very rim of eternity, she watched her broken body below begin to stir. It rose on fractured arms, its head pivoting from an impossible angle and turning to look at her. The scarred face, freshly bruised and reddened with blood, grinned upward.

"So long, Sweet Cheeks," Leonard's gruff voice issued from the throat of Rhoda's body. "Have a nice afterlife."

The Skull Merchant

"Again the Vulture of Temptation soared to the highest heaven of his contemplation, bringing his soul down, down, reeling and fluttering, back to the World of Illusion."
— Lafcadio Hearn, "The Tradition of the Tea Plant"

Desert owls were unlike the owls of Ring Gargery's homeland. These desert birds were half a size larger, earless, colorless, and twice as bold as the familiar jumbi owls that populated the shores and countryside along the Redgauntlet River. When approached, jumbis fluttered off with a panicky *whoot whoot*. Their desert cousins, on the contrary, adopted a still and studying stance, their hooded, glassy golden eyes fixed on Ring as if deciding whether to ignore him or eat him.

"There's a bird after my own heart, Lativius," Ring said as they rode their horses into the shade of a narrow path between two mountains.

In the near distance, across a flat pan of black sand, a desert owl atop a tall, thin spire of rock already eyed their approach. "A bird like that fears nothing and no one."

"Ye do know that owl includes us in the things he doesn't fear," Lativius said. "Judging from the size of his talons, there's no reason he should."

The riders were boys, little past their fourteenth birthdays, wearing the plain robes in which they'd departed their home in Hastur some weeks ago. Ring, on a white stallion, Lativius Bendel on a brindled mare. They wore scraggy, adolescent beards and the pinched visages of desert ramblers. Already the sun had baked their bronze skin a darker brown and dried it tough as tannery leather.

Since breaking camp on the snowy fields of Carcosa, just inside the Ligeian border, the boys had traveled weeks into Valdemar, where the blazing sun soon evaporated the snow and the cold, and all that stretched before them to the horizon and beyond were sullen outcroppings of desert rock and gnarled trees, and black sand that radiated pitiless heat. The trail they'd followed had led them west through an oasis and past several streams, but the deeper they sojourned into the desert, the stingier the land became in giving up its water. They learned to keep an eye out for the slightest trickle of wetness.

For the past days, they'd taken to rationing water in miserly sips. Now their flax bags were almost empty.

As Ring cantered across the black sand's surface, with Lativius close on his heels, a voice broke the desert stillness.

"Excuse me, sirrahs."

The utterance startled them, coming as it did from behind. They spun around, gripping their fighting sticks from the sheaths on their saddles.

On the black sand, there rested the burnt and blistered head of an old man buried to the chin. "Could I trouble ye to dig me out?"

The boys climbed down from their steeds, holding the fighting sticks loosely. Ring walked up to the head and crouched. "Looks like ye've fallen on hard times, good sirrah. I don't imagine ye did this to yerself."

Lativius stood beside Ring, fingering the bloodhawk feather he wore on his breast for luck. "We're deducing ye caused people some trouble and this is what ye earned for yer efforts," Lativius said.

The elderly face, red as a ripe tomato and blistered with pockets of ooze, spoke from a bone-dry throat, through lips split and ruptured. "Come on, sirrahs, have a heart. Get me out of here, and I'll tell ye the whole story."

Ring and Lativius exchanged looks.

"Tell ye what," Ring said, "we'll spare ye a drop of water, benevolent souls that we are. But we're not digging ye out until we know what ye did to get yerself buried like this."

Lativius fetched a woven-flax water bag from his horse, brought it to the gaffer, and squirted water into his gaping chops. He gulped like a ravenous boar.

"Alright. Alright. Enough of that," Ring said. "Let's hear yer story."

The old man squinted up at them. "My name is Worthy Kane. I'm a merchant from Bethmoora, in Usher. I sell skulls. Well, I used to. Before they made off with them."

"Skulls?" Ring frowned. "What kind of skulls?"

"Oh, the people kind."

"And for what purpose does anyone want to buy a human skull?"

"Why, to honor their ancestors, of course."

Lativius gave Ring a puzzled look.

"You know, to display."

The boys were familiar with the practice of collecting and displaying the skulls of family members. At Gargery House, for instance, the bony domes of sixteen former relatives graced an ornate wooden shelf. It was how they'd honored the dead in the olden days before cemeteries took hold. But civilization had advanced since then.

"Why would anyone want to buy the skull of a stranger?" Lativius asked.

Here Worthy Kane noticeably winced. "Well, let's say someone may have misled them to believe that the skull in question was the recently discovered skull of one of their dead ancestors."

Ring grinned. "And, in this scenario, you'd be the one doing the misleading?"

Worthy blew out a gust of air. "Well, what's the harm? They're happy to be reunited with long-lost cousin so-and-so, and I make a little coin on the side. So there's basically no victim here."

"How did you ever get anyone to believe you had their ancestor's skull?"

"Well, I just poked around a little. Found out about the history of some folks. The tricky part is not attracting too much attention. Once word gets out someone is selling skulls, it's best to be off to another town. Before someone starts asking too many questions."

Ring, still grinning, stood up beside his friend and drew in the black sand with his knotty fighting stave. "I don't know, Lativius. It seems to me that those fleeced of their coins by buying skulls they've been led to *believe* are dead ancestors but really aren't are the victims here. Do you agree?"

"Aye. No question."

The old grifter grew alarmed. "I don't have any money left to give you. They took it all from me, the fiends, along with my skulls. But I could read yer fortunes. I learned how years ago from a cunning man in Carcosa. I can tell ye anything about the future you want to know."

Ring drew a row of straight lines in the sand as if ticking off a passage of time. "One more question. From where did you get the skulls?"

Worthy's face turned noticeably sour. "Different places."

"You dug them up from graves, didn't you?"

"The old ghoul!" Lativius said.

"I may have gathered a few that way," Worthy answered glumly. "It's not like they're handing out fresh skulls in the market. Ye have to get them from somewhere."

Ring chuckled. "Ah, let's dig the old bastard out."

"May Dagon bless you," Worthy crooned. "May yer patron god Hastur awake from his slumber to pat yer backs and cross yer palms with gold."

Ring had a small spade in the roll behind his padded wooden saddle. They took turns digging until the old grifter could free himself from the black sand's clutches. He crawled out awkwardly, his thin old arms and legs coated in black dust.

By then, the sun had climbed to its zenith.

"Could ye spare a few more drops of that water?" Worthy asked.

Ring looked at Lativius, who shook his head. "Our flasks are all but empty, I'm afraid," Lativius said.

"Oh," Worthy replied, "I know where ye can get more. As much as ye like."

Ring eyed him skeptically. "And where's that?"

Worthy pointed to the far distance. "Just beyond those mountains, there's a well filled with the sweetest, coldest water a person could ever want. I'll show ye."

Across the wasteland, past black sand and rocky terrain, lay a low range of mountains. The range curved toward them with a distinctly taller and sharper peak at each of the forward edges of the curves. The formation resembled the jawbone of a lion.

"Alright," Ring said. "Lead on."

The boys stashed away their fighting sticks and mounted their horses.

"Well, if one of ye could give me a lift, we'd get there quicker."

"We're in no hurry, and it looks like ye could use the exercise," Lativius said. "Ye heard the man. Lead on."

The owl, still squatted on his needle of rock, watched as the three of them journeyed off.

WHEN IT COMES TO FIGURING DISTANCE, the desert can fool you. Everything is either nearer or farther than you think it is. In the case of the mountain range, it was farther, of course.

Here, the merciless sun had cooked the land until it was hard and dry, and it had begun giving up rocks of all sizes, including tall, rugged outcroppings of vermilion stone. Grains of sand skittered across the landscape and swam in dusty whorls in the daylight.

Worthy Kane, amazingly spry and resilient for his years, led them across the plain without complaint, at one point, snatching up a lizard from the hardpack and happily chewing off the creature's head. He held up the lizard to the boys, offering them a bite, which they declined. He chomped some more, spitting away the bones until the whole lizard was gone.

Along the way, they passed road markers of pink sandstone. Each bore a carved symbol and an arrow that pointed them onward. The symbol was a man with the head of a wolf and the tail of a serpent. It was the likeness of the demon god said to guard over the Valdemar Desert. Tutor Will Boyle had taught Ring about the animal-headed gods worshipped throughout the cities of this forsaken kingdom. He knew they were formidable and not to be taken lightly.

By the time the three arrived, they were bathed in sweat—the horses, too—and as they made their way through the mountain pass, evening approached. The boys were tired, their horses were tired, and they could only imagine how tired Worthy was, but upon spotting a slab of stone in a sandy clearing, the old grifter scrambled to it. He pulled back the flat rock and unveiled a wet hole with water rising to the brim. The hole was big enough to climb into, but instead, he filled his cupped hands and drank deeply.

Ring and Lativius joined him.

Ring tasted the minerals the cool water carried up from its depths, the traces of salt and sulfur, and maybe even some of the smoky darkness that rose from far below where the sun never reaches and all is enshrouded in mystery.

Ring and Lativius drank until they could drink no more, then they hauled over handfuls for their horses to drink. When they'd finished, the boys spoke to their horses in low voices and petted the animal's necks and muzzles.

Next, the travelers stripped off their clothing and scooped water into their faces, rubbed it into their hair, sent great handfuls of it cascading down their fronts and backs, and rubbed their torsos and limbs until all sweat and grit were cleansed away.

Still naked, Ring returned to Phantom, his stallion, and took down a copper cooking pot from the horse's back, carried the pot to the water hole, and filled it. He submerged his robe in the pot and vigorously agitated it in the water. Then he wrung it out and put it back on. The other two did the same. The robes dried almost instantly.

He emptied the pot in the thirsty sand and filled it again, brought a sack of dried beans from Phantom's back, and dumped a healthy measure of the beans into the pot. They gathered sagebrush and dried logs and branches. Ring was about to strike sparks from a piece of flint to start a fire when he sensed movement behind him.

He turned and spotted in the sky, just beyond a craggy column of scarlet sandstone in the far, far distance, two tiny, circling silhouettes.

"What are those?" he asked.

Worthy frowned. "The people here call them dragon hawks. They're the biggest damn buzzards you've ever seen. Tall as a man when they're walking upright, with a wingspan three times their height. And I'll tell ye, dragon hawks are about the scariest-looking beasts in the desert."

Ring watched them for an instant, then struck the flint.

As night fell, they gathered around the fire, eating the cooked beans with their hands, while the horses fed on the low saltbush that rimmed the base of the mountains.

Their talk came round to Worthy's promise to read their destinies.

"Come on, ye old ghoul," Lativius said. "What do the stars foretell for yer young liberators? If the Netherworld is to claim us, at least vow not to sell our bones to some fishmonger's wife as the remains of her storied great uncle."

"Alright, let it never be said that Worthy Kane wasn't good as his word."

He moved over to Lativius' side. "Turn around and face me," he said.

Lativius did, and they sat cross-legged across from each other.

"Alright, give me a coin." Worthy held out a hand.

"I'm not giving ye a coin," Lativius said.

"Ye have to. It's the way it's done. Otherwise, I can't do it."

Ring motioned with his chin for Lativius to pony up.

Reluctantly, Lativius stood, walked to his horse's saddle, and pulled down the coin purse that held all the wealth they possessed. Then, he sat down again, fished through the pouch for a copper paldin, and held it out.

As Worthy took it, Ring imagined that very hand of the old fellow's scrabbling in the cemetery dirt for profitable skulls.

"Alright," Worthy said. "A silver coin might be more fitting, but this'll work." He breathed onto the shiny surface and polished it with the sleeve of his robe. Then he flipped it over and repeated the routine.

He held up the coin, so the setting sun caught on it and beamed light back into his face.

"I put five fingers on this coin to conjure five devils to fly through time," Worthy said. "Guided by Mother Fortune, let them hasten through the misty banks, through the mizzle and the murk, to bring back a glimpse of destiny."

He pressed the paldin to his forehead and closed his eyes. For several moments, he said nothing, his sunburnt, blistered old face clenched in concentration. Then his breath wheezed in and out. His eyes opened, his face went blank, and he whistled softly. The hand with the coin dropped to his lap.

"What?" Lativius asked. "Did ye see something, ye old ghoul?"

He was slow to answer. "Aye, I did see something. But maybe it's something ye'd rather not know."

"What do ye mean?" Lativius said.

He looked uneasily from Lativius to Ring and back again.

"Ye were blinded by the glint of gold and forsaked yer confederates for personal gain. A scheme that ends badly for ye, I'm afraid."

Lativius appeared thunderstruck.

"He would never do that," Ring protested.

Worthy shrugged. "I can only tell ye what I saw."

Lativius rubbed his scruffy jaw. "Go on. Anything else?"

"I saw the dead stir in their sleeping places and rise with open arms in welcome."

"The dead? Welcoming me?"

"And then ye lifted to the clouds and flew off to the next world."

A look of bitter defeat swept Lativius' face.

Ring stepped forward. "Don't listen to him. He's gotten it all wrong. His old brains have probably boiled from him being too long in the sun." He clasped his friend's shoulder.

"My fervent hope is that yer right, Sirrah Ring," Worthy said. "But I saw what I saw."

That night passed largely in silence. Ring poked the fire with a stick. Worthy went quickly to sleep, curled up in the desert's black sand.

Lativius watched as the stars broke through from the other side of the heavens.

"LATIVIUS, WAKE UP!" Ring jostled him. "The old bastard is gone."

Morning glared down on them, its breeze already prickled with sparks of heat.

"Gone? Gone where?" Lativius sat up and rubbed the sleep from his eyes.

"His footprints lead that way." Ring pointed past the hardpack into the distance. "I'm not sure what he's up to, but I'll wager he's up to something."

"How long ago did he leave, would ye say?"

"While we were sleeping. Sometime in the night." Ring bit his lip.

Lativius rose to his feet and began searching the nearby sand. "Where's the coin purse?"

"Don't ye have it?"

"I left it here. By the fire. When he read my future."

"Dagon help us."

Worthy had distracted them with the story of Lativius' betrayal. He'd waited till they were asleep, then seized the opportunity to fleece them of their riches.

"At least he left us the horses."

They collected their things from the campsite, filled their flax water bags, then swung upon their steeds, and cantered off in search of Worthy and their missing paldins.

Worthy's trail disappeared on the hardpack surfaces but always turned up again in the sand beyond. They paused occasionally to let their horses feed on sparse patches of bristlegrass and tanglehead. Their newly washed robes had begun soaking through with sweat.

"Do ye think I'd ever do that?" Lativius asked. "What the old ghoul said."

"Of course not. He made that up to get us off our game."

"But don't people say there's a darkness in every man's heart, Ring? Aren't we all capable of doing the unthinkable, if pressed far enough?"

"Maybe. I only know that ye've always been a loyal friend to me. I don't see that changing."

They rode in silence for a long while. The shadows shrank as the sun climbed. The heat beat down on them and their horses, and they stopped at last in the shade of a rocky outcropping for a drop of sweet water.

Lativius pinched the sweat from his eyes. "Ye got to hand it to the old ghoul. He made some distance from us."

Ring shielded his eyes as he peered into the sky past the black side of a hill. "What do ye suppose that is?"

Lativius squinted. "Crows, from the look of them. Maybe ravens."

"What do ye suppose they're circling?"

They looked at each other. "Let's see."

Up till then, they'd resisted galloping so as not the stress their steeds in the heat. But now, they leaned far forward in their padded wooden saddles, touched their heels to their horses' sides, and swept across the dusty plain and around the jutting hillside.

Before them lay, facedown in the sand, a gangly old bag of bones with a crow resting on one of his shoulders. They scrambled down, fighting sticks in their hands. Ring chased off the bird and then, with one sandaled foot, kicked over the body.

It was Worthy, collapsed in a heap, his face slack, his sunburnt skin taking on a bluish cast. Ring felt the old grifter's neck for a heartbeat. There was none.

Their purse rested beside the body, some of the coins spilled out in the sand. Lativius collected them and picked up the pouch.

Suddenly, Phantom reared, ripping at the air with his front hooves. He whinnied, and his eyes rolled wildly. The brindled mare also panicked as the air filled with a powerful *whoop-whoop-whoop* and black sand flew. The boys spun around and froze at the sight of a full-grown dragon hawk hovering three strides from where they stood, its enormous wings thrashing the air.

Their jaws dropped.

It landed just beyond Worthy and eyed them malevolently.

The creature stood taller than they did, with an enormous wingspan and a massive torso that rippled with phenomenal strength. The red flesh of its bald head shivered with rage. The sight of the beast's size alone was enough to cripple a person with fear. But, from nature's armory of horrors, the dragon hawk had also received a bluntly downward-pointing beak and long, flashing talons. The beak looked sharp enough to slice through muscles and strong enough to crack open bones to feed on marrow. The talons were razors with grips powerful enough to carry off a calf.

Batting at the air threateningly with their sticks, the boys scurried backward toward the horses.

Another dragon hawk fell from the sky, and landed beside the first. They snapped their heads toward Ring and Lativius, glaring at the boys and screeching, *Ack-ack! Ack-ack!*

The fighting sticks trembled in the boys' hands. They turned and ran to the mounts, latching onto their backs just as the horses were about to bolt away in fear. They held on for dear life, letting the steeds run wild until the dragon hawks were far behind.

Glancing back over their shoulders, they saw the great buzzards grasp Worthy's body at either shoulder and lift it from the ground.

Ring and Lativius slowed their steeds until they halted. The boys turned and watched as the skull merchant rose high into the air beneath the great wings of the dragon hawks and disappeared in the clouds.

"What do ye think killed the old ghoul?" Lativius asked, his calm restored.

"Hard to say. Maybe his heart just gave out."

"At least we got our money back."

"Aye."

"And the other business? About me betraying my comrades for gold and me dying and flying off into the sky?"

Ring smiled.

"Don't ye see, Lativius? It wasn't yer future that Worthy saw. It was his own."

My Dark Friend Déjà Vu

"'It almost seems as if I'd been here before, or dreamed I had. I seem to faintly remember, like a far-off nightmare, running, running, running endlessly through these dark corridors with hideous creatures on my heels....'"
—Robert E. Howard, "People of the Dark"

Women with large hands have always attracted me. The meatier the fingers, the fuller the palms, the better. It started in grade school when I first came upon a picture of Da Vinci's *Mona Lisa* in an art-class textbook.

Most would have it that Mona's most striking feature is her eyes, which seem almost alive in the conveyance of their gaze. It's true her eyes are both knowing and mysterious and can be read to communicate almost any intention, from wisdom to yearning, especially when combined with her famous half-smile. Still, I was drawn at once and irrevocably to the sensual quality of her hands.

You must understand that I was quite young when I first came upon her picture. In third grade, perhaps. Well before I understood sexuality in any real sense. However, at that moment, on some primal level, I came to understand the feathery touch of arousal.

Her right hand rests casually atop her left wrist. Her fingers are unadorned with rings or other jewelry. Her nails are trimmed, her knuckles soft, her skin unblemished by wrinkle, discoloration, or flaw of any kind. Not everyone can see that her hands are unusually large, but I can. To my eye, they are beautifully immense.

Some suggest that her hands serve merely as a counterpoint to her face, and people will see what they wish in the composition of any artwork, but I have long suspected that Da Vinci shared a secret side of himself in this portrait. I believe he shared his fetish for large hands with all the world, though only those likewise attuned could see it. That was his genius.

Unobserved, I tore the picture from the textbook, and carried it with me in my wallet for many years until the folds tore through the grains of the paper and obscured the details to the point where it lost its value to me. By then, I'd saved my allowance to purchase a full-size poster, which I hung on my bedroom wall. My parents were surprised by my interest in this masterpiece but viewed it as perfectly harmless.

Sometimes I would sit in my room for hours and stare at her hands.

Now I own an expensive print of Mona (from an art house in Italy) that adorns my living room. Yet, I've kept the original poster from my childhood, and it still hangs on my bedroom wall, a curiosity from my past that has followed me from dwelling to dwelling all these many years.

Granted, there may be something androgynous about this predilection of mine. All the articles I've read on the subject say abnormally large hands on women likely result from fetal exposure to higher-than-average levels of testosterone in the womb. But I could care less where this feature comes from or why I find it so attractive. All I know is that I do.

As they say, the heart wants what the heart wants.

In everyday life, I have occasionally encountered women with large hands, and it saddens me how so many of them self-consciously hide these assets by keeping them balled or pocketed or otherwise out of sight. However, a few do display them proudly, openly, with long, polished nails and elaborate bracelets and finger bands that lure my eye.

These are the women worth possessing, especially when they are young and fresh and ravishing in an elegant sort of way, as was Karilla Mason.

I suppose it's a cliché to say Karilla radiated beauty. Still, whenever she stepped on the stage in supporting roles at the

Chanhassen Dinner Theatre or the Pantages Theatre or the Ordway, she held every show-goer in the ample palm of her hand. As flirtatious dairymaid Meg Brockie in *Brigadoon*, she dazzled the critics. As farm girl Gurtie Cummings in *Oklahoma!*, she stole every scene she was in. As hyperactive Ursula Merkle in *Bye Bye Birdie*, she brought to her character a sense of urgency that made her an instant crowd favorite.

A favorite of mine, as well, in no small measure because of her stupendous hands, with which she gestured liberally.

No matter how trivial her role, no matter how prominent or intimate the stage, she always left a mark on the audience: an inordinate accomplishment for one so young. When I was cast to play Tevye opposite Karilla's Golde in Chanhassen's *Fiddler on the Roof* production, she was just nineteen and about to embark on her first professional dramatic lead. Perhaps the most pivotal role of her career.

This gave me an excellent opportunity to observe up close those amazing hands of hers.

Not only were Karilla's prehensile appendages immense and impeccable, but her ring fingers and index fingers were exactly the same length, which I found fascinating. To the touch, her hands were smooth and warm and moist. It was a thrill to encase them in mine whenever our roles called for it.

I desperately wanted to feel their caress on my naked body.

I know. I was far too old for her by conventional measures. But the theater realm is a magical place where time is reckoned differently, where years are added or subtracted from every visage with the sweep of a makeup artist's brush. When actors assemble under the bright lights, all the world shrinks to the dimensions of the stage, and the only other living souls that exist are your fellow performers. Again and again, this singular camaraderie has proven—in my experience—to be quite the powerful aphrodisiac.

It didn't hurt that I was an actor of some renown on the Twin Cities theater circuit, who'd appeared, to rave reviews, as Billy Lawler in *42nd Street*, Nathan Detroit in *Guys and Dolls*, and as the iconic Phantom in *Phantom of the Opera*. I'd also gathered something of a following playing the masked mascot Captain Awesome in TV commercials for Galactic Pizza in Minneapolis, and I briefly starred as

Dr. Amos Malrooney in the short-lived daytime soap opera, *Another Life.*

Of course, I played down my celebrity, though I could tell Karilla was quite pleased to be starring with me in *Fiddler.* I didn't want her thinking I had big head (though all actors do). Instead, I concentrated on my craft, on becoming the best Tevye I could be. I took a dash of Zero Mostel, added a hint of Chaim Topol and just a smidge of Herschel Bernardi, and the rest was all me. With a slight stoop and an altered cadence, of course.

During rehearsals, I was generous and encouraging with Karilla, coaxing from her moments of sheer brilliance. I knew in my heart I would get from her the most remarkable performance of her life. Oh, how her face lit up whenever I praised her.

"That was wonderful, darling," I would say to her. "Maria Kamilova couldn't have lent more passion to that scene."

"You're too kind, Justinian," she would reply in her tinkling, bell-like voice. "I feel we have a real chemistry as Tevye and Golde."

I grinned and nodded. Yes, I still had the old magic. I could feel it fizzing from my pores. If I proceeded with care, taking this fair maiden would be as easy as plucking a grape from the vine. Or so I thought.

But an obstacle stood in my way: my failing health.

Sadly, carefree living had taken its toll on me. Smoking, drinking, drugs, carousing, they all played into my condition, but what was I to do? Live like a cloistered monk? Rob my existence of the simple pleasures that made life worthwhile? I made up my mind long ago that I would rather die in a blaze of glory than in the huddled whimper of temperance.

So, I ignored the signs and hid them from others as best I could.

Increasingly, I'd catch myself suspecting I was repeating the events of my life. I'd walk into some little shop on Grand Avenue in St. Paul or in Uptown Minneapolis for the very first time, and I'd feel a dread certainty that I'd been there before. I know, déjà vu, everyone gets it at one time or another, but I felt its intrusion multiple times a day, and though I tried getting used to it, it always left me slightly disoriented.

An anomaly of memory, some would have it. The mind takes in the same impression twice and fools itself into believing the experience is being repeated. That's why when one has déjà vu, it's impossible to recall when the initial incident took place. Most have the fuzzy notion that it was in a dream.

Some opine déjà vu is a trick of genetics. The LGII gene on chromosome 10 may be the culprit, though nothing definitive has yet been determined.

I was also aware that this experience could be a symptom of a neurological disorder, but I didn't explore this possibility too deeply.

For the most part, these feelings were fleeting, but sometimes they lasted as long as two minutes.

Do you have any idea how eerie it is to relive two full minutes of your life?

Sometimes déjà vu would strike repeatedly, relentlessly buffeting my awareness and leaving me dazed.

Other times, these sensations had the glow of precognition attached to them.

Let me give you a taste of what that's like.

Imagine yourself in my place, and you are in a conversation with another actor at a reception, and you know at once what the other fellow is going say just before he says it. He offers you a food you've never had before, and you already know with certainty you won't like it. Nevertheless, you try it anyway and all but gag. He introduces you to his wife, and you know beforehand the scent of her perfume. Not only do you know what she's going to say, but you know how she'll say it: what her accent will be, which words she'll emphasize, what expression will accompany her words, and so on. Your thoughts about her will be the same as the last time you've met her, though, of course, you've never met her before.

Or if I'm driving, I may know a car is in my blind spot an instant before I see it emerge. Or I'll expect my cell phone to ring, and almost instantly it will. When I'm reading, not only will whole paragraphs seem replicated, but I usually know ahead of time how the book will end.

You see how this can become bothersome.

And, if that wasn't bad enough, once or twice a year, my déjà vu would trigger full-blown migraine headaches. If you get them, you know how paralyzingly painful these can be. I suffered through headaches so severe they affected my vision, bending and twisting the light, casting arcs and afterimages and halos, and all sorts of bizarre reflections. These hallucinations would begin as slight distractions, quiverings across the zones of my perception; here one minute, gone the next. But gradually they'd overpower me with screaming, spotlight intensity: blinding me to all reality. And I'd pause in their glare like the proverbial deer in the headlights, unable to move or think.

At first, I could tamp down the effects of the headaches to a certain degree with massive doses of ibuprofen. But soon, I was keeping vials of sumatriptan on hand for emergency injections. This became necessary to calm my mind to the point where I could at least function, albeit exclusively indoors with shades drawn and lights out.

Luckily, the headaches and accompanying hallucinations never manifested while I was on stage.

In fact, no one I worked with had a clue about my ailments. If I missed a step here and there because of the déjà vu, it was the creep of age gaining on the old thespian—nothing to be concerned about. When the headaches hit, I played it off as a touch of the flu. To them, I was still the great Justinian Gaule, leading man, a little long in the tooth, but still possessing an actor's command of the stage—and a sailor's zest for the nightlife.

And, of course, I always had an understudy to fall back on should the headaches ever appear on a performance night.

My understudy in *Fiddler* was a Puerto Rican fellow named Oliver Skinner, half my age and twice as good-looking. An up-and-comer, as they say. Oliver was a good-natured sort. Although I'd never worked with him before, I'd seen his Corny Collins in *Hairspray* at the Orpheum Theater and caught his performance as Pharaoh in *Joseph and the Amazing Technicolor Dream Coat* at the Chanhassen, and was suitably impressed by his work. Also, we may have once shared a few bong hits at a house party in Northeast Minneapolis.

At the final dress rehearsal for *Fiddler*, Karilla and I were performing the scene where Golde tells Tevye that their daughter

Chava has run away with her lover, Frydka. It's a powerful scene. Tevye angrily vows to turn his back on Chava. Golde, heartbroken, storms offstage crying.

As Karilla scampered off, she suddenly became not one but three Goldes, running behind one another. Then five, then seven. All identical and in a perfect row. Beneath me, the stage began to sway. Lightheaded, I looked out on our bald director Yanis Dubs and the smattering of others who were attending the rehearsal. Most looked back at me, puzzled. Yanis looked mortified.

I knew that to stay in character, a stern expression was needed from me in this dramatic moment, but my facial muscles acted on their own. I couldn't control them. They formed into a maniacal grimace, and, the next thing I knew, the stage lights began to dance and shiver. My vision blurred. Panic like sweeping tides churned within me. Thunder bolted down, smacking between my eyes and tearing through my brain in a flood of agony.

My footing faltered, and I tumbled into a bottomless void.

I awoke in a hospital. A well-fleshed male nurse with close-cropped hair and sleepy eyes entered my tiny room with a tray. "That's good timing."

"Where am I?" I asked.

"North Memorial," came my reply. "How do you feel?"

"A little dizzy. Thirsty. How long have I been out?"

"Two days." He set the tray containing flavored gelatin, plain yogurt, and a cup of weak coffee on the bedside counter. "You had an episode in Chanhassen."

I reached for the coffee. My hand trembled.

"Sometimes I get migraines. Is that what happened to me?" I asked.

"I can't really say. A doctor should be making the rounds shortly. He can answer your questions."

"I was onstage. At a rehearsal."

"Yes. Your clothing suggested as much. We don't get many Russian peasants around here."

"What day is it?"

"Wednesday."

Judging from the nurse's reaction, my face must've become a mask of distress.

"Don't worry," he said, touching me lightly on the back of one arm. "Your vitals are fine. The doctor will probably send you home today."

"I must be released by tomorrow. I open on Friday at Chanhassen Theatre as Tevye in *Fiddler on the Roof.*"

He looked at me doubtfully. Friday was just two days away. "Let's see what the doctor says."

What the doctor said, after examining my eyes with a tiny flashlight, was, "A week of bed rest." Then, putting down the flashlight, he eyed me as if I were a bug in a spider's web.

"But the nurse said my vitals are fine."

The doctor, who was tall and extremely thin, looked at my chart and frowned. "They are now, but they weren't when you were admitted. Your heartbeat was erratic, which is potentially life threatening. You had profuse sweating, labored breathing, and displayed an overall twitching, all of which are symptoms of a seizure. Do you have a history of epilepsy in your family?"

"Not that I know of."

"While you were out, we ran some blood tests and did some imaging, but the results were inconclusive. I'd like to do a lumbar puncture and a full CT scan."

"How long will that take?"

"We can probably get you out of here by tonight if nothing serious shows up on these other tests. But you'll have to take it easy. I understand you're an actor?"

"That's right."

"Well, the show's going to have to go on without you, I'm afraid. At least for a week."

"But I play Tevye at—"

The doctor held up a slender hand. "Mr. Gaule, you suffered through a serious event. Some kind of seizure that knocked you out for two days. This is nothing to play around with. At the minimum, you need a week to give your body time to heal." He paused and crossed his arms. "You might want to give some thought to retiring from the stage. Maybe find a less stressful pastime. You're nearly sixty. Maybe travel? Think about it."

Then he left, having taken a wrecking ball to my life's greatest joy and all my ambitions.

That evening, I was back in my own home. The tests had all been negative. Though I reclined on my couch, I was quickly on the phone to the director. I got his secretary.

"Yanis Dubs' phone. Marjorie speaking."

"This is Justinian Gaule. I'm starring in *Fiddler on the Roof*, and I've just been released from the hospital. I need to talk to Yanis."

"Oh, he's not available just now, but I can tell you he's aware of your condition."

"What?"

"After your collapse on the stage, I was on the phone to the hospital, getting updates. We learned you were unconscious for two days. How are you feeling?"

"I feel fine." A lie, of course.

"Well, Yanis has decided to go with Oliver Skinner, for the first week of the run anyway."

"That's not really necessary. I feel fine, I tell you."

"Mr. Gaule, there are insurance considerations here. What if you fainted and hurt yourself onstage? The theater could be legally responsible."

"But you don't understand—"

"I'll have Yanis give you a call as soon as possible. For the time being, though, he's going with Oliver. He suggested you bring a doctor's note explaining your condition. Once you have a clean bill of health and a chance to rest, he's open to possibly bringing you back on."

"*Possibly?*"

"Well, let's say probably."

After some well-wishing banter, Marjorie hung up.

That night I dreamt I was at a wedding. At the front of the church, waiting with the minister and the wedding party, stood Oliver Skinner, dressed as Tevye. He winked at me.

The minister, stony-faced, held what I recognized as a forked scepter of Pluto, a Satanic symbol.

The organist began to play, not "Here Comes the Bride" but a more raucous number, a garage-band anthem from R.E.M.'s early days: "It's the End of the World as We Know It." Oliver, the minister, the wedding party, and the assembled guests all turned to face me and joined in singing, "It's the end of the world as we know it." Over and over.

The church rang with their voices, which resounded like the peals from angry bells.

Down the aisle, trailing behind her the full cast of *Fiddler* in costume, came Karilla Mason, dressed as Golde, clutching to her bosom in her exaggerated hands a bouquet of black carnations. When she came to my pew, she paused and looked my way. Her eyes flared open, and her mouth widened. Then she and the others joined in the haunting but hearty refrain, "And I feel fine."

And I feel fine.

I looked down at my hands and watched as they faded from sight. I knew then that at the end of my world lay nothing but dissolution and memories lost to the passage of time.

All the next day, I stewed on my fleeting fame.

Yanis never called, as I knew he wouldn't. As far as he was concerned, my star had tarnished. I could hear the rag-tagged and the bobtailed masses already: "What was the name of that actor? The one who played Sam Wheat in *Ghost: The Musical* at the Old Log Theater in Excelsior? Justin something-or-other?"

If William Powell, Wallace Beery, Greer Garson, and Claudette Colbert were all but unknown to modern audiences, how long would it be before they forgot me? A nanosecond?

There must be a way to circumvent what appeared to be an abrupt end to my brilliant career.

Somehow I had to win back the role of Tevye. It was my only hope to at least delay the inevitable. After all, they couldn't forget me while I performed before their very eyes over their platters of slow-roasted prime rib and vegetable lasagna. I *would* be Tevye, I vowed. I must find a way.

Time was not an ally. Tomorrow was opening day. If I was to act, it needed to be tonight. Slowly, a plan unfolded in my mind. A sinister plot hatched by a desperate man.

A few phone calls garnered me the address I needed. My nemesis lived in a section of St. Paul known as Tangletown, a leafy pocket of winding streets in the Macalester-Groveland neighborhood. Houses there tended to be larger than average and, though most of them were built in the early 1900s, they were magnificently well-preserved.

I waited past nightfall. Then, ignoring my doctor's advice, I took an Uber to Grand Avenue and walked the short distance from there to Tangletown, until I came to the turreted Victorian abode of Oliver Skinner. The street was dim and vacant, and I was confident no one saw me at that late hour as I approached Oliver's house and crept toward the heavy shadows of bur oak that lined one side.

The night's exertions, thus far, had left me winded and a little dizzy. I could feel the sweat breaking on my brow. The headlights of the occasional passing vehicles in the street flickered in intensity. The dark of the trees' shadows reached out to me.

As I collected my breath and strength, I peered through a picture window into Oliver's dining room. He walked past in his robe, smoking a cigarette and thumbing through a copy of a script. *Fiddler*, no doubt. Studying Tevye's lines for tomorrow's opening. He paced back and forth, wearing an expression of intense pleasure.

He moved sleekly, spryly in the loose folds of his robe.

I, on the other hand, was old and sick, and knew I couldn't overpower him if I played fair. But all's fair when defending what's left of one's life. Isn't it?

The night air was not exactly cool but sort of coolishly tepid on my face. Still, it felt good.

I'd brought along a dagger that I'd "liberated" from a production of *Hamlet* years ago at the old Guthrie Theatre in Minneapolis. Oh, I wasn't the title character, not that time, but I was Polonius, the prince's chief counsel. The prop had been judged too deadly to use on stage and had been discarded in a pile of damaged costumes and broken scenery pieces, where it probably would have been hauled off as junk anyway.

Now I felt the press of it against my thigh.

Maneuvering into a seated position, I drew the knife and examined it in the light from the window.

The dagger was polished steel, its slender blade beveled from a central ridge and honed sharp at both edges. It tapered to a devilish point. The handle widened slightly at its pommel. The crossguard was a full four inches long. When gripped by the handle, it stretched beyond the user's knuckles. This was probably for dramatic effect.

At last, Oliver had finished his cigarette and stubbed it out in a glass ashtray. Then he turned off the lights and vanished from view.

Feeling somewhat rejuvenated by then, I rose to my feet and slinked around toward the back of the house, clutching the dagger in my fist, looking for a way inside.

A screened porch, moonlit, jutted from the backside of the building. Inside it, I moved carefully in the semidarkness, making sure the floorboards didn't squeal. Silhouettes of patio furniture hulked around me, but a clear aisle led to the backdoor. I approached it, and, sure enough, the knob twisted and the door quietly opened onto a pantry area. I stepped through into the kitchen and the dining room beyond, where I'd watched Oliver pace.

I wasn't sure where Oliver had gone after smoking his cigarette, but it was stage left.

Some moonlight entered the picture window, but the oak trees blocked much of it. I gave my eyes a chance to adjust to the house's black shadows. Gradually, I could make out that past the dining room lay a living room full of angular furniture and squat end tables. I entered it cautiously.

In a far corner, past a floor lamp and a closet, a hall entrance beckoned. Yes, this corridor was likely where he went. I stole into it, coiled and ready to strike should his form suddenly appear before me in the gloom.

Three open doorways loomed ahead. One to the left was a bathroom. The other two, to the right, appeared to be bedrooms. Holding my breath, I looked in the first. It wasn't a bedroom at all, but a storage area full of exercise equipment.

No one in there.

As I approached the second door, I could hear Oliver breathing.

A peculiar glee seized me as I neared this threshold with the dagger's metal handle fisted. Neither off the stage nor on had I ever played the assassin. I'd always assumed this work would be grim, but—perhaps because I knew that freeing Oliver's soul meant I would regain the cherished role of Tevye—I found the experience exhilarating.

Just inside the doorway, a silhouette on a mattress squirmed beneath colorful sheets.

I sprang to the bed, bringing down the dagger's blade with every ounce of power within me. To my surprise, as the back of my hand and forearm went wet with blood, a second figure bolted from the bed. The room filled with light.

"Justinian! What have you done?" Oliver, his robe opened on his bronze nakedness, raced toward me and grappled away the dagger.

In a daze, I looked down to see whose gore dripped from my arm.

And beheld the large, magnificent hands of Karilla Mason, holding her chest, blood pumping through her fingers. Karilla, my real life Mona Lisa. Her glazed eyes looked up at me, as if she was unable to understand who I was or what had just happened.

I rose to my feet. The floor began to rock. The bed, the lamp, and all the other furnishings in the brightly lit bedroom swayed, leaving behind trailing afterimages. Golden shafts of light and sweeping auras assailed from every direction. The walls began to heave. Skeletal shapes from childhood dreams fluttered and drifted in the air.

I felt my legs failing me under the onslaught of this sensory overload. I struggled to maintain my balance. Then, before I tipped into the boundless abyss, I watched the spark die from Karilla's eyes, not once, but over and over.

My dark friend déjà vu, coming round to call on me again.

Now I spend the days in my new forever home, where I dream up plays that will never grace the stage, and audiences made up of ghosts. Here, everyday, I deliver a performance that brings the house down.

I could almost be happy here, performing in my make-believe world, but sadly those eyes of Karilla's continue to haunt me. While I'm queued at the cafeteria line or shuffling to the showers or just staring at nothing through the barred window of my hospital pen, they suddenly appear, staring back at me.

Just as the life winks out of them.

The Last of the Sebeka Mungers

"The thousand injuries of Fortunato I had borne as I best could, but
when he ventured upon insult I vowed revenge."
—Edgar Allan Poe, "The Cask of Amontillado"

W hat Ma knew of her husband's lineage was what she got
out of him when he was "in his cups," as she put it. She
never talked ill of the dead, of course, but Petey figured
those cups of which she spoke were probably brimful of
Wild Turkey bourbon. Randal and he had found a pile of empties
hidden in the tool shed.

"Your pa came to this area from St. Paul on the K-branch of the
Great Northern Railroad," Ma would say. "He was seventeen at the
time. He planned to travel through to Seattle, Washington, and find a
job out there, but then he met me at the Pioneer Store in Sebeka, and
his plans sort of changed."

She smiled at this part of the story, and her wizened gray eyes
glistened like tinsel on a Christmas tree.

"We married within two weeks, and he moved in with my family,
who owned this farm. Back then, we raised chickens and milked cows,
and your pa, who I don't think ever even saw a live chicken or cow up
close in his entire life before then, learned what it took to work a
spread. He and your grandpa took care of the animals and crops, did
the maintenance, and so on. But, of course, this was back before the

barn burned down and your grandparents died, and the farm just kind of went to seed."

Petey thought that sometimes when she looked out the kitchen window, she still saw the farm as it was back then.

"Your pa never talked about his family, except when he was in his cups," she continued. "His father was a grocer, I think. Anyway, your grandpa on that side of the family died young, and Grandma Munger raised your pa mostly by herself. Then she passed on. It seems to me you had a great uncle or cousin or something named Wally somewhere, but he'd be dead by now, I would think. In any case, he never married, far as I know. And he never contacted us.

"When your father was in his cups, he'd talk mostly about how his pa used to beat him when he was little and how even at a young age, he wasn't sorry to see that cruel bastard planted in the ground. Those were his words, not mine. The way he told it, when his ma died, he had no family left to turn to. That's when he came here."

"So Petey and me could be the last of the Mungers?" Randal said.

"Far as I know, far as your father knew, the last branch of the Munger tree ends with you boys, at least where your father's family is concerned. As I said, you might have a very old cousin or something floating around out there somewhere, but you're the last of the Sebeka Mungers, anyway."

"What about other people named Munger?" Petey asked. "We must be related to them."

"I suppose that's true, but I'm not sure how. I guess all of humankind is related to one another if you go back far enough. But for all practical purposes, you boys are the end of the line."

Back then, when they'd had that conversation, he and Randal were still fledglings, and Ma still possessed the vim of a young woman.

Looking down at Ma now, in her black dress with her hair all done up, lying in the frilly fabric like she was taking a catnap, Petey's heart about burst with sadness. He put a hand on the polished wood of the casket lid. "I know she's gone to a better place, but I still can't believe it. I don't know how to go on without her, Randal. What're we supposed to do?"

This degree of helplessness might've seemed like strange talk coming from a man almost fifty years old, but the few visitors at the mortuary knew the Mungers well enough to understand. Shirleyanne Munger's adult children, still known as "the Munger boys" around town, grew up with Shirleyanne as their only constant companion. She'd raised them, homeschooled them, and now she'd left them on their own for the very first time. It was an odd situation all around, but it was the sort of oddness a small town tends to absorb with little reaction.

Petey, who worked among the folks of Sebeka as a handyman, was the better known of the two boys, and he got along well enough with most people, strictly on a business basis, of course. Inexpensive and dependable, Petey's work was always in demand.

Randal, though, preferred subsistence farming on the old homestead. He kept the pantry and the root cellar full of potatoes, rutabagas, carrots, onions, green beans, and corn, some of which he canned in quart Mason jars, along with cucumber pickles, cabbage, and stalks of rhubarb. This left him ample time for daydreaming, his favorite pastime. Randal seldom ever left the farm. Some of the folks at the funeral parlor didn't even recognize him, it had been so long since they'd seen him last.

"It's going to be alright, boys," chubby Ralph Peterson said. He worked his tongue as if he had something stuck in his tobacco-stained side teeth. "Things will keep purring along like they always have. You'll miss her, we all will, but you'll see. Time heals all." This was the sort of empty talk the bereaved come to expect from visitors largely untouched by their loss, but coming from Ralph Peterson, the words had a smug ring to them.

He clapped a flabby hand on Randal's shoulder and gave him a studied look as if he'd just shared with Randal the wisdom of Solomon.

Petey could tell Randal didn't think much of Ralph's advice, and Randal didn't like being touched by people like Ralph, who had, after Pa died, low-balled the Mungers on what he paid to lease their back ninety acres. But Randal let it pass.

"Thanks, Mr. Peterson," Randal said. He called him Mr. Peterson even though Ralph was five years his junior.

"We're real sorry about your ma, boys," Pearl Peterson, the chiseler's wife, said, wearing a somber and courtly black dress and veiled hat. Pearl was pretty in a round-faced kind of way. "Shirleyanne was a fine lady." A tear ran down Pearl's cheek. She always was too classy for that skinflint Ralph. She took the boys by the hand and gave them each a heartfelt squeeze. She smelled like peaches.

The Petersons moved past the coffin, across the room to where the sign-in book lay and the framed pictures of Ma were all on exhibit.

"How Pearl ever got involved with that money-grubber, I'll never understand," Petey said.

Mayor Anderson swung by. He was a good guy, well-liked by most. He knew how to be sympathetic, even though he barely knew the Mungers. Rosa Garcia from down the road dropped in with some of her Sodality friends to pay their respects (not that Ma ever bowed to that thieving, miter-capped Roman). And, of course, Ma's sister and her family—Aunt Minnie, Uncle Chester, and the girls—drove in from Sioux Falls, South Dakota. But by noon, the mourners had all come and gone, and the boys held down the fort until around three o'clock, when they told Zim Greavor, the funeral director, that he could close up shop for the day.

Tomorrow she'd be cremated. It was her wish, and she'd wanted the boys to spread her ashes on the old homestead, which, aside from town, was the only place she'd ever been or ever wanted to be.

AFTER MA DIED, the farm just wasn't the same. For one thing, her way of explaining things was what kept them levelheaded and got them through trying times. For another, she pretty much directed them in their work and kept everything running smoothly. Her presence had filled the farmhouse with lightness and good humor and made getting up in the mornings a joy.

Now, Randal didn't feel much like weeding the garden, and Petey couldn't drag himself to his next handyman job.

Soon they were running short on cash, and the bills started coming in with writing in red ink, and all they could manage to do was mope around the house and yard, drinking coffee boiled on the woodstove with eggshells to allay the bitterness.

One day an envelope arrived with the bills. Its return address read: W. Munger, Moose Pass, Alaska. When Randal carried it in, his hand was shaking. "Petey, I think we may have a letter from our only living relative."

Petey took the envelope and studied it. "He lives in Alaska?"

"That's what it says."

"Well, let's open it then."

If only they hadn't.

They sliced open the envelope with a kitchen knife, pulled out the pages, and smoothed them flat on the table. Petey, who was more of a reader than Randal was, cleared his throat, picked up the letter, and commenced reading:

Dear Peter and Randal,

I read recently about the death of your mother. You have my condolences.

I came upon her obituary accidentally while searching the internet for tax information on some property I sold years ago. Up until then, I wasn't sure I had any living relatives anywhere. But I suspected I might.

My fervent hope is that you two are the last of us Mungers. I'll explain in a minute.

The obituary said Shirleyanne Munger died peacefully and left behind two unmarried sons. It said her husband, Enoch, preceded her in death.

Although I never met your mother, I'm sure she was a loving and pleasant woman. The Mungers always had the knack of marrying well, though these marriages generally ended in tragedy.

I only met your father once, when he was a baby. That tells you how old I am.

Unfortunately, it's my sad duty to add to your grief by sharing some news of which I'm sure you are unaware.

You may know that you two and I are the last of this branch of the Mungers, and by the time you read this, I will have passed on to the majority, and you two will be all that remains of our clan. I wish I could tell you our family has epitomized the ideals of love for our fellow human beings; that we were generous, caring people who helped the poor and afflicted, and so on, but the truth is very much the opposite.

This is what I know about our family for sure.

Your great grandfather, Günter Munger, was a factory worker in Heidelberg, Germany, who was better known as the Werewolf of Heidelberg. Between 1919 and 1928, he strangled two dozen women and had sex with their corpses. He then sold their flesh at a sausage stand he operated on weekends at the Heidelberg train station. When he was caught and imprisoned, he killed himself with a bedsheet, though this may have been during a vain attempt at autoerotic asphyxiation.

His wife had died after giving birth to their second son. The boys, Stefan and Günter Junior, were raised by their father until the police captured Günter for killing all those women. Then the two, who'd witnessed unimaginable depravity growing up in their father's home, went to live with Günter's brother, Hans, and Hans' family in Mannheim.

Hans Munger was a physician at University Hospital from 1917 to 1938, though he forged his medical degree, and it's unclear whether he actually knew anything about medicine or not. During his career, he treated thousands of patients, prescribed medications, even assisted in many surgeries. Unfortunately, those in his care had a higher-than-expected mortality rate, and some nurses even hid patients from him. More than twenty of his terminally ill patients died after making Hans the sole beneficiary of their estates. He also sold drugs stolen from the dispensary to street dealers.

Hans lost his position after being caught ejaculating on the face of a twenty-three-year-old woman he incapacitated with morphine.

Also living with Stefan and Günter Junior in those days were Hans' wife, Anja, and their two children, Astrid and Dirk. Anja was kind-hearted and well-liked, though a bit dim-witted. Astrid, on the other hand, grew up to be a hellion. She eventually worked as a prostitute in Berlin and died syphilitic from a heroin overdose.

Dirk, Stefan, and Günter Junior joined the German army in 1939. In September of that year, Germany invaded Poland, and World War II got underway.

Military life didn't suit Dirk very well. He was constantly in trouble for petty larceny, being late to formations, having a sloppy uniform, etc. When he got orders to report to the Russian front, he instead went AWOL and headed back to Mannheim. He used his service Luger to shoot to death his father, his mother, then himself.

Stefan, on the other hand, excelled under military discipline and mastered the use of the bolt-action Mauser rifle to such a degree he became a sniper. He used to brag that his aim was a hundred percent deadly whenever the target was closer than five-hundred feet. In 1943, he went to the Eastern Front, where he killed more than three-hundred Russian soldiers, earning him the Knight's Cross. In December of 1944, he was transferred to northern France for what history has dubbed the Battle of the Bulge. In that campaign, the last great battle of World War II, the German army was forced to retreat, and on May 7, 1945, Nazi leaders surrendered.

After the war, Stefan, your grandfather, married Hannah Müller. They had a baby boy named Enoch. That boy, of course, was your father. The three of them immigrated to America and ended up in St. Paul, Minnesota.

I only had the chance to see the boy once before they left because I had to go, as well. I was wanted as a war criminal and had to flee for my life, along the ratlines through Rome to Genoa, then on to South America.

You see, I was your grandfather's brother, Günter Junior. I started going by my middle name, Walter, after we moved in with Uncle Hans.

My time in the military ended in Auschwitz, where I served as an assistant to the Angel of Death himself, Josef Mengele. My work included collecting eyes from the dead for research on pigmentation, finding twins and pregnant women for use in Mengele's experiments, and administering the cyanide-based insecticide Zyklon B in the gas chambers. I was very good at my job. I couldn't even estimate the number of deaths for which I was personally responsible.

After many years living in Argentina, I set sail to Mexico. I made my way north through the continental United States and Canada to Alaska, where, they say, it doesn't matter who you were but only who you've become. But, take my word for it, you can reinvent who you are for others, but not for yourself. There is no escaping what you know is your own truth.

Sometimes I still hear the wailing screams of the faceless women my father brought home, still picture my uncle's helpless patients in the charge of a madman, still hear the ruckus and smell the faint wisps of deadly fog escaping through the walls of the death chamber at Auschwitz. And I would be lying if I said these memories didn't bring with them a tinge of maniacal delight. I've learned to hide displays of these feelings, but I cannot hide from myself what I am.

I am a Munger, son of a slayer, nephew to a sociopath, cousin to a murderer, brother to an assassin, assistant to the Angel of Death. In short, I am a monster, and I fear that the monster's blood courses through your veins, as well, Peter and Randal. I pray that I am wrong.

Do what you will with this information, my nephews. But, as I shrug off this mortal coil, I can only hope that you choose to join me and spare the world any further pain the presence of our dreadful family may bring.

In closing, let me leave you with a saying from the old country: Ich drücke dir die Daumen, which means "I'll cross my fingers for you."

Sincerely,

Uncle Walter

Petey looked up from the letter and saw Randal lost in thought.

"What do you make of this?" Petey asked.

"I don't know. Do you think it's true?"

Petey shrugged. "Ma never told us much about the Munger side of the family. But this all sounds a little ... farfetched, don't you think?"

Randal frowned and nodded slowly. "But what if it is true?"

"It's not our fault what our ancestors may have done."

"So, we just ignore it?"

"We could try to find out if it's true."

"And what if it is? What do we do then?"

"I don't know. Make amends, I guess. For the terrible things in our family's past."

Randal made a face. "If this letter is true, we're talking maybe a thousand or more people dead because of the Mungers. How are we supposed to make amends for that?"

"Well...."

"And what if we're monsters, Petey? Deep down, I mean. Have you never had a shameful thought? Never wished anyone dead?"

Petey felt a stillness come over him. "What you think is one thing; what you do is another." But there was no surety in his voice. "We never bothered no one, Randal. Just minded our own business. All our life."

"But what if that's not our true destiny?"

"What do you mean?"

"I mean, wolves are wolves, and sheep are sheep. Neither can become the other by wishing it."

"No," Petey said. "I guess not." He scratched his chin.

ONE THING THE LETTER accomplished was to snap the Munger boys from their lethargy. Petey lined up new handyman jobs, and Randal weeded his neglected garden. To the outside world, all signs pointed to the boys having more or less recovered from the loss of their mother and getting on with their small existence.

But what no one could have imagined was what seethed beneath Petey's and Randal's outer shells as a result of reading Uncle Walter's letter. It was as if a dab of murky darkness had been added to their compositions. Not much more than a drop or so, to be sure, but enough to slightly alter their perceptions and take their thoughts on darker turns.

Petey was adjusting the pneumatic closer on Rosa Garcia's screen door when, out of the blue, he asked her, "Mrs. Garcia, do you know anything about my father's family?"

"Your mother never talked much about them." He could tell at once she was hiding something.

"I know, but have you heard *anything* about the Mungers? You were probably her closet friend."

"We were friends. Your mother was a good woman."

"Can you tell me what she did say about them?"

Rosa looked like she'd just stepped in a cow pie. "I don't like gossip. Gossip is the voice of the devil."

"You do know something, then."

He watched her frame her thoughts carefully before she spoke. "All I know is that your mother had some suspicions. About your father and grandfather."

"What kind of suspicions?"

She paused a long time. "Wicked ones." Rosa looked genuinely pained by this revelation. "That's all I'm going to say."

Petey finished fixing the door. "I'll do the rest of the work tomorrow if you don't mind, Mrs. Garcia. I have something else I need to take care of today."

It was fifteen minutes from Rosa's front door to the parking lot across from St. Helen's Episcopal Church in Wadena. The 1950 rust-bucket Chevy 3150 pickup that Petey got around in had belonged to his father. The engine was prone to missing and sputtering, and it got just under eight miles to the gallon, but it kept stubbornly running year after year (with Petey's assistance), well after the truck's odometer froze at 999,999 a decade or so ago.

He walked across the parking lot in his overalls and flannel work shirt to the First Street entrance of the Wadena City Library, a one-story brick building. Inside, he located the bank of computers, signed the user log, and sat down in front of a screen.

He peered at it a moment, reacquainting himself with the computer's workings. He'd played around on computers in the library before, years ago, but never with a specific purpose.

Petey clicked the little arrow in a couple of squares and pulled up the Google search engine. He typed: ENOCH MUNGER ST PAUL MN.

At a quarter to five, the librarian reminded him that it was almost closing time. He looked up dazed. He'd been on the machine almost four hours.

"Thanks," he said absentmindedly, standing up and shambling from the building.

On the drive home, the facts he'd learned about his family that day swam around in his brain, trying to interlock with one another. The only mention of Enoch Munger that he could find was in Hannah Munger's obituary. He learned from this that his grandmother was survived only by his father. His grandfather had passed years before in a house fire.

There was ample information elsewhere, though, on the other members of the Munger clan. Uncle Walter's horror stories about the Werewolf of Heidelberg, the insane doctor of Mannheim, the familial slayings by Dirk Munger, and Uncle Walter's shameful role in the holocaust all proved to be true. If anything, Uncle Walter had spared Randal and him most of the grisly details.

When Petey pulled the Chevy 3150 pickup onto their homestead land, he stood outside the old house and stared at the horizon. Smoke from forest fires clear up in Ontario feathered the air and made the sun a faded-orange glow. Randal stepped from the front porch and joined him. They looked at the smoky skyline together in silence.

"I went to the library in Wadena," Petey said at last. "Near as I can tell, what Uncle Walter wrote in that letter, it's all true. Every word of it."

Randal nodded. "I figured it was."

"I wish I didn't know."

"Me, too."

"The weight of all that evilness, it bears down on a fellow."

"It does."

Randal put an arm around him. They spent a long time looking at the sanguine orb of the setting sun. And when they considered how much wickedness and barbarity took place beneath it every waking day, they saw it was a miracle the very earth itself wasn't awash in the blood of humankind.

At last, they went inside, where Randal had a pot of vegetable stew simmering on the cookstove. They ate in silence, neither knowing what more to say.

That winter, Randal passed away. Petey found his brother flat on his back in the snow behind the old shed, looking up at the winter sky in wonder. Petey had half a mind to lay down beside him, hold his hand, and await himself the trumpeting of the angels. He didn't, of course.

But many a time, in the coming days, Petey reflected on whether or not he'd made the right choice.

He busied himself in his handyman work, and when he wasn't working, he discovered newfound solace in the slow, comforting burn of Wild Turkey whiskey.

He ordered a book in the mail that someone had written on the Werewolf of Heidelberg. It was translated from German and read a little rough in spots, but he learned from it that old Günter was not the first entry in the Munger hall of shame.

Günter's father had been a crooked policeman known for his quick and often questionable use of firearms. He'd abandoned his family, running off to Bavaria with a cabaret singer. One of the father's brothers was a shadowy figure who worked in a slaughterhouse and, eventually, went to prison for beating his wife to death. Günter's father had one other brother. Little was known about this one, except he was so badly disfigured that the neighborhood children ran shrieking at the sight of him.

Petey tracked down a few other books. One, on Josef Mengele and his hideous experiments, devoted an entire chapter to Uncle Walter and his role in the Nazi death camp.

Some nights he would read from these books at the kitchen table, and some nights he would read from the family Bible, but mostly he would just stare into the shadows, sipping Wild Turkey and remembering what it was like in the old house when Ma and Randal were still there with him.

Back when his family was just a rural curiosity, not the tail end of a trail writ in blood and gore.

That little drop of murky darkness he had felt upon first digesting Uncle Walter's letter became a steady *drip-drip-drip*, fouling him at his core. His long-dead relatives began reaching for him from their graves, their touch icy yet somehow comforting. He could either be with them or free-float through the rest of his life. Maybe it was just the loneliness that got to him, but loathsome as they were, his wicked family at least moored him to something.

THAT SPRING, Ralph Peterson's check arrived for the upcoming year's rental on the Mungers' back ninety acres. Only, it was made out for $8,000 instead of the usual $9,620.

"What gives, Mr. Peterson?" Petey asked on the phone. "Seems to me you're $1,600 dollars short on the rent for my land."

Ralph cleared his throat. "Well, you know, Petey, it's been a tough year for farming. The truth is, I feel a slight adjustment is necessary. Given the state of things, and all."

"You agreed to pay $106.89 an acre, which is already only half of what that land is worth."

"Land is worth what people are willing to pay for it, son. Maybe that's the businessman in me talking, but I paid what I think is a fair price."

"You agreed to pay $9,620 a year. That's the deal. Far as I know, that's the same price you paid thirty years ago. Maybe I should be figuring in a little extra for inflation."

Ralph was silent for a moment. Then he said, "Listen, Petey, it's just you on the homestead these days. It's not like you're splitting the money with your mother and brother anymore. $8,000 is still a lot of cash for a freewheeling bachelor like yourself."

"So, you're going back on your word. That's the way it is with you, huh?"

Petey could picture Ralph Peterson's flabby face going red.

"If you don't like my offer, you can tear up the check. That's your right. But I'm standing firm on the $8,000. It just ain't worth it to me to pay more."

Petey hung up on him.

It was just like that chiseler to try to take advantage of Petey, now that Randal wasn't there to back him up. Well, Ralph Peterson was going to regret this, Petey vowed.

In the end, he cashed the check. The electric co-op wanted its money, and the taxman waited just around the corner. But every night when he sat at the kitchen table with his books and his Wild Turkey, Petey stewed, the anger gurgling up in him like hot lava.

He knew how the Werewolf of Heidelberg would handle a miser like Ralph Peterson: slice him up into steaks and grind the leftovers into sausages. Dr. Hans, if he weighed in on this, would probably favor a little surgery of his own. And Uncle Wally? Hell, he'd just scoop out Ralph's eyes, draw a circle in the dirt and play himself a game of marbles.

Some nights he felt the still air stir behind him, pulsing like the beating wings of an angel. The Angel of Death—not Mengele but the real angel—swooped up from its deathly hollow to keep company with him and his wicked thoughts. And to whisper in his ear.

One night he had just cracked open a fresh bottle, bought with the last of Ralph Peterson's blood money when he heard the crackle of a car on the gravel driveway. He stepped out onto the porch and made his way through his weedy and overgrown yard.

Pulling to a halt in a shiny black sedan was none other than Ralph Peterson himself.

The fat man climbed out awkwardly and closed the door. He carried an envelope in one flabby hand.

"Hey, Petey," he called, nodding in his straw gardener hat.

"Mr. Peterson," Petey said grimly.

"I just came by to clear the air." He closed the gap between them, huffing a little. "Pearl's been on my case ever since I sent you that check. Says I wasn't being fair to you. With your losses and all. I told her I was just being a businessman. But you know women. You can't reason with 'em."

Ralph pulled out a sweat rag and wiped his neck.

"Anyway, this is the rest of your money. $1,620. Just like we agreed on." He handed Petey the envelope. "I'll have to make do somehow, but what's fair is fair."

Petey's lips curled back over clenched teeth. "That's awfully decent of you, Mr. Peterson."

"Well, I'd cross the devil himself before I'd get on the wrong side of Pearl. She might not look it, but she can get mean as a snake when she puts her mind to it."

"Why don't you come inside for a drink?" Petey's words seemed to come from somewhere beyond his body. They resounded in the falling night, flat and dull as a well-traveled Lincoln penny. "We'll drink to bygones being bygones."

Ralph mopped his chin with the rag. "Well ... maybe just one. I didn't think you were a drinker, Petey."

"Not much else to do out here by myself."

"I hear you, son."

They went inside, and Petey found a pair of pint Mason jars in the cupboard. They sat at the table in front of the cookstove. Petey poured them each a generous snootful. "Sorry. I don't have nothing to mix it with except water. You want water?"

"That ain't necessary."

They sipped.

"Anyway," Ralph said, "I just wanted to bury the ax. No hard feelings?"

Petey's eyes took on a shimmer. "I was just wondering how a cranky old businessman like you could get himself such a sweet bride as Mrs. Peterson. You got yourself a good one there."

Ralph took this as a compliment. "I guess that's true enough." He set his gardener hat on the table.

The Wild Turkey bloomed in Petey's belly, blending with the drops of darkness inside him that had by then become maybe a hundred drops. Maybe a thousand. The injuries visited on him by fortune and fate, and the savage legacy of his twisted forebears had, since Randal's passing, altered him in some fundamental way. His innermost workings had become bent and blighted and almost unrecognizable. But that was on the inside. On the outside, he looked the same as always.

"It's too bad you can't take it with you," Petey said.

"Excuse me?"

"The money, I mean. The fruits of your labor. It doesn't quite seem fair that a person works all his life to accumulate wealth, only to leave it behind when he departs this Earth."

Ralph gave him a puzzled look.

"You can't take riches through the pearly gates, can you, Mr. Peterson?"

"I guess not."

"Odd, isn't it? How we work ourselves to death just to survive, then we die anyway, and death is the same whether you're a well-off farmer or a pissant handyman. Don't you think, Mr. Peterson?"

"I'm not sure I know what you're getting at, Petey."

"Doesn't it seem odd to you that when we pass on all we take with us is maybe a good feeling about having gone to church or helped someone change a tire or whatnot. In a sense, our whole lives come to nothing, as they say."

"Well ... that's a dismal outlook, isn't it, son?"

"It's true, though. You can't deny it. We die with the same nothing we were born with."

Ralph drained his glass, then wiped his forehead with the sweat rag. "Well, it's been a real joy talking with you this way, Petey, but Pearl will be expecting me home for dinner." He started to wobble upward from his chair.

"Hold on, Mr. Peterson. What's your hurry? Have another drink. It'll do you good."

Ralph settled his weight back into the chair. "Well, maybe one more. Then I'll have to head home. You understand, don't you?"

Petey grinned, not exactly pleasantly. "Course I understand. Even a simple man like me understands that family is all that makes life worth enduring."

Ralph eyed him, looking slightly wounded. "Son, it's not too late for you. You could get yourself a widow or a divorcée to settle down with. Your best years could still be ahead of you."

"Mr. Peterson, my best years are so far behind me I can't even see the trail of dust they left."

Petey held up his mason jar of Wild Turkey and tipped it toward Ralph. "To the best years of our life."

Ralph lifted his jar and joined in the toast.

But before Ralph could say anything, Petey was on his feet, hunkered down on him, rawboned fingers coiled in boney fists. Petey's knuckles rocketed toward the fat man, the punch landing below one ear in the thick folds of Ralph's neck, whiplashing his head sideways. Ralph dropped his glass on the table, splashing Wild Turkey on his straw gardener hat and sweat rag. The chair skittered backward on the floor's worn linoleum.

"This here's been a long time coming, Mr. Peterson," Petey said flatly.

Clasping his neck, an expression of stunned horror on his face, Ralph looked up dully as the second blow came, tearing open his lips and rocking him backward to the floor, the wood chair busting to pieces beneath him in a thunderous crash. Ralph groaned as he tried to push his great bulk up from the floor, but Petey was quickly on him. Again and again, the angular fists rained down on Ralph, bruising and opening runnels of blood in the once smug face, pounding as the slumped head rolled from side to side.

Petey felt the bloodlust of a hundred years in the rapid smack of his flailing fists.

When he'd finished, it was hard to say which was worse off, Ralph's face or Petey's knuckles.

WHEN RALPH HADN'T COME HOME by seven o'clock, Pearl Peterson tried calling on Petey's house phone, then tried on Ralph's cell phone, but got no answer from either one. She called Rosa Garcia and asked her to check in at the Munger's and see if Ralph was still there. It wasn't like her husband to be late for dinner. She was starting to worry.

Rosa could have walked to the Munger homestead from her place, but it was getting dark, and she was getting old, and it seemed far easier to tool over in her late-model Honda Civic. When she arrived, she saw Ralph's immaculate sedan in the driveway next to Petey Munger's rusty old truck. The lights were on in Petey's kitchen, but things looked pretty quiet overall.

She made her way to the porch and was about to knock on the screen door when she saw through it why everything was so quiet inside.

"Oh, my!" she said, pulling the screen door by the handle and stepping into the kitchen.

The surrealism of the scene brought a sudden clarity to her vision. The horror of it kept her from drawing a breath.

On the floor in a pool of blood lay Ralph Peterson, his face looking like someone had taken a two-by-four to it. He wheezed up bubbles through his ruined lips.

And from the kitchen rafters dangled the form of Petey Munger, his neck stretched by thick rope. The handyman's eyes and mouth hung open, emptied at last of his troubled spirit. A housefly circled his nose.

On the kitchen table, speckled in blood and spilt whiskey, on a piece of typing paper was scrawled the message: MAY GOD HAVE MERCY ON US ALL.

It was signed "Petey, the last of the Sebeka Mungers."

The Pact

"Happiness is in the happy. But honor is not in the honored."
—Thomas Aquinas

Six mirrors lined the little round room, facing the center where Alessandro Yezdan stood at the altar, slicing the palm of his hand with a keen-edged black dagger. As blood welled up in the open cut, he made a fist and squeezed droplets of the vital fluid into a smoking, brass-plated censer. The blood sizzled on the glowing embers of incense.

"From the wide, ancient skies of Baala Sheem, where storm gods unsheathe swords of lightning, I call upon Valafar, succubus supreme in the nightmare army of Thamuz, queen of falsehoods."

He picked up the handbell from the altar's surface and shook it three times. Its peals echoed jarringly in the tiny chamber.

"Valafar, who causes all shadows to fall, come from your coven of three, from the deep roots of your shoreless void to the side of your True Believer. I beg you, come to me."

Alessandro, with his heavy eyebrows and hooked Italian nose, lifted bulging eyes skyward and dropped to his knees. His pockmarked face was the color of faded leather, and his grimace revealed stumps and crags of rancid brown teeth.

In the open portal overhead—hazy with the remnant smoke of late-summer fires blazing many miles to the north—appeared a great fluttering hawk who landed on the rim of the opening and peered down at him malevolently. From her sharp, curved beak, the bird dropped a tender twig of green leaf onto the altar, just as the book said she would.

Alessandro stood, picked up the sprig, and added it to the contents of the smoldering censer.

Outside, thunder bellowed. A hard rain began to fall, drumming on the rooftop of his suburban home on Boone Avenue North in New Hope, Minnesota. Inside, the censer erupted in a flash of flame that quickly permeated the room with the charged scents of petrichor and ozone.

He looked up, his sight swimming with flickering black spots.

A bolt of lightning silhouetted the hawk, limning her predatory beak and talons. She leaned her feathered crown in as if deciding whether or not to strike at him.

Now came the tricky part: the sloughing off of his earthly form so that he might communicate in the astral realm with the summoned entity. This was where things could go terribly wrong if fate so willed it.

True, he had slipped from his skin bag before in nighttime forays to ethereal dream worlds, but this time it was different. This time, he knew from Crowley's book that Valafar would hold the reins on his very survival. She could either extend a span for him to cross over to her, or she could cast him into the black abyss where he would plummet forever.

Or, the book had pointedly warned, she could simply eat him.

Rolling the dice on his destiny, he lifted himself from the world of solidity and substance, shedding his homely skin with practiced ease.

But when he emerged, it wasn't anything like the dream realm he'd entered before. Here he was not weightless. Here he was not free to roam unguarded through courtyards and houses and straying city streets, expansive as the horizon, careless as a gypsy moth. Instead, here he felt the significant burden of the cosmos on his insignificant mortal shoulders.

He tremored before stars that blinked down at him like a million eyes, before twirling planets of murky haze that pivoted toward him on their axes, before howling cosmic winds and stinging sands and bursts of panicky shadow that flapped past him on all sides. And from the center of this tumult, on a silver trail of moondust, approached a figure grim and serene. She took the form of Diana, consort of Lucifer, huntress of celestial woodlands and plains, and her beauty was almost blinding.

"Who calls to Valafar from the world of men?" Her voice, dark and full, reverberated in his ears over the cacophony.

"I ... I." He struggled to lift his voice over the din. "Alessandro. Alessandro Yezdan."

She stood not a dozen yards from him, her slender feet poised at the silvery path's end, just beyond where the awful black chasm began its yawn toward Alessandro. He stared at her, at her arched eyebrows and the clean line of her nose, at her pert lips and her elegant neck and shoulders, at the citrine hair elaborately pleated and braided.

"No one has called to me from your world for some time, Alessandro." She tilted her head slightly. "Have you come to barter?"

Overwhelmed, he stammered out meaningless sounds before successfully seizing control of his voice. "Yes ... yes, exactly." The book had said to set his fears aside and make his case as clearly and concisely as possible, but now that seemed far easier said than done, especially amid this celestial roar.

Here is my chance, he thought. *Don't blow it.*

Grappling through his terror, he launched hesitantly into his story, gathering strength as he went: "That is, my father was a military man—a sergeant in the Army. I always wanted to be like him, but I hadn't the strength of character, and he saw through all my flaws, and I'm afraid I was a disappointment to him.

"I tried joining the military, but I washed out in basic training and returned home a failure. That failing haunted me for all my life. I went to college for a while, but that didn't stick either. I ended up drifting from one dead-end job to the next through the course of my entire life. I never married. I never made a mark on any kind upon my world."

He eyed the endless blackness that lay just beyond his feet and realized that if therein lay his fate, it would perhaps be appropriate.

"Go on," she prodded.

"On his death bed, I'll never forget the look on Father's face. It told me that, in his eyes, my life amounted to nothing. Absolutely nothing. And he was right. After his funeral, I decided to try one more time to make something of myself. It was too late to impress him, but I could still make my mark if I could only find a way."

Alessandro had long toyed with the esoteric. With tarot cards and Ouija boards, and mass-produced paperback books on magic. He'd put these in the same category as slasher films and lurid novels: merely entertainment, not to be taken too seriously. But what if there *was* something legitimate to the occult? What if beyond the physical world there lay a dominion he could tap into for his self-betterment? If indeed true, he reasoned, then pursuing this path would be his most direct and potentially fruitful course of action.

"I saw no other option," he said. "I'd already passed the age of fifty and could feel the press of mortality. So, I decided to devote every free moment to the study of forbidden knowledge. I investigated book after book, the older, the better, and learned many things, but not the path to the total reformation for which I yearned. Then one day at a book fair, I came upon a slim volume called *The Secret Teachings of the Hermetic Order of the Golden Dawn*, alleged to have been written by Aleister Crowley, the self-proclaimed wickedest man in the world. Though familiar with his other books, which I'd found largely incomprehensible, this was one I'd never heard of before, and at first, I doubted its authenticity. The seller, who had no idea who the Golden Dawn or Crowley were, said he'd bought it as part of a lot at an estate sale in Bemidji. I took it off his hands for five dollars, thinking there might be something of value in it even it turned out to be a swindle. The seller, frankly, looked relieved to be rid of it.

"When I brought it home and had a chance to study its yellowing pages, I saw that it was part of a very limited edition, one of a hundred, which would make it the rarest book in my collection. It could be the only remaining copy in existence. As I thumbed through the profusely illustrated pages, it struck me that this was exactly what I'd been searching for."

He'd constructed his circular altar room in the attic of his house following the precise instructions in the book. He'd practiced the rituals laid out to establish and strengthen his esoteric powers. Over time, he learned to influence the weak-willed. He learned to bend fortune his way in minor circumstances. He even learned to make himself invisible to others for brief periods. When he felt sufficiently secure in these skills, he turned his attention to summoning.

"It took me more than a year of studying the step-by-step instructions of Crowley's book to give me sufficient power and courage—pitiful as they may be—to stand before you now, Valafar."

With a wave of her hand, she silenced the maelstrom around them and formed a rickety bridge that spanned the abyss and provided him with a way to her. "Approach," she said, gesturing with her chin and stepping back.

Without hesitation, Alessandro moved forward. He knew from the book he had to trust the bridge to hold, no matter how flimsy it seemed, no matter how great his fear of falling. He had to walk with headstrong purpose, or all his work would have been for naught. So, boldly, he marched across the span even as it swayed and groaned beneath him. Even as he passed through the moist and fetid breath of gaping eternity below.

As his feet came to rest on the far lip of spongy soil, he stood before her, not sure what to do next.

"I don't grant favors, Alessandro. I only make pacts. You understand that, don't you?"

"Yes."

"I can do things for you, but only if you do things for me."

"I understand."

"And you must be aware that what I demand of you may seem beyond what you are capable of providing. But if you fail to remit my chosen tariffs, the consequences for you will be tragic in the extreme."

"I understand."

She appraised him skeptically, then said, "You want to be a military man?"

"I want to be an *important* military man—a general. I want to be famous and admired for my wisdom and daring. I want to be wealthy and enjoy the rewards of being a wealthy man. I want powerful allies, a beautiful wife, and a lovely family. I want to be handsome and to live a long life. If you can grant me all this, I'll repay you anything you wish."

"Very well," she said. "But I warn you: do not fail to deliver on that promise."

That said, she waved her hands, and Alessandro Yezdan stepped into his all-new life.

THE JOHN F. KENNEDY Conference Room is in the basement of the West Wing of the White House. In it, around a long, paper-cluttered table, sat some of the highest officials in government, and Alessandro knew the name and function of every one of them.

There was, of course, the President, white-haired in an open-throated polo shirt, studying a missive at the head of the table. A long-faced fellow bent over the President's shoulder and pointed at something on the page the President was examining. That was the national security adviser. Whatever he was conveying to the commander in chief was lost in the general hubbub of grave conversations among advisers, assistants, and military personnel assembled around the table.

"We're getting reamed in the press," the oval-faced Navy captain with the gray crewcut said, leaning in on Alessandro's left. "Fox News is having a field day with this."

Alessandro nodded. "Invasion is always more inspiring than withdrawal."

"The President will have to take some kind of action."

Alessandro again nodded. "My guess is a drone strike on an ISIS-K target."

These words came assuredly from Alessandro's lips, but sometimes he still had the sense that his words belonged to someone else.

Raw news feed of the Kabul airport filled one of the room's large video screens with images of nervous soldiers and terrified Afghan civilians. The camera broke to a close-up of a weeping, hysterical Afghan woman, her voice mercifully muted. It didn't take much imagination, though, to speculate on what she was saying. Given a chance, the Taliban would kill her and possibly her entire family because she had worked for the Americans. She needed to get out of the country; to the U.S., to Italy, to anywhere not governed by fundamentalists intent on turning the hands of time back five-hundred years.

The final withdrawal of American troops from the decades-long war in Afghanistan couldn't have gone more miserably. As the negotiated departure date approached, Taliban fighters had marched across the country taking back city after city, barely firing a shot. No one had expected them to have such an easy time of it. The Afghan people, by and large, just rolled over.

It was the fall of Saigon all over again.

To make the situation worse, within days of the official deadline for withdrawal of American forces from the country, a suicide bomber had detonated an explosive device at the Kabul airport, killing thirteen service members and dozens of Afghan civilians. ISIS-K, an Islamic State group not affiliated with the Taliban, claimed responsibility for the attack.

The President looked up from the page, said something politely dismissive to his national security adviser, and focused down the table at Alessandro. The President waved him over.

"Yes, Mr. President?" he said, standing at parade rest beside the most powerful man in the world.

The President beckoned him closer. "I've got more problems than Carter has little liver pills." He shook his head. "I'm not complaining, you understand. My father always said, 'Never complain, never explain.' But I'm telling you, Al, I've got a roomful of smart-asses here who want me either to carpet-bomb Kabul, or wait until we get the last of our folks out of Afghanistan and then carpet-bomb the whole damn country."

"Yes, Mr. President."

"It's all bullshit, of course, but I understand how they feel about those troops being taken out by that ISIS-K suicide bomber. I feel just awful for those young people who were killed and injured, and I feel for the families. Who wants to be the last American soldier killed in Afghanistan?"

"No one, Mr. President."

The dark blue eyes he leveled at Alessandro looked almost black. "What do you think we should do? Tactical strike?"

"Yes, Mr. President. I'd use our on-the-ground intelligence to pinpoint an ISIS-K target and launch a drone strike. Keep the Taliban out of it, as much as possible. That would be my advice."

The President paused, thinking things over. Then he said, "I think that's what I'm going to do. I'll need you join me at the press briefings on this afterwards."

"Of course, Mr. President."

THE GOVERNMENT SEDAN rolled through the open, wrought-iron gates of the stone mansion on 30th Street Northwest. Four stories tall in the fashionable Beaux-Arts style, the residence featured a heated walkway, a custom-etched exterior, and an entrance that led through four towering columns and an arched, dual-glass door. At night, with its massive windows all lit up and the tracings of its indirect lighting glowing softly, the house was truly magnificent. Worth every penny of the $18 million Alessandro paid for it.

"Have a good night, Jim," he said to his driver. It had been three years since Alessandro had started his new life, but he still marveled at the idea of having his own driver.

"You, too, sir."

The glass doors opened on a reception foyer of polished white marble whose rotunda ceiling rose clear past the second story. An immense overhead chandelier lit the way up a sweeping, carpeted staircase to the bronze doors of five bedroom suites and the master suite. On the main floor, to the left, lay two living rooms, two dining rooms, a library stocked with all of Alessandro's favorite books, a theater, and a kitchen with restaurant-caliber appliances, a well-stocked pantry, and a walk-in refrigerator.

To the right, a double-glass door opened onto the outdoor terrace and the heated, enclosed swimming pool. The Caribbean calypso music favored by Karen drifted in from the outside, as did the splashing of Tim and some of his friends in the pool. One of the children laughed.

As was his habit, Alessandro jingled the keys in his pocket as he walked. ·

Next to the pool, on handmade poly rattan lounge chairs rested Karen and Jane-somebody, the mother of Tim's swim friends. The women sipped cocktails.

He stepped out to join them, still carrying his black briefcase, and smiled. "Evening, ladies."

Karen, in her orange mesh bikini with open side panels and a zippered front, padded over and kissed him full on the mouth. She tasted warm and inviting.

"We saw you on TV, General," Jane-somebody said. "You're quite charismatic on the screen."

"Thank you, Jane." He swung his free arm around Karen's bare shoulders and turned toward his son in the pool. "And how are you this evening, sport?"

Tim wiped water from his eyes. "Great, Dad. I got an A in spelling." Beside Tim bobbed two skinny, tow-headed boys who stared in admiration at Alessandro.

"That's wonderful. Evening, boys."

"After school, we had éclairs," Tim said.

"I'm afraid we have a weakness for pastries from Boulangerie Christophe," Jane said. "I hope we haven't spoiled his dinner."

"Not at all," Alessandro replied. "Trust me, when it comes to food, Tim is a bottomless pit."

"Aren't all boys his age?" she said.

One of Tim's friends seemed particularly taken with the General. A year or two Tim's junior, the boy's name was Justin. He'd been over to the Yezdans' before with his mother, Jane, and his older brother, whose name escaped Alessandro. Justin's pale, freckled face flashed a grin that featured a missing front tooth.

Alessandro was about to turn from the boy to the women when a chilling voice spoke in his head, and it was all he could do to keep the horror from showing in his face.

THE FIRST TIME Valafar had spoken to him after the summoning was nearly two years ago. It was regarding his chauffeur's tomcat, a kitten barely off his mother's teat. A soft and furry tan bundle of precocious energy with lively green eyes and a petite pink tongue that licked Alessandro's thumb when Sergeant Philips handed him over at the end of the workday.

"He's a beauty, Jim," the General said. "Should make a wonderful pet."

Jim's face glowed with pride. He had the neat, scrubbed look of a Nebraska farm boy, and any praise from the General pleased him greatly. "It's for Sarah, our oldest, sir. She's been bugging us to get her a kitten, and we thought, well, she's old enough now, almost ten, and owning an animal will teach her some responsibility. I picked it up at a pet store while you were in your meeting today. I hope you don't mind."

"Not at all."

But, in truth, the General did mind. It wasn't because his driver had abandoned his post, so to speak, but because when Alessandro petted the little tom, a dreadful sensation washed over him. Valafar, who hadn't communicated with him since he'd summoned her more than a year before, had just made her presence known.

The voice out of nowhere startled him. "Kill the cat," she whispered. "I want his bloody entrails on my altar."

At first, he tried to believe he'd imagined it. After all, why would the succubus supreme in the nightmare army of Thamuz want this adorable little fur ball snuffed?

But in his heart, he knew what he heard, and he'd heard correctly.

Perhaps she loathed the kitten's naked sweetness. Perhaps it was a test of Alessandro's resolve. Either way, he knew the deed must be done, even as he handed the tom back to Jim.

Secretly, he'd always hoped Valafar would never actually exact a toll on the new life she'd awarded him. Or if she did come calling for her remuneration, it would amount to some petty charge: a minor inconvenience; a new ceremony perhaps, or a renewal of his dark vow. He now realized how foolish he'd been to think she'd expect of him so little.

But in a sense her demand was *little, wasn't it?* Miniscule, really. What was the life of this cat compared to the reward of living in his personal wonderland? Besides, to deny her was unthinkable.

What was the phrase she had used? "If you fail to remit my chosen tariff, the consequences for you will be tragic in the extreme."

As he sat in the back seat of the limousine, headed home, he made his plan.

In the coming days, he encouraged Jim to talk about the kitten, to reveal tiny facts about the kitten's routine: where he slept, where he ate, where they kept his litter box. Bit by bit, Alessandro assembled a workable blueprint.

Then, at last, came the news for which he'd waited.

Sarah, an earnest if not particularly talented pianist, was to perform with a dozen other classmates in a school recital.

"She's playing that John Lennon song, 'Imagine.' She's been practicing it all week, driving us buggy. I mean, it's a nice tune and everything, but the way Sarah plays it, it's almost like a funeral march." Jim smiled slyly. "And she plays it *over and over*. But, after Friday night we should be finally done with it. Hopefully. For a while, anyway."

"I'm sure she'll be great," the General said. He now knew that Friday night the Philips house would be empty, except for the kitten.

That night, while thumbing through *Lolita* in the larger of the two living rooms, Alessandro looked up at Karen and nonchalantly suggested that Tim stay overnight at a friend's house on Friday, and he encouraged Karen to go out that night with some of her gal pals for cocktails.

"You deserve a night out," he said.

He'd knock around the big house by himself, maybe in his underpants and robe, he joked. Read a book or watch a movie.

Karen readily agreed, and made the necessary arrangements.

When Friday evening came, Jim dropped the General off at his front walkway. Before closing the sedan's door, Alessandro leaned in and said, "Tell Sarah, good luck at her recital tonight."

"I will, sir."

He shut the door with a solid thud and watched as the car drove out through the wrought-iron gates, which then closed automatically behind it.

Once inside the house, he found Karen's note attached to the refrigerator. "Enjoy your peace and quiet tonight, General." She addressed him by his rank when she was feeling playful. They must've just missed one another.

He changed clothes quickly, replacing his dress greens with blue jeans, a coal-black flannel shirt, and a Washington Nationals baseball cap. In the garage, he fired up the midnight-blue Toyota Camry they used for around-town driving and slid off into the night.

The Philipses lived in a duplex townhouse on 38th Street Northwest, just eight minutes from where Alessandro and his family lived. It must've been a struggle for Jim to afford such a place on a buck sergeant's salary, but it was a rental, and Alessandro had the impression that Jim's father helped them out financially.

He drove past the white-sided home, which attached at the hip— Chang and Eng style—to another white-sided home. The neighbor's townhouse was an exact mirror image of Jim's.

Alessandro had never been to Jim's house, but he knew from a Google Maps street view that parking was in the rear, off an alley. He pulled up to the curb on the side street near where the alley emptied in the general direction of Stoddert Elementary School, the site of the piano recital, and waited.

Ten minutes later, just as the first of the street lights came on, a silver 2008 Dodge Grand Caravan with a dented passenger-side front quarter panel pushed out of the alleyway and onto the side street where Alessandro sat hunched with the baseball cap tugged down over his eyebrows. He waited (*One Mississippi, two Mississippi*) until the Dodge was long gone, then snuck out onto the street and entered the alley.

He had to be mindful of cameras. Nowadays, many homes came complete with surveillance, especially in decent neighborhoods. He used his old trick of turning himself invisible for brief periods of time, but he wasn't sure the trick would work with electronic eyes, so he plotted his course to give the cameras as little to look at as possible.

It wasn't like when he was a kid, busting into neighbor's houses. Back then, a home intruder could take his time, riffling through drawers of panties or searching closets for hidden stacks of *Playboy* magazines or similar treasures, and as long as he got in and out cleanly, he would never be caught.

Halfway down the alley was the car pad where Jim parked the Caravan. A plash of oil marked the spot where it had sat. He walked briskly past into the backyard and followed a pathway to the rear door. Jim had once let slip that they kept a spare latchkey under the back mat and, sure enough, there it was.

Alessandro fetched it and twisted it in the backdoor lock.

Something of the old thrill came back to him, walking into a vacant house with mischief on his mind. It was odd how the memories of his real past and the General's fictitious past overlapped. His clearest remembrances of the latter were of West Point, where he'd never actually been, and his infantry years in Iraq and Afghanistan, where he'd never actually served. He remembered his wedding in Topeka, his honeymoon in Hawaii, the day Karen's water broke and Tim was born. He recalled writing the book, *A Pleasure to Serve*, full of the General's war stories. It was the bestseller that first brought him to the White House's attention. He'd followed it up with the sequel, *Don't Call Me a Hero*, which not only topped *The New York Times* Bestseller List, but also earned him a nomination for a Pulitzer. The book money paid for his mansion.

Between the lines, though, were shreds of his true life: the bug-eyed boy with jagged teeth ridiculed on the playground, the lonely bookworm who composed a fantasy existence based largely on stolen erotica, the window-peeper, the liar, the petty thief. All of this was him as well, though these memories were more distant and were wholly unavailable to the rest of the world.

Dying day radiated through the window coverings and blinds of the kitchen. A light shined over the stove. He crept past an island of cabinets into the living room. He listened. A soft mewling came from beneath a coffee table. Stalking from the shadows came the tomcat, blinking at him with oversized green eyes.

"Here, kitty, kitty," he said.

Carrying the tom under his shirt's dark flannel, he locked the door and replaced the key beneath the mat and crossed the yard into the alley. With the visor of his baseball cap pulled nearly to the bridge of his nose, he walked casually to the street entrance and around the corner to where the Camry rested against the curb.

He pulled out onto the road and was back to his empty home in under ten minutes.

THAT MONDAY MORNING, Jim arrived promptly at 5 a.m., long-faced and quieter than normal.

"Something bothering you, Jim?" Alessandro said as he slid into the backseat. "Did the recital go alright?"

Jim glanced back in the rearview mirror. "The recital went just fine, sir. There were lots of parents there, and the girls and boys performed amazingly well. Sarah's 'Imagine' was a hit with the audience."

"Good." He set his briefcase on the seat beside him. "Was there something else, then?"

"It's just that damn cat, sir. While we were at the recital, Benji just disappeared. I can't for the life of me figure out how he did it."

Alessandro tried not to let the tug in his belly affect his expression. "Did you look in the closets? When I was a boy, I had a tabby. She used to swipe at people's ankles from under the couch. We found her hiding all the time. In closets, under furniture, behind dressers. Once, we found her in the clothes drier. Still have no idea how she got in there."

"Well, sir, we couldn't find him anywhere. We looked off and on all weekend."

"I'm sure he'll show up, Jim," the General said, ending the conversation by opening his briefcase and examining his notes for the morning's staff meeting. The typed words seemed to be sliding around on the paper.

As it turned out, for all the skullduggery involved, taking the kitten had turned out to be the easy part of the operation. Dispatching him, well, that was another matter.

Alessandro had carried the cat up to the fourth story of the mansion, to the locked storeroom that concealed at its rear the round, mirrored altar room where he worshiped Valafar. Once a week, without fail, he went to his hidden chamber and recited the "Song of Subjugation" from *The Secret Teachings of the Hermetic Order of the Golden Dawn*: "From the limits of this hollow tube of human language, I call to the reaches where truth manifests from untruth, where the old gods are and always were, where the mighty and marvelous Valafar of the Three Devils resides in all her magical aspects. Beneath the black sun, beyond the realm of disorder, I gladly take up the yolk of servitude and subjugation. All work I do in your honor. With every breath, I praise you." And so on.

Having said all the words, Alessandro set the kitten on the flat of the altar, where he purred softly and looked wide-eyed around the room in all its reflections. As the General shook the handbell, the kitty cautiously roamed the altar from end to end, past the smoldering censer and the cutting edge of the black dagger.

It suddenly occurred to Alessandro how difficult it would be to kill this harmless creature.

In his military past, he recalled firefights in the mountains and deserts of Iraq and Afghanistan where enemy combatants clutched at their chests and tumbled under the onslaught of the M14 carbine rifle barking in his hands. He'd even earned medals for some of these battles and had written about them in his memoirs, but those experiences belonged to the General, not Alessandro, not really. Instead, they were the airy and pale memories of the artificial background required for him to inhabit his new role.

In truth, Alessandro had never before taken the life of any living being.

But he'd promised Valafar to obey her every command, and she had been quite specific in this case. "Kill the cat," she had whispered. "I want his bloody entrails on my altar."

He felt helpless to do anything other than heed her.

He tried tapping into his intellectual side, logic being a time-tested defense against sentiment, but he kept thinking about that tabby he'd owned as a boy. That was a real memory, not a manufactured one. The cat's name was Jinx. Often Jinx would follow him around the house, rubbing up against his leg or making a nest of his lap. He remembered how Jinx had vibrated while purring, how he would lick Alessandro's skin and somehow made the boy feel blameless and normal and unconditionally loved.

One day Jinx had wandered off and been hit by a car. Alessandro found him in the street, two blocks from home, looking more like a rug than a cat. The boy had felt collapsed and defeated.

The General now picked up the kitten on the altar top. He was going to say something to him. Something like, "You're going to a better place," but that seemed like a lie. So, instead, he gripped the cat's neck in two hands, apologized, and suddenly twisted.

He heard the neck snap, felt the dead weight drop. Something inside of him rose in concert, as if gravity had suddenly failed. As if the wringing of the poor animal's neck was such an outrage, it triggered some whorl in the binding threads of reality.

Then he picked up the dagger and began carving, moving as if in a dream, hot tears running down his cheeks.

THE DRONE ATTACK the U.S. launched in Kabul had appeared at first to be a brilliant success. Two ISIS-K facilitators were believed to have been in the targeted car, which was thought to carry munitions, perhaps for another airport bombing. However, satellite images later suggested that the car may have, in fact, been carrying an innocent civilian and that there were no bombs aboard. Of course, the keyword was "suggested." There was nothing really to disprove the Joint Chiefs' initial assessment. No one would ever know for certain, one way or the other. Probably.

"The President's approval ratings are tanking," said one of the generals coordinating the airlift of U.S. citizens from Afghanistan. This man had an oversized jaw and eyes that were too tiny to be trustworthy. In his Pentagon office, he put a hand on Alessandro's shoulder. "Let's hope we don't end up taking orders from that *other guy* again. We might all have to retire in disgrace."

Technically, the officer was probably being insubordinate, but his concern was understandable.

While the electorate largely supported the withdrawal from America's longest war, the way the U.S. handled it was not popular at all.

"Best for him to dig in on getting everyone vaccinated for Covid," Alessandro said, jangling the key ring in his pocket. "Get people's minds off foreign affairs."

Ultimately, the Kabul drone strike had proven a total disaster. In passing days, *The New York Times* confirmed that the victim of the drone-launched Hellfire missile hadn't been an ISIS-K bomber but a 43-year-old aid worker with a carful of topped-off water containers. Also killed in the fiasco were ten members of a family, including seven children. These revelations came in the wake of mounting criticism of the President for the way he'd conducted the entire evacuation.

America's longest war had ended in a debacle, leaving the fates of hundreds of Americans and maybe thousands of Afghan collaborators uncertain.

"People have to realize that war is a messy business." The shiny-faced Marine major shook his head. "It's not like cutting a cake at a birthday party."

Alessandro nodded, though the birthday cake analogy alluded him.

Truth be told, his mind wasn't entirely in the game.

Even with the passage of two years, he never gotten completely over slaying the kitten at Valafar's command, but he'd almost forgotten the intensity of the pain it had brought him. How the snapping of one feline neck and a little post-mortem butchery had filled him with revulsion and bitter self-loathing. How the sacrifice had cost him countless nights' sleep and a king-sized chunk of his humanity.

He had nearly forgotten all that when Valafar's second directive reopened his wound.

As he walked the Pentagon corridor to his office, absentmindedly clinking the keys in his pocket, the General's thoughts drifted to the previous night's calypso music, to Karen and Jane in colorful bikinis, to the laughter of children splashing in the water.

To Tim's pale and freckled friend, Justin, smiling a gap-toothed smile, as Valafar commanded in Alessandro's ear, "Kill the boy. Bring me his greasy heart on a platter."

The words had stopped him cold.

Behind the General's stoic expression, electric fear and dread ran rampant throughout his frame. He fought the urge to retch. Alessandro watched that carefree child beam up at him, unaware that the face he smiled into was that of Death itself.

But what could he do? It would be folly to ignore her demand.

Alessandro closed his office door behind him and sat down at his desk.

He wasn't sure how to even begin to meet Valafar's monstrous dictate.

That night at dinner, he gently prodded Tim for information.

"So, tell me about your friend, Justin," he said, scooping butter-bean casserole onto his fork.

"Justin's a good egg," Tim said, using the slang he'd picked up from some old gangster movie on television. "He has an Xbox and a million games."

"A million, eh?"

"Well, practically." Tim skewered a clump of cavatappi noodles onto the tines of his fork and took a big bite. "He has all the cool ones," he said around his mouthful.

"So, you like him for his toys?"

Tim chewed noisily. "Justin's my best friend. We're blood brothers. We swore a pinky oath." His eyes displayed to his father the gravity of this confession. He swallowed. "Sometimes we camp out in his backyard in a tent, when Mom lets me sleep over."

"Sleeping on the ground is good for the soul," Alessandro replied. "That's what we say in the infantry."

"Yeah, it's pretty cool. We play Scrabble in the tent at night, using flashlights. Sometimes we tell ghost stories."

"Maybe you should have another campout at Justin's," Alessandro suggested. "Before it gets too cold."

Tim's face lit up. "Could we, Mom?"

Karen smiled. "I'll call Jane tomorrow and see if we can set it up."

Alessandro nodded, stabbing into his casserole, his mind drifting to bleaker ruminations.

OF ALL THE CHANGES he had to get used to when stepping from his former life of disappointment and ruin into that of a military celebrity, the hardest to adjust to wasn't his sudden good looks nor his role as a White House advisor nor his history of triumphs on the battlefield nor his famous friends nor his vast wealth nor even having become overnight a father. It was Karen.

Valafar, to all appearances, had chosen the spouse for him perfectly.

Karen was astonishingly beautiful, beautiful in every classical sense: her hair, her face, her neck, the sweep of her shoulders, the contours of her flawless body. She could mesmerize him with the swell of her calf or the flex of an elbow, with the delicacy of her fingers when she gestured or the sensuous spread of her smile. Her posture was always impeccable.

Additionally, she was intelligent: knowledgeable but never overweening, opinionated but not overbearingly so. Content to link arms with him in formal settings, to banter good-naturedly with his work partners in informal ones, and to step back when he spoke, so as not to deflect from him the spotlight of attention.

She was the textbook definition of a caring mother and a faithful friend. And her willingness to please him sexually knew no bounds. In fact, she sometimes frightened him a little with the ease with which she bent to his every desire, no matter how debasing.

But there was something in her eyes that wasn't quite right. Something beyond their shimmering luster that occasionally revealed to him a glitch in her design: a hint of troubling vacantness at her core.

Whenever she showed it, he looked away.

Despite this, Alessandro knew in his heart that he did not deserve such a near-perfect mate. He knew it by the contrast she presented from the girls and women of his previous life: the sweaters, the pimpled, the ones with misshapen jaws, askew eyes, and chewed lower lips. The stammerers, the unbathed, the shoddily dressed, the socially inept. He had not been forced into celibacy by his former appearance, but he'd been limited to congress with those unfortunates whom his bulging eyes and pockmarked face didn't wholly revolt.

He could never shake the notion that Karen was out of his league.

"Well, it's all set," she said Wednesday night, looking her stunning self over a plate of cooked quinoa, black beans, corn, and chopped cilantro. "Justin's mom will pick you up after dinner on Friday."

"Alright!" Tim beamed up at her. "Woo hoo. Thanks, Mom."

"Be on your best behavior, son," Alessandro advised. "We wouldn't want Jane getting upset with you."

"Yes, Dad. I'll be good."

"I know you will. I'll get some pastries for you to bring along to share with your friends."

"Could you get some éclairs? I love éclairs."

"Sure."

"That's very thoughtful of you, General," Karen said, baring her perfect teeth.

Thoughtful, yes, but not in the way she assumed. Jane's family, he knew, was fond of pastries from Boulangerie Christophe. That Friday, he ordered a dozen of their richest pastries and had Jim pick them up. They came in a box with the trademark "C" on the lid.

Once alone with the box in his Pentagon office, Alessandro pulled from his top drawer a vial of pills, a spoon, and several of the pink sugar packets that he'd swiped from the food court. Cracking open several capsules, he mixed the contents with the sugar and a little water until it formed a thick paste.

The temazepam had originally been prescribed to him back when the kitten killing was still fresh in his mind and insomnia plagued his every night. Although the chronic disorder had left him after he used up his initial prescription, he kept a supply of the powerful sleep agent on hand for occasional sleepless bouts.

Using a pastry-filling injector, he added a healthy squirt of the temazepam mixture to each of the bakery delicacies. He wasn't sure if the drug had much of a taste, but if it did, he calculated the sugar would temper it.

That night, the Yezdans finished their meal and were clearing the table when Jane arrived to fetch Tim. After pleasantries and displays of gratitude all around, Tim was out the door wearing a backpack loaded with clothes and toys and carrying the box of tainted sweets.

Alessandro and Karen waved as the car departed through the wrought-iron gates.

Closing the door, he embraced his wife, held her tight, and kissed her. Her lips were cool and tasted of pleasure.

He led her up the stairs to their bedroom, where he made love to her on satin sheets, her legs wrapped around his, her lean body writhing wickedly under him.

They had just finished when the temazepam he'd slipped into her dinner coffee began to take effect. She grew drowsy, then curled up next to him and fell asleep with her head on his chest. He lay there for a long time, trying to read a new translation of Franz Kafka's short stories, stroking Karen's perfect hair.

When midnight struck, he rose, took a shower, then donned his dark clothing and crept out into the night.

THE YARD HAD NO FENCE, just a hedgerow along the back property line. From there, crouched in deep shadow, Alessandro could see the tent where the boys slept and the rear of the house where Jane and her husband slept. He thoughtfully fingered the keyring in his pocket.

The evening's full moon hid behind rafts of clouds, and all lay dark and quiet in his field of view, except for a tiny amber safety light that glowed over the house's rear door.

It isn't too late, he told himself. *I could still turn around, climb back in the Camry, and be home and in bed in a matter of minutes. Forget the whole adventure. Throw myself on Valafar's mercy. What's the worst she could do to me?*

The thought froze him, quite sure that the demon's worst was more horrific than anything he could imagine. An eternity, perhaps, trapped in a vile, gurgling slush of worm-laden carrion? Or maybe being torn apart daily by mad dogs and winged harpies in a tomb of flames? Or possibly being slowly reduced to bones by the incessant bites of flies and wasps in a lonely pit somewhere beyond the reaches of time. Valafar had no mercy, he was quite sure, and her wrath would come at him unflinchingly in some genuine pre-Medieval, Dante's *Inferno*, apocalyptic-vision-of-St.-John shit storm. His would likely be a fate whispered of by the Old Ones, a fate for the ages.

For the first time, he wished he'd never seen that Crowley book, never called up that devil, never agreed to that pact. But it was too late now to back out.

He wiped his lips on the black flannel sleeve of his shirt and inched toward the tent.

Blocking out all discursive thoughts, he moved like a straw man—like an automaton—oblivious to reason, unencumbered by conscience. He opened the tent's outer flap and peered in through the unzipped screen on three apparitions sleeping fitfully in sleeping bags on the tent's plastic floor. He pushed his way inside, into the chemical smell of the confined space, and let his eyes adjust to the dimness.

One of the figures stirred and sat up briefly, looked his way with a curious glance, then lay back down and returned to sleep. *Tim.* His Tim, having viewed through the gossamer veils of slumber into the face of his father the executioner. Upon awakening, would the boy remember having seen him? Would he be able to separate the sight from the phantasms of his dreams? And, even if he convinced himself that what he'd glimpsed he'd dreamt, would a part of him always wonder whether his father was indeed the monster who claimed the life of his little chum?

Alessandro fought down the sickness that threatened to boil up from his gut.

Leaning over, he located Justin, carefully lifted the slender boy, sleeping bag and all, and carried him from the tent.

In the backseat of the blue Camry, Justin rolled uneasily from side to side. He let out a sudden belch, and the air instantly filled with the unmistakable scent of vomit. In the rearview mirror, Alessandro glanced at the boy and saw Justin having difficulty breathing.

Keeping a steady foot on the pedal, he watched the road, watched the boy, then decided to pull over. He parked in a vacant church lot, opened the driver's side door, and went around to check on his passenger.

In the dome light, Justin lay with his cheek to the seat, his lips, face, and throat measurably swollen. The upward side of the boy's face festered with hives, and his breathing grew shallower by the moment. He tried speaking in his sleep, but the words came out all slurred and mumbly.

He must be having some dreadful reaction to the temazepam.

For an instant, Alessandro half considered speeding Justin to the nearest hospital. It was the only decent thing to do. But as he shifted into drive, he remembered Valafar's vile command: "Kill the boy. Bring me his greasy heart on a platter." Desperately, he worked to smother his surge of empathy. *I made a pact, and I must keep it. The boy must die. There is no other way.*

There is no other....

He drove and wept, feeling as much a helpless prisoner as was the shanghaied boy.

THE NEXT DAY was a Saturday. Karen slept in till an uncharacteristically late nine o'clock. Normally when she woke, she came instantly alert, as if someone somewhere threw a switch on her from "off" to "on." This day, though, she moved more slowly, less assuredly, taking pains to focus on the simplest tasks.

After-effects of the sleep drug, Alessandro thought, glad to be averted even in this small measure from the dark memories that had kept him awake all night.

She hunted up a robe and wrapped it around herself.

"Toast and coffee okay?" she asked, brushing back a swirl of disheveled hair.

"That would be great," he replied, trying to look cheerful.

She shuffled out the bedroom door on unsteady legs.

On the wall opposite the bed was an expensive Salvador Dali print. Though Alessandro found the surrealist an oddly troubled and dislikable man, Dali's talents as a painter were beyond reproach. At its best, his art opened for the casual viewer doors of perception on fantasy realms that were bizarre and yet strangely grounded in reality. The General had always found the paintings fascinating, even back in the bad old days when he was still bug-eyed Alessandro.

This one in particular—*Dali at the Age of Six When He Thought He Was a Girl Lifting the Skin of the Water to See the Dog Sleeping in the Shade of the Sea*—had a sort of Alice in Wonderland charm to it. A naked tot hovering over a sandy stretch and holding a conch shell raises a corner of calm surface water and peers beneath it at a snoozing, brown-and-white hound. It was as much a portrait of innocence and curiosity as of magical realism.

This morning Alessandro imagined he was that child, only his sea was turbulent, and beneath it lay horrors more reminiscent of H.P. Lovecraft than Lewis Carroll.

He rose lethargically from bed. He knew Karen would bring the toast and coffee to him on a tray, but he'd save her the trip. He hoped that once he got moving, his coursing blood would wash away the wretched shame of his transgression. He glanced down at the boxer shorts and T-shirt he'd worn to bed last night, half expecting them to bear the stains of his villainy.

He plodded across the room, somehow out of sync with his moving limbs. His head, groggy from lack of sleep, was like a balloon that swayed side to side in uncertain breezes.

He paused to examine himself in the full-length mirror near the bathroom door, and he didn't like what he saw: bloodshot eyes, pale skin, a vacant, zombie-like expression. *Who was this stranger?* he wondered. He inspected his hands, half expecting them to still be dripping red.

As he made for the room's exit, the shrill ring of the landline telephone stopped him in his tracks. Karen's voice came from the kitchen, at first relaxed, then tightening, moving up a register. "Oh, Jane! Are you sure?" He could only imagine the terrified voice on the other end of the line. "He's probably just wandered off somewhere," Karen said, trying to soothe her friend. "Of course, I'll be right over."

By the time he reached the foot of the stairs, Karen was already there.

"Oh, Alessandro," she said.

"Bad news?"

"Justin's missing."

"Justin?"

"Yes. You know, Tim's friend. Who he spent the night with?"

"Oh, right. Missing? What do you mean missing?"

"I mean vanished. From the tent where they were sleeping last night."

"Is Tim alright?"

"Tim's fine. Shaken, I guess."

"We'd better go get him." Usually, he felt secure issuing a call to action, but not this time. Still, he knew to act. She'd expected him to act.

They took the lipstick-red Prius Prime he'd given her for her birthday. He'd wanted to buy her a Lexus hybrid or Tesla, but she was firm in her desire for the Prius, and he always tried to give her what she wanted. His wife was something of an environmentalist but not an outright tree hugger. She said she just wanted to leave the planet as unadulterated as possible for Tim when he grew up.

The Prius offered a smooth, quiet ride, with effortless steering and a power setting for added zip. The styling was a bit futuristic for his taste, but the seats were comfortable, and it was tough to beat the JBL sound system, though they elected to ride in silence for this drive.

A pair of squad cars, one with lights flashing, sat in front of the house. They pulled up behind them and hurried up the walkway to the front door. Alessandro knew his feet were roving, was aware of holding Karen's hand, but felt once removed from his bodily senses, and everything around him had a dreamlike cast.

A policewoman wrote on a pad of paper, nodding as Jane babbled frantically. The cop looked up at Alessandro and recognized him. An expression of awe crossed her face. *This was what the boy had died for,* he told himself. *For fleeting glances of admiration from total strangers.*

She tipped her cap to him and said, "General," then went back to taking Jane's statement.

Tim rushed up to Karen, burying his tear-streaked face in Karen's sternum, hugging her for dear life. "It's alright, honey. Justin will show up. He's probably just wandered off." She rocked slowly on the balls of her feet, offering soft words of hope that Alessandro knew were lies.

HE WOKE TO THE SMELL of garbage and sewage. The concrete beneath him was damp and had seeped through his trousers. He tried to get his right hand underneath to push himself to his feet, but his palm slipped in something oily, and he came down painfully on his elbow. Rubbing the injury, he noticed the knuckles of his hand were split open and swollen. His fingers were bloody, but not with his blood alone.

Looking up, he saw he was in an alley.

A low-pressure sodium street lamp threw its glow across a loading dock in the distance, where a stone-gray rat, alerted to Alessandro's presence by his movement, sat on haunches and peered at him. From behind came the *thump-thump* of loud music, deadened by a brick wall. He listened keenly and recognized the strains of the Pretty Reckless. "Death by Rock and Roll." He tried getting up again and, this time, rose feebly to his feet.

A wave of dizziness swept him. For an instant, everything went blurry. When his focus returned, he saw a bloody mound stir beside a dented trash can, heard a groan.

He remembered the argument but not the fight. Some trust-fund monkey had said something vile about the President, and Alessandro had come unhinged. He could feel his face flushing and the veins rising from his neck.

Responding with a stiff finger poked into the punk's chest, he'd said, "Some people struggle with life-and-death decisions while clowns like you sit around jacking your jaw and playing with yourself."

After that, he wasn't sure of his exact words, but he remembered the rage, the all-consuming fury that blotted out mercy and reason. He remembered hauling the punk by the collar out the back door, and then ... nothing more.

He was surprised no one had called the cops. Or maybe someone had, and they just hadn't arrived yet.

Straightening his clothes, he clambered from the alley's mouth onto the sidewalk, feeling for his keys.

Back home, he found Karen waiting for him in bed, reading the latest book from Lisa Scottoline.

"Alessandro?"

He looked at her lying there, deserving better.

"Got into a little scuffle with a yuppie in a bar," he explained. "It looks worse than it was." *Tell that to the punk I left in the alley.*

She gave him an exasperated look. "I'm worried about you, General. You don't seem to be yourself lately."

"Don't I? Then who do I seem to be?"

"Alessandro, you know what I mean."

"I wish I did."

He went into the bathroom, spit blood in the sink. He wiped a washcloth down his face and stared at himself in the mirror. He looked like a wax statue.

It had been a month since he'd offered up the platter with the still-warm heart on it, and Valafar had materialized, this time as a crimson-eyed alligator, twenty feet long, winged and wearing a jaunty top hat. The breeze of her flapping wings blew back his hair.

She'd brought her predatory, V-shaped snout within inches of him and had bellowed ferociously, baring her sharp, jagged teeth, her breath gushing out at him, hot and rancid.

For his part, he stood like a guilty schoolboy in the principal's office.

She moved her neck in a way that he doubted a genuine alligator could, then looked at him slyly, side-eyed. "I'm impressed, my darling. You've served me well."

He set the platter with its diabolic offering down on the altar amid the blood and gore that was once his son's young friend.

Freeing the heart from the boy's cavity had been a challenge. He'd torn at the flesh like a rabid animal. He could still hear the cracking of bones, still feel the slime on his hands as he clawed in the visceral ooze, searching its warmth for the no-longer-beating nub of life. When he'd yanked the heart out, it made a sucking sound.

"I warned you, Alessandro, that I don't grant favors. I only make pacts. That I could do things for you, but only if you did what I asked of you. This time you've done well. I'll be back again for more."

"I understand," he answered, and for the first time, he'd felt the true weight of his obligation to the demon.

She'd snapped up the heart and departed in a flash, taking with her the hollowed-out corpse, the remnants of flesh, the shards of bone, and every last drop of blood from the altar, the floor, the mirrored walls of the circular room, and even from Alessandro's clothes and hands. *Every bit of forensic evidence gone lickety-split.* She'd left him clean—clean and empty.

Who am I now? he wondered. *As Karen had rightly observed, certainly not myself.*

The cops had never even considered him a suspect in Justin's disappearance. *And why would they?* Wasn't he a presidential aide, a decorated hero, a leader in the fight against the enemies of democracy? Besides, his wife was his alibi. She'd fallen asleep with him in bed and woken with him in bed and had no reason to believe he'd ever gone anywhere.

Instead, the police grilled the parents, the boy's father especially. Alessandro could only imagine the hell they were suffering through.

Tearfully, on the boob tube, Jane pleaded for her son's return. The media swarmed the organized searches and prayer vigils, reporting on the story until there were no more facts to be had. Until the public lost interest and moved on to a new atrocity, which always lurked around the next corner.

The cost to Alessandro was not just the numbing guilt of having committed a horrendous act, not just the memories that ate clean through him like malignant rust, but something more. Something that showed in Tim's eyes when they fell upon him.

His son had sat up and viewed him in the dark of the tent, before falling back asleep. Alessandro could see the boy trying to piece together the remembrance of that moment, which had since apparently drifted and merged into the shadowlands of dreams and slumber.

Alessandro sensed the curious workings of Tim's mind as the boy grappled with this half-forgotten memory.

GOING STRICTLY by floor area, the Pentagon is the world's largest office building. Located in Arlington, Virginia, fifteen minutes from the White House, it's made up of seven floors, five aboveground and two below, and employs 26,000 people, mostly military personnel. It's designed so any point in the building is reachable from any other point in the building within seven minutes.

Opened in 1943, it was the first desegregated building in Virginia.

On Sept. 11, 2001, when al-Qaeda terrorists flew American Airline Flight 77 into the Pentagon, the plane hit a part of the structure that had just been renovated, and only about 800 of the 4,500 workers assigned to that area had moved back into their offices. Because of that and structural reinforcements in the newly completed section, thousands of lives were saved.

Including those on the plane, the crash claimed 184 people. They are honored with a memorial just southwest of the building.

At the Pentagon food court, Alessandro—his newly bandaged right hand clutching a copy of *Suttree* by Cormac McCarthy—had hoped to be left alone to stew in his misery, but, of course, that wasn't happening. Pulling up across from him at the round, polished-steel table came the shiny-faced Marine major from the office next to his. Strangis, that was the man's name. Joachim Strangis. Alessandro had once let slip that his hometown was New Hope, Minnesota, and Joachim said his brother Bruno lived there, and somehow that cemented a camaraderie between them, if only in the major's mind.

"Looks like you got winged there, soldier," Joachim said, setting down a tray full of chicken nuggets and french fries. "Did the missus catch you with your hand in the cookie jar?"

Alessandro set down the book and flexed his bandaged paw. "Carpentry accident. Karen wanted a new bookshelf in her office, and my hand slipped. Sliced my knuckles open on a metal bracket."

Joachim popped a nugget in his mouth and chewed side-to-side, camel-like. "Listen, it's none of my business, and you can tell me to screw off, but I couldn't help noticing you looking a tiny bit frayed at the edges, General. Maybe you should take that family of yours on a little vacation somewhere. Get in some R and R."

"Maybe you're right, Joachim. Maybe I need a break." He pushed away his half-eaten salad. "How are things going with you?" he asked, feigning interest.

The major was more than eager to talk about himself. About his burnt-orange Mustang GT and his latest gal pal. That was one thing about Joachim: once you set him up, he could go on talking forever, mostly about himself. Alessandro half listened, half stewed.

If this idiot could see he was at loose ends, how many others had noticed as well? He needed more bounce in his step, more light in his eyes. Stop being General Gloom-and-Doom. He had to somehow put the boy's death out of his thoughts and focus on living the high life. *That's what it's all about,* he told himself. *What's done is done.*

Just then a fork clacked at another table, and it reminded him of the sound of Justin's breast bone snapping. Anxiety spurted up from his gut in a shot, and his head began spinning.

"General, are you alright?" Joachim asked with a look of concern. The major jolted backward, drawing attention from other tables.

Alessandro feebly held up his left hand. "I'm fine. Just a little lightheaded." He massaged his temples.

Joachim went to fetch a glass of water. The eyes of maybe a dozen people focused on the General uncertainly. "It's okay," he said to them. "Just a little indigestion is all."

He rose from his chair, and it skittered back on the linoleum too loudly. His brow instantly dampened, he trembled, his heart hammered in his chest.

Picking up his book, he pushed his way through a knot of gawkers and moved in slow strides, his breath rapid and shallow. He was aware of Joachim calling to him from behind, but Alessandro was afraid if he paused now he'd lose all command of his body and collapse in a heap.

Chills raced up and down his spine, and now his whole frame shivered. He moved through the corridors of mask-wearing faces, several greetings going unanswered. Picking up his pace, he came at last to the door of his office, which he opened and then closed behind him, engaging the lock, turning off the overhead lights.

He sat behind his desk and loosened his tie.

Joachim rapped at the door. "Are you alright, General? Do you want me to get someone?"

"No. I think I might be coming down with something."

"Not Covid, I hope."

"Not Covid, I don't think. A cold or maybe the flu. I'll call up the motor pool and have them send over my driver. I'm going to call it a day."

"Alright, General. Might be a good idea to see a doctor, as well."

"Thanks, Joachim."

Glad to be rid of him, Alessandro focused on his breathing, on slowing it down, smoothing it out. *One Mississippi, two Mississippi.* That's when the waterworks began. He buried his face in his arms and wept uncontrollably.

Was any of this worth the life of an innocent boy?

By the time his car arrived, Alessandro had things, at least outwardly, in hand. Jim, surprised at being summoned midday when there were no meetings scheduled, eyed his boss warily. "Where to, sir?"

"Home," he said bluntly.

When the driver timidly asked him if anything was amiss, he replied irritably: "Just drive, sergeant."

The jitters stayed with him all day and all night, distracting him from the life that had once seemed so important to him; from Karen and Tim, from the mansion with its elegant rooms, from the pool and all the other trappings of fame and fortune. These benefits paled when weighed against their cost to him of becoming a monster.

The next day, he took a "mental health day" from work. He still needed to get his feet back under him. Word had already spread through the Pentagon about his episode, and the National Security Adviser suggested he take a whole week. More, if necessary.

He spent the day in bed with the remote, flipping through channels, finding nothing of interest. When he tried to read, he found himself rereading the same paragraph of *Suttree*, over and over: about dusk on the Tennessee River; about the kudzu and dusty vines along a dark wall of hillside.

When Karen came up with a breakfast tray, Alessandro left it untouched.

"You have to eat something, General," she said.

"I'm not feeling well. You can leave the coffee but take the rest of it away."

"Do you want me to take your temperature?"

"No. I just need to rest."

He slept in fits and starts, fidgety and agitated. The anxiety came in waves now, with spells of emptiness broken jarringly by crashing breakers of terror. What he'd done to that little boy was beyond forgiving.

As Karen slept beside him that night, he stared at the ceiling and peered into his mirrored room, into the frightened eyes of his young victim, into the gaping maws he'd opened in Justin and, ultimately, in himself. The boy had lost his life, and Alessandro had lost his humanity. Restless in the dark, he wondered who had gotten the worst of that bargain.

THE NEXT DAY, by the break of dawn, he was out of bed and dressed in civilian clothes. He'd achieved an hour or two of dreamless sleep, and, though the waves of anxiety had grown wider apart, when they surged and plunged again, they obliterated whatever traces of serenity he had managed to gather.

He needed to get out of the house before his bed seduced him into endless lethargy. He left Karen—who was still asleep—a note saying he'd gone to get some fresh air and not to worry. As fate would have it, they were the last words he ever communicated to her.

Driving into the beginnings of rush-hour traffic, he followed the roads northwest to Georgetown, and hunted up a Starbucks. Then he sat on a nearby bus bench, sipping an almond-milk latte and watching the stirrings of the new day all around him, a dispassionate observer with a revoked membership in humankind.

Commuters got on and off the buses, hurrying toward various agendas. Some sat briefly on the bench with him but at a distance, no doubt wary of his haunted demeanor.

One of the commuters left behind a copy of the *Post* beside him. Alessandro read of the President's freefall from grace: the withdrawal of forces from Kabul had created a vacuum that the Taliban quickly filled, eager to institute their stone-age ideologies; American citizens were rebelling in defiance of reason against mandates requiring Covid vaccines and the wearing of protective face masks indoors to slow the spread of this modern plague; and violent crime and inflation were on the rise, as was, according to pundits, the political trajectory of the Orange Man, who's every action seemed to challenge the foundations of democratic rule.

Alessandro wasn't sure how long he sat on that bench, but it was long enough to afford him multiple crashing waves of malaise.

Returning at length to his midnight-blue Camry, he reentered traffic, crossing the Potomac into Arlington, Virginia, and drove to Springfield Mall. He walked around for a while, fiddling with his keys and killing another hour or so.

He arrived at the Regal Cinema just in time for the one o'clock showing of the new James Bond movie. Donning his face mask, he bought a ticket and, since he hadn't eaten anything yet that day, a box of Dots and a small popcorn at the understaffed concession stand.

In those awful, plague-blighted days, theaters were struggling to get back customers who had a general distrust of crowded venues, and the theater room Alessandro entered was a little less than a quarter full. He settled in a few rows back from the screen, near center, and rocked stiffly back in his seat, looking forward to doing nothing mindful for the next three hours.

The house lights dimmed, and the coming attractions commenced when an unmasked Hispanic woman in a checkered skirt and a denim jacket began moving down the row toward him. He watched her out of the corner of his eye to see whether he would have to stand up for her to pass him, if that was her intention. But as she approached, she gestured for him to stay seated and attempted to clamber over his knees, spilling some of his popcorn into his lap.

"Balls!" she said. "Sorry, sorry, sorry."

Her hair was black, cropped, and very straight, and she had a cute, upturned nose that somehow softened the sharp ridges of her gaunt features. A brown mole marked one cheek. The fact she wasn't wearing a facemask, though the theater rules stipulated they were required of all attendees, made him feel uneasy.

Then, ignoring the ample choice of seats beyond, she sat immediately next to him. When he looked at her curiously, she winked.

Opening an oversized shoulder purse, she withdrew a silver flask, unscrewed the lid, and took a deep swallow. Before putting it back, she offered it to Alessandro, who declined with a polite wave of his hand.

She looked about thirty. Up close, he noticed a frayed section on the hem of her skirt, and the cuffs of her jacket were also starting to go. When she crossed her legs, she showed a lean but healthy expanse of calf and lower thigh, lightly downy with pale hairs. As the movie started, she fished pinches of candy corn from her bag and nibbled them one at a time. Whenever she caught him looking at her, she smiled.

Now Alessandro had two diversions: the film and the woman, to whom he found himself oddly attracted. But neither she nor the motion picture could wrestle him entirely from the terrible grip of his emotional barrages and the soul-sucking emptiness between them.

No Time to Die, Daniel Craig's final outing as 007, filled the screen with generous doses of car chases, fistfights, stunts, bellowing machineguns, and pyrotechnics; about what he'd expected from the action picture. Though, between the girl and his fractured state of mind, he barely followed the thread of the plot.

When at last the credits rolled, and the house lights came back on, he expected her to leave, but she remained seated, smiling at him. "My name is Moina. Why don't you buy me a drink?"

Figuring he had nothing better to do at that moment, he agreed.

They ordered Jamesons and Gingers, and sweet-potato fries at a booth in a rustic mall restaurant called the Yard House, basically a beer-and-streak joint. A soccer match played on the TVs.

"So, tell me, Moina, what's your story?"

"Pretty much the same as yours."

"How can you say that? You know nothing about me."

"When I look at you, I know who you are," she said. "You may wear designer jeans, but the look in your eye is that of a broken man. Whatever's gotten to your soul has bit in for all its worth."

"What makes you such an expert?" he asked.

"Years of practice." She sipped her drink.

He introduced himself as "Al" and said vaguely he worked at the Pentagon. Told her he was married with a kid. She didn't seem particularly interested in these attachments, asking him instead what it was about his life that had him in such a funk. But when he deflected the question, she let it go.

"Tell me this, Al," she said, chomping a fry in half. "What do you do to beat the blues?"

"Drink, I guess. It takes a bit of the edge off. What do you do?"

She ate the other half of her fry and licked salt from her fingers. "You name it," she said.

Moina didn't own a car. She'd taken the bus to the mall from downtown Washington, D.C., where she lived. She'd come to apply for a job opening at a store called Five Below, where all the merchandise was five dollars or less. After a second round of drinks, he offered to drive her home, and she accepted.

MOINA LIVED in a homeless encampment in a park at 12th Street and Massachusetts Avenue Northwest. It was one of several such gatherings of the hopeless in the district, and was located just yards from an elementary school.

Alessandro had read about this camp. The park service was threatening to shut it down. That action would have the effect of relocating these unfortunates down the road somewhere, where their presence would no doubt be as unwelcome as it was at their current location. A cynical game of kick the can, most observers agreed.

On the drive over, Moina managed to wheedle from him some minor details about the angst that consumed him.

"Let's just say, I used to be a different person years ago," he said. "You wouldn't have recognized me. I owned little and my future looked bleak. So, I did something to turn my life around—never mind what—and then suddenly I had a great job, a great house, a beautiful wife. People respect me. But the thing is: this new life of mine came at a price, and it turned out to be a high one. It involves a debt I might never be able to repay. And the terms are brutal."

"Balls," she said.

"In order to become who I am, I needed to become something I never wanted to be. Understand?"

She nodded thoughtfully. "If you're going to dance to the music, you got to pay the piper."

The tent city thronged with early-evening activity. A Black man in a black hoodie pulled a child's wagon (a Radio Flyer classic like the one Alessandro had owned as a boy in New Hope), packed tight with clothes, a broken chair, and a waterlogged sleeping bag. An emaciated woman with messy gray hair popped her prune head out of a tent and looked at Alessandro as if he might be the devil himself. A pair of sketchy youths in oversized shirts and pajama pants talked too loudly and laughed too excitedly.

The stench of the unwashed was almost enough to make him gag.

He had no business being here, he knew. *I have to get back home. Karen will be worried.*

But there was no real urgency in these thoughts. He'd reached that point where putting one foot in front of the other took all the determination he could muster.

Moina led him past mounds of plastic bottles, cast-off clothing, knurls of buzzing flies, trash, excrement; down a narrow foot path between rows of nylon tents.

She stopped at one that was occupied. Holding the flap open for him, she stooped and stepped in.

On a worn mattress laid on top of a tarp sat one man and kneeled another. The seated man had a hypodermic needle in his neck, and the kneeling man was injecting him with something.

"Fentanyl," Moina told Alessandro.

"I got more," the kneeler said to Moina in a thick Southern accent as he sank the syringe's plunger.

She turned to Alessandro. "What do you think, Al? Takes the edge off."

The kneeler pulled the needle from the other guy's neck, and that guy went kind of wavy.

"What do you say, Al?" the kneeler repeated. He looked all of twenty-five, white, tubby, with a cocked baseball cap and a Ludacris T-shirt two sizes too big. "It's good shit. Rock your world, bro. Only five clams for a taste."

Alessandro took out his wallet. "No needles," he said.

"I got patches, too. Forty bucks each."

Moina looked at him hopefully.

"Sure. Why not?" He bought two, one for Moina and one for himself. Moina peeled the packs open and applied one of the patches under his shirt. Then she attached one to her shoulder.

"Thanks, Pookie," Moina said to the dealer, then led Alessandro from the tent.

Midstride, despair reached out and grabbed him by the throat. Moina's denim jacket and checkered skirt faded into the distance. The night's growing darkness encased him. Once again he was climbing the stairs, the weight of Justin's small frame against his chest, the boy shuddering like a frightened animal. Up to the fourth floor to its hidden room of mirrors. Setting Justin down on the altar top, the boy's head lolling, eyes rolling, spittle-foam forming on his bluish lips. *I did this.*

Scalding tears ran like lava down Alessandro's cheeks as he stumbled in the dark, tripping on a shopping cart and losing a shoe.

"Who are you?" he shouted, rising to his feet, shaking with rage. "What have you become?" His hands clenched so fiercely that his fingernails drew blood from his palms.

He stumbled past shadowy forms, through concentrations of tents all around him, past piles of rubbish and the other discarded leavings of the pitiful and the pathetic. *Aren't I now also one of them?*

Numbness bloomed from the spot of the patch, and euphoria tingled in this temples. His breathing slowed. His panic began to recede. Sitting down in something cold and wet, Alessandro looked up at the rising moon and the star-spangled vault of the heavens.

A calmness overtook him.

If he could've died by pure volition, he would have gladly given up his ghost right there, in the enveloping embrace of the powerful opioid.

HE CAME TO ABOUT SIX HOURS LATER, hugging an overturned cooler, a pair of straggling tent dwellers walking around him. Karen had texted him urgently several times during the night, but he continued to ignore her messages.

It was still dark. His pants were wet. He tried to locate his missing shoe, but it was nowhere to be found, so he walked from the encampment in one socked foot, covered in mud, and still woozy from the fentanyl. He hadn't eaten anything since the platter of sweet potato fries, and his stomach growled.

He located his Camry where he'd parked it, a ticket now pinned to his windshield by a wiper blade. At least they hadn't towed it.

He pulled up to an intersection stoplight, and when the light turned green, he hesitated. *Left or right?* He realized he had no interest in getting back to where he lived.

A car came up behind him, and the driver tapped the horn.

Alessandro turned left and drove for several blocks, still not sure where he was headed, but it felt good to be driving for the sheer joy of it, window rolled down, classic rock playing softly on the radio. It's been a hard day's night. *Yes, it has.*

It felt good to feel a little good again.

He drove and he drove, west on K Street to a gas station where he topped off his tank and cleaned up as best he could in the bathroom before buying a pocketful of candy bars that lasted him till Buckhannon, West Virginia, where he loaded up on sneakers, jeans, and a couple of shirts at the Walmart Supercenter, and a tall cup of black coffee and an avocado wrap to-go from the Daily Grind on Main Street. His next stop was a pizzeria on Maxwell Street in Lexington, Kentucky. While he was there, he stopped at an ATM and withdrew the one-thousand-dollar daily limit. Then he gave his cell phone to some homeless guy.

That night, in a hotel room in St. Louis, Missouri, Alessandro, exhausted from driving all day, slid into a dreamless sleep. It was the way he'd slept when he was a child, unaffected by the complexities of life. A deep swoon of a sleep that nuzzled him in its silken cradle.

Suddenly, his eyes opened in the dark room. A chill traveled the ridges of his spine.

Someone was in bed with him. A small, light body that unmistakably lowered the mattress beside him.

He reached to the nightstand lamp, and it turned on.

Justin. The boy slept fitfully on the adjacent pillow, hair tousled, breath whistling through his missing front tooth; pale and freckled, just as he had been at the pool party in that mansion that now was so far distant.

He pulled the covers up over the boy's chest.

It all made perfect sense to him. Justin was now his to carry.

He turned off the light and fell back asleep.

IN COMING DAYS, they searched for him, of course. The police, the FBI, military investigators, civilian volunteers. He was, after all, a big deal: the presidential adviser who vanished like some schlocky magician's assistant. But he was always a step ahead.

He sold his car in Denver, caught the 8:05 a.m. California Zephyr to Sacramento. Kept cashing out at ATMs until finally a machine denied him access to his funds and refused to give back his debit card, which was just as well since his movements could be traced through bank transactions. By then, he'd doubled back via Greyhound bus through Salt Lake City, Utah, to Billings, Montana, where he bought a fake ID from a college kid that was good enough to get him onboard a 737 flight from Billings Logan International Airport to Sioux Fall, South Dakota.

All the way, Justin tagged along with him, never speaking a word.

They spent the first week of winter in Montgomery, Alabama. By then Alessandro had grown a scruffy beard and had taken to wearing nut-brown sunglasses and a blue-black Panama hat. He liked the way Southern women addressed everyone as "sugar" or "hon," and at a tavern called Ric and Moe's, he hooked up with one of them, a bony, middle-aged blonde with a flat, hard face and a twitchy smile. Rose Ellen, she called herself.

He took her back to his hotel room along with a fifth of Famous Grouse Blended Scotch and a six-pack of club soda.

Justin sat in an armchair, looking out the window the entire night.

Then, he and Justin skipped around through southern towns: Atlanta, Orlando, New Orleans, Houston. Sometimes he introduced himself as Oscar Dawn, sometimes as Win Meadows. They traveled by cab, bus, train, and once even by boat when they rode the Key West Express ferry out of Fort Myers, Florida.

He still had his bad days, when the remembrance of his past deed ripped through him, when the blood reappeared on his hands, and Justin gave him that dark, taut look that said, "You have taken from me what you can never give back."

Though rarer than before, these grim passages now sometimes went on and on.

On days like that, he'd weep and blubber and drink himself into oblivion. In New Orleans, he scored some OxyContin and holed up for three days in the Commons Club on Baronne Street, eating out of vending machines when it occurred to him to eat at all. In Houston, he bought a 9mm Ruger semi-automatic pistol from a bartender and took it back to his hotel room, where he'd pressed the muzzle to his temple several times but couldn't pull the trigger.

Most days, though, he maintained his equilibrium. Constantly moving helped: fresh sights, new people, and untried-before experiences kept his mind occupied, for the most part. Having Justin along also helped somehow, though he could never pinpoint exactly why this was true.

He saw Karen on TV at a bus terminal in Atlanta, tearfully begging him to come home. She missed him. Tim missed him. Apparently, a lot of people missed him. But the him they missed was an illusion whipped up by a demon who haunted the world from another dimension. They had no idea who Alessandro was. He barely knew himself anymore.

Still, from time to time, he'd think about the family he'd abandoned, and missed them, as well.

Spring arrived. He and Justin found themselves in Oklahoma City, sitting outdoors at a coffee bar on Northeast Sixth Street when Alessandro struck up a conversation with a tall foreign-exchange student from Amsterdam. She had a closed copy of *Slaughterhouse-Five* by Kurt Vonnegut on the table in front of her.

He asked her what she thought of the book, which he'd read years ago in his pockmarked pre-General days.

She found Vonnegut's tale endearing if somewhat sterile.

Her name was Anna, and she looked to be in her mid-twenties, far too young for him, he thought, but he wasn't sure she felt the same way. Anna was taking classes in literature at Oklahoma City University, a private school associated with the Methodists, though nothing about her struck him as overly religious. Her hair was like Moina's, black as a moonless night sky, and her pretty green eyes shined on him with genuine interest.

He told her he thought *Slaughterhouse-Five* was the author's masterpiece and especially liked the way it jumped around in time with a fluidity that never confused the reader.

"It's so rare to meet an American outside of university who can talk knowledgeably on literature," she said, joining him at his table. "I got the impression most Americans don't read books anymore." She had a Dutch accent but spoke English impeccably.

Because they were outdoors, neither of them wore a facemask, not that this state required them anyway.

The two talked about Billy Pilgrim, the everyman protagonist of Vonnegut's novel, and about Kilgore Trout, the comically sad-sack cynic who often reappeared in Vonnegut's books.

"Are you from Oklahoma, Oscar?" she asked, eyeing him evenly.

"No, I'm just visiting from New Hope, Minnesota." He spun a vague story about taking a vacation from a brokerage in Minneapolis, then quickly changed the subject back to literature.

They talked for an hour or so about popular authors such as Joyce Carol Oates (who they both loved) and Charles Bukowski (who he liked more than she did), and about politics (hers, in true European fashion, being noticeably left of his), and when Alessandro rose to leave, Anna got up with him.

They crossed the patio to Northeast Sixth Street, and headed toward Embassy Suites, where he was staying, though neither mentioned any potential destinations. It was a sunny afternoon, if a bit chilly. He jangled the keys in his pocket and couldn't help noticing that she had a way of swinging her legs when she walked that struck him as impish.

He was about to respond to a comment she made about the Orange Man when another voice spoke to him, a deep commanding one he knew only too well: "Slay her. Cut the tongue from her head and feed it to me."

A sudden frost sprouted from his middle. He felt his face drop, and he nearly stumbled from his feet.

"Are you alright?" she asked.

That question seemed to be on everyone's lips these days. "No, I'm not alright!" he wanted to shout. "I'm as *un*-alright as a person can be!" But, instead, he excused himself; said he wasn't feeling well and it was nice talking with her, and he hoped she enjoyed her studies in America. The words spewed from his lips in an almost incomprehensible torrent, like verbal raw sewage.

He glanced at Justin, who had been following behind them, and the boy looked back at him with a piercing gaze.

"Are you sure?" Anna asked hesitantly.

But all Alessandro could think to do was to get as far from her as his legs would carry him. Away from this precious life that still held so promising a future. His clumsy footsteps quickened.

Back at his hotel, he loaded his suitcase, paid the bill, and walked with Justin to the downtown Amtrak station, where he bought a ticket at the kiosk for St. Paul, Minnesota. This time he knew where he was headed, where he'd always been headed. His path may have been tortuous, but he realized it led all along to a final destination. To a certain house on Boone Avenue North in New Hope where a bug-eyed boy had long ago made a pact with a devil.

Alessandro was going home.

THAT NIGHT, the house stared back at him vacantly, a dull coat of whitewash on it and the lawn's grass untrimmed. In the yard, a FOR SALE sign listed Bridge Realty as the broker. Also in the yard, the birch tree he had climbed as a child, now sickly with falling branches.

He pulled the key ring from his pocket, the one he was always absentmindedly fingering. He wasn't even sure what half the keys were for anymore nor which life they were a part of: Alessandro Yezdan, the repellant failure, or Alessandro Yezdan, the national hero. But he spotted the one he needed, a flat silver one with Axxess+ stamped on one side and the numerals 66 stamped on the other. He held it up for Justin to see. The boy nodded.

Alessandro carried the key and his suitcase to the front door.

There was no guarantee the silver key would still unlock the building. It was, after all, forever ago that this structure had been his home. Savvy owners of newly purchased property knew to change the locks to guard against former key-holders invading their privacy. But it was worth a try.

It fit smoothly into the lock cylinder. He felt the rotor turn and the bolt draw. Then the door opened soundlessly.

The place was empty, and it looked as if it had been empty for a long time. It wasn't dusty, but it had a closed-in smell and feel to it that told him it should have been.

He set down the suitcase and closed the door behind him.

In the dark, Justin and he walked across the dim living-room floor to the tarnished wooden staircase. They climbed the worn steps to the upstairs hallway. There he pulled down on the ceiling lever that opened the attic hatch and released the sliding ladder. Climbing the first few rungs, he turned to see if Justin was following, but he wasn't. Instead, the boy looked up at him and grinned. It was the first time he had smiled at Alessandro since that night in the swimming pool. Back then, the gap-toothed grin had expressed innocence and delight. Now, it looked more like a sneer. Justin's eyes shone in the dark as the boy stepped backward, and the hallway's deep shadows swallowed him.

This final leg of the journey, Alessandro would cover on his own.

He crossed the attic's floorboards. When he'd lived here, the room was a jumble of books and trunks and extra furniture. He remembered this was home to the Christmas tree from January to November, and to the camping equipment they never got around to using, and to the golf set that was missing a putter. Now all these things were gone, and the room was bare. But the round mirrored chamber at the attic's center remained.

He supposed the former owners and the realtors didn't want to bother with taking it apart.

He opened it. Inside, it was more or less as he'd left it. Someone had boarded the open ceiling, no doubt in an attempt to keep out the snow and rain, but tendrils of moonlight wormed between the boards, revealing that the mirrors and altar remained intact.

Mounting the altar, he reached up and pulled down the boards from the skylight. They came free, accompanied by the kindly squeal of carpenter's nails tugging from roof wood.

He cleared the portal, and the crisp night breeze swept in.

He looked around for the black dagger and located it, surprisingly, on the floor beneath the altar, the same black dagger he'd left behind in D.C. The handbell, and the brass-plated censer, however, were long gone. Likewise, *The Secret Teachings of the Hermetic Order of the Golden Dawn*—the book of rites allegedly written by Aleister Crowley—was missing. He hoped it hadn't been turned over to some thrift store or secondhand bookshop where it could further spread its arcane wickedness. He hoped that whoever removed it had burned it or at least thrown it away.

Making do with the tool at his disposal, he picked up the dagger and cut his palm, squeezed blood from his fist onto the altar, and repeated from memory the summoning prayer: "From the wide, ancient skies of Baala Sheem, where storm gods unsheathe swords of lightning, I call upon Valafar, succubus supreme in the nightmare army of Thamuz, queen of falsehoods." He raised his face to the open sky. "Valafar, who causes all shadows to fall, come from your coven of three, from the deep roots of your shoreless void to the side of your True Believer. I beg you, come to me."

A low rumbling sounded, and from a distance came a rushing of wings.

Bodies began dropping on the rooftop outside, too heavy to be birds, too light to be humans. These beings chattered, and, as their numbers grew, so did the sound of their chattering, until all he could hear was the constant gabble of what must have been a hundred creatures milling on the shingles of the roof. They sounded as if they were jostling one another, rolling like bowling balls just beyond the ceiling. They scuffled and shrieked and laughed—yes, laughed!—a peal of high-pitched mocking that came from no beast this side of the Netherworld.

He froze in terror as the first one inserted its head through the skylight and peered down at him, its features vaguely simian, though hairless and wrinkled and asymmetrical, appearing as if crudely fashioned from some castoff scraps of cracked black leather. Its nose consisted of little more than naked holes punched in its face. Its long chin framed enormous teeth, and its dark eyes gleamed like jeweled slits and betrayed an intelligence beyond that of a simple animal.

It dropped to the altar top and a second one appeared at the skylight. It, too, hopped in.

Two more appeared at the opening.

These creatures were less than three feet tall, with leathery black wings folded at their backs. They walked bipedally, slightly crouched, swinging sinewy arms that ended in long, curled fingers. One of them picked up the ceremonial dagger and examined it curiously.

One by one, they fell from the sky into the small room. First, they landed on the altar. Then, as that surface became overcrowded, they dismounted onto the floor, edging toward Alessandro from all angles. Their primal smell soon overwhelmed the mirrored chamber.

Forcing himself to snap from the grip of his terror, he reached clumsily behind him to open the door. All at once, every cracked black face in the room turned and hissed at him. Several creatures took wing in the air around him, and four alighted on his arms, effectively pinning them to his sides. The touch of these gristly fingers on his bare skin sent billows of revulsion through him so powerful he nearly blacked out. He tried making himself invisible from the glaring slits of their eyes, but even if the trick had worked, it was too late.

They landed on his shoulders, on his chest, on his head, their leathery bodies swarming him from all directions. At first, the great weight of the creatures had him staggering. Then the flapping of their wings began lifting him.

He tried breaking free, but it was no use.

Up he soared, past the altar, through the open passage into the night sky. A dozen or more of the creatures carried him, over rooftops and steeples, beyond parking lots and congested roadways, through banks of clouds, toward the chill and the twinkle of distant stars. The other creatures flocked behind and around him, howling and jabbering excitedly, showing their teeth.

How much of this is real, and how much an illusion? he wondered. And it was only the belief that what he experienced was at least partly a mirage that kept him from losing his mind and howling and jabbering manically in concert with his tormentors.

As the air thinned, he went increasingly lightheaded until he flitted at the brink of unconsciousness, at the barest horizon of perception.

When everything came back into focus, he found himself before her, slumped to one knee at the mossy edge of a black cliff that looked out on soulless eternity.

"Why do you call to me, my darling, without my tribute in hand?"

This time Valafar took the form of a giant insect, with gaping mandibles and powerful pincers, with spiky barbs running down her back, and clawed feet, and the raised tail of a scorpion, with long legs and quivering antennas, and swollen compound eyes that studied him impassively, as she slowly floated toward him from the void.

"What you ask of me," he said, in a gasp, "I can no longer bring myself to do."

Her great alien head twisted stiffly. She rubbed her front legs together. "Cannot or will not?"

"Will not, then." His voice cracked with this defiance.

"But what of our pact?" She was still drifting toward him.

"I already have innocent blood on my hands." His mouth and lips went dry, and anxiety trembled from his nerve endings through his muscles and his guts. "I can't be responsible for any more carnage."

"But haven't I upheld *my* end of the bargain?" She paused within an arm's length of him. Her giant insect head began to quiver, to fall in on itself, to reshape itself into the sleek and spotted head of a leopard, a transformation terrifying to witness.

The leopard head propped on the hard-shell body of the insect.

"Y-y-yes. You've been n-nothing but generous in the life you've given me. And I understand that, at the least, I will lose all of it by terminating the pact."

Now the leopard's head began to waver. The color of its fur changed; it sprouted a tawny mane and took on the characteristics of a lion. This shape-shifting both mesmerized and horrified Alessandro, who was too stunned to move.

"At the least," the lion's mouth said. "I should think, at the *very* least."

He had no reply for this unspoken threat.

Once again, the outlines of the head pulsated, and the flesh of the furry face collapsed and folded and reformed, this time into the shaggy contours of a wild boar, its deep-set eyes glaring at him, its huge, canine teeth jutting from its jowls. She grunted at him.

"How shall I repay your betrayal, Alessandro?" Valafar flexed her brawny boar's neck. "I know: I could turn you inside out and have you live for all eternity that way. Or maybe I should make of you a limbless, bouncy sex puppet to keep me amused? Have my minions queue up to have a go at you. What a long line *that* would be." She chuckled.

"Ask of me anything short of murder, and I will obey. But I cannot take another innocent life. I don't have it in me."

"Very well," she said, stretching so that her snout was bare inches from his nose. "As you wish."

Her insect arms whipped out in a blur, seizing him and drawing him in tight. She planted her tusks deep in his neck and made wild suckling and chomping sounds as his heart pumped madly. His insides—his muscles, veins, ligatures, organs, bones, and marrow—began melting. They turned first to a viscous sludge, then to a free-flowing stream that gushed from the lesion in his neck into his tormentor's mouth in gouts of searing pain.

Valafar swilled this liquefied ooze deep into her ravenous gullet, relishing every drop.

He tried to scream, but the hole in his throat allowed only a faint sputter.

His fingers and toes went numb and began to shrivel. His nose withered, as did his eyes, tongue, and ears. Blood ran freely from every orifice.

He felt a shoulder drop, then the other one. His sexual organs pulled up into his pelvis, where they blended with the offal swirling up from his thighs. His knees collapsed. His chest caved.

He should have been long gone by then, off to the realm of darkness from where no mortal returns. He ached for his final glint of consciousness to wink out and leave him in peace, but, even as the dregs of himself found their way into the demon's maw, he maintained his sense of awareness. Even as the final wag of flesh disappeared into the monster's cavernous mouth, Alessandro's sense of being remained.

Valafar had reserved this final, delicate morsel of him for dessert.

Still Life

"I have made my bed
In charnels and on coffins, where black death
Keeps record of the trophies won from thee."
—Percy Bysshe Shelley, "Alastor, or The Spirit of Solitude"

More coffee?" Lilly Barnes held out the glass pot.

"Why not?" the customer said, leaning back sheepishly as if caught by the waitress doing something embarrassing. He smiled at her over his plate of half-eaten steak.

She knew he was appraising her as men do. Finding her, perhaps, a little on the plump side but otherwise vaguely alluring. She had the waitress thing going for her. Men are drawn to women who see to their needs, whether nurses, barmaids, or waitresses. They liked being served.

"I seem to be a little out of it today," he said.

"Daydreaming is allowed," Lilly replied. "All the best people do it."

She filled his cup, then filled the cups of a couple of old-timers at the counter, one eye on the clock.

Twenty minutes till her shift was over, but business was pretty sparse. After the lunch crowd, things had slowed way down. Just five customers in the entire diner, most picking at their food, one foot already out the door.

"Hey, Rich," she said, stepping through the swing doors to the kitchen. "Think you could handle things if I slip out a little early? I've got some errands to run."

On a stool near the grill, he looked up from the *Sun-Times*. "What do you think about this serial killer in Indiana?" Rich was only thirty, but his walrus mustache, thinning hair, and old-fashioned eyeglasses added ten years to his appearance. "The cops say it's the work of the Midwest Butcher."

"People have been talking about it all day. It's sad. Real sad. How 'bout it? Can I go?"

"The cops say he killed this guy, chopped him up, and parts of him he probably ate." When she didn't react to this, he repeated: "*Ate.*"

She almost said, "There's no accounting for taste," but didn't. Instead, she said, "It's a real tragedy, Rich. I feel sorry for him and his family. Can I go now?"

He closed and folded the newspaper. "Sure. Big plans?"

"You know me. Always got something going on."

He did know her. He knew her from two years' worth of bantering and chitchat, from the bits of information she'd let slip out about the workings of her personal life. She knew some things about him, as well. Knew he lived with his cat in a two-bedroom condominium, that his parents resided in his hometown of Indianapolis, that he collected baseball cards, and that he sometimes watched her from across the restaurant when he thought she wasn't looking.

Sometimes the people at work know you better than your own people.

They knew each other well enough, anyway, to know that neither one of them had anything going on that day nor nearly any other. But he played along with her.

Lilly's first stop was the Barrytown Ben Franklin store, where she spent most of her tip money on watercolor supplies: a tube of burnt umber; a small, stiff-haired flat brush; a 2H sketch pencil; and a twelve-sheet pad of ten-by-fourteen, one-hundred-and-forty pound, hot-press paper.

Next stop: the liquor store for a bottle—no, make it two—of Riunite Lambrusco red.

She lived on the outskirts of town, close to Fairview Garden Park, a secluded wooded area near the bridge on Main Street. The house had belonged to her folks, but it passed to her when they passed to the majority. Her father hung on the longest, roaming around the place in his underpants and robe until last year when she'd found him posted in front of the TV with a half-eaten bowl of soggy cornflakes in his lap.

A former coworker of her father's from Gilbert's Printing in Vandalia, her dad's brother's family (who flew in from Florida), the Jennings from down the road, Rich and Namadia from the diner, and Lilly herself, of course, were all who attended the final planting of her father next to her mother in the dark loam of eternity.

Now the old homestead was hers alone, and she had the rest of today, all of tomorrow—Saturday—and half of Sunday to dabble in her watercolors. She'd have to be back at the diner to help clean up after Sunday brunch, a popular draw in Barrytown.

Setting her bags on the kitchen counter, she stepped to the fruit bowl on the table just beyond her easel. Clamped to the easel was a sheet of ten-by-fourteen hot-press paper that bore a spidery outline of the aforementioned fruit bowl. But there was something not right about the drawing. Some mistake in the proportions. Unsatisfied with her rendering, she frowned at it, then removed the sketch and replaced it with a fresh page from the pad in the Ben Franklin bag.

A blank sheet of paper represented a clean slate of boundless opportunity, but it always intimidated her a bit.

She poured herself a glass of Lambrusco and began organizing her supplies on the near edge of the table.

Late afternoon brought with it a wonderful golden light that streamed through a side window over the sink, maybe four feet away from her easel. Outside stretched a view of the backyard, spacious and unmown. No fences out here, and the nearest neighbors were the Jennings, a quarter-mile down the road on one side, and, on the other side, Fairview Park, which she could just see the entrance of from a near corner of her backyard or from the top of the driveway.

Lilly sharpened her new pencil.

The sunlight lit up the bowl, which, after much deliberation, she'd settled on placing at just the right angle to catch the amber light along the front of the bowl's glass rim. She'd arranged the fruit just this morning: a jumble of apples, pears, and bananas, with a single orange on the table in front of the bowl. She considered adding a patterned tablecloth but decided the bare table's reflective wood texture better suited the mood for which she was aiming. Beside the bowl, she'd place a white saucer with bread crumbs on it.

In the background, a square of framed shelves, used normally to display her mother's Precious Moments collection, had been emptied of all but one figurine—a round and smiling pink pig, bonneted, with gold coins at her feet.

Lilly wanted her painting to be an exploration of color and light.

Years ago, when she was still in high school, her parents had taken her to an exhibit of Patrick Heron's work at the Walker Art Center in Minneapolis. She'd found Heron's Matisse-inspired paintings radiant and visually delightful. His use of color and form dazzled her, especially on his still lifes, which blended representative and abstract techniques in novel and startling ways. In the museum's gift shop, she'd bought a book of his prints and studied it in the car all the way back to Barrytown.

She wanted this painting to be a study in the Heron fashion; her fruit bowl to become an allegory for the color and space of her world; her brush strokes to contain the glimmer of what it was that connected her small life to all the rest of humankind. When she died, she wanted this painting to sum her up so she might, in some sense, continue to exist.

Didn't every artist strive for a taste of immortality?

She sipped from her glass and began sketching.

UNKNOWN TO HER, an assassin came that night to Fairview Garden Park and forced at knifepoint a young hotel manager named Pamela Bates to drive into the very entry Lilly Barnes could just see from her backyard or the corner of her driveway. A monster he was— a madman, a ravisher. But Lilly did not witness that car drive into the woods that night.

Instead, she was absorbed in her pencils, her paints, and her bowl of fruit.

She tried to think like Heron and find meaning in wild flushes of color and playful voids and imbalance. She toyed with form, exploring non-figurative aspects of the apples, the pears, and the bananas. During different phases of her progress, the errant orange went from an angry, fiery orb to a pale silhouette; the saucer of breadcrumbs from a linear glare to an irregular, soft-edged, phantom-like presence. The background and foreground fluctuated in and out of focus.

As the blush of late-afternoon sunrays yielded to the silvery glow of moonbeams, she examined her finished product with the critical eye that always found fault. Tonight was no exception: her mechanical skills, as usual, left much to be desired; her color choices were sallow and sickly, and she'd captured nothing of the essence of her study. The work was flat and unimaginative, just as her art teachers had always implied. *This is why I'm a waitress and not a painter.*

Only mildly dejected (because she'd secretly suspected all along her painting would be inadequate), she emptied the last of a bottle of Lambrusco into her wine glass, carried it into the living room, and turned on the TV. She'd mount the painting in a cheap frame and give it to one of her cousins as a Christmas gift.

IT'S DIFFICULT TO GAUGE the exact moment that Pamela Bates shrugged off her mortal coil, though it was sometime after her shift at the Barrytown Snuggle Inn ended at 10:30 p.m. The coroner would estimate her time of death at two o'clock in the morning. By all accounts, she must've reached by then that stage where death is preferable to the agony her life had become at the hands of the Midwest Butcher.

Lilly fell asleep watching a rerun of *Jordon's Crossing* on the same couch her father had died on, and she had a most unusual dream.

In her dream, a great fluttering of birds' wings from outside roused her from the couch. She scrambled for the window over the sink and, looking out, witnessed an immense migration of starlings skyward from her backyard. There must've been two-hundred birds, at least. For an instant, their ascendency blacked out the moon and the stars.

Lilly stepped outside, her feet naked in the cool evening grass. A howl, like that of a wolf, arose from Fairview Garden Park. It scattered the birds off into the far horizon.

Now standing in the moonlight of her backyard, Lilly spotted a moving spark of light near the park's edge. Wandering toward the glow through the tall grass of her unmown lawn, she struggled to make sense of the vision, its radiance too indistinct and still to be anything as mundane as reflected headlights or a flashlight beam. It was more like ethereal candlelight shining in a mist.

She walked toward it, through a meadow of grass and weeds and clawing undergrowth. The light drifted with her approach, leading her through gathering clusters of white oak and birch, past the hoots of a great horned owl, past the flickering swoops of brown bats and the rustling scamper of small, crawly creatures hidden all around her in the gloom.

She followed the misty light down a labyrinth of trails to a stony creek that ran with shallow water. And from the striped shadows at the creek's bank rose a woman's shriek of anguish so loud it shook leaves from branches, quaked the ground, and sent ripples across the water's surface. So heartrending was the cry that it clutched Lilly's heart in its icy grip and froze her in her tracks.

Blood, black in the moonlight, flew in oily jets as a razor-sharp blade flashed in the night. A crazed figure—part monster, part man—slashed and whittled at shuddering flesh pinned beneath its savage form.

Lilly realized that it was from this woman's flesh the light had arisen and called to her.

Sensing Lilly's presence, the hulking attacker whirled, now smiling at her with a mouthful of jagged iron instead of teeth, its semi-human face bespeckled with droplets of blood, its eyes rolling wildly, holding out the blade to her, not in a threat, but an offer. *Here, take it and join me in my madness. Feel the power terror wields. Watch as your victim's eyes go glassy and dim.*

She mustered the strength to move forward toward the fiend. She reached out her hand and, in a silvery thread of luminescence, touched one finger to the treacherous razor's edge.

Something akin to a lightning bolt jolted through her hand and up her arm, through her shoulder, and across her chest and back. Epiphany-bright whiteness flooded her skull. It seared her with its heat, blinded her with its dazzling brilliance, burning away some substance within her and replacing it at its scorched margins with a gush of corruption so vile her body quivered to contain it. Pockets of her skin bulged out as her spirit tried to expel this poison before it could permanently settle within her, before it could claim her. But it was too late for that.

She awoke on the couch, trembling, the recollection of the dream echoing in her like a haunting voice from her past.

Lilly sat up, soaked in sweat. *What time was it?*

Milky daylight spilt through every window. The TV screen displayed long-dead actors Paul Lynde and Elizabeth Montgomery exchanging sitcom quips.

Lilly rose on shaky feet, aware that something in the house had changed.

She trudged her way to the kitchen and, as the fog lifted from her brain, she saw what was different. The bowl and the fruit and the plate with the breadcrumbs had been swept to the floor in a jangle of glass and bruised produce, and on the table's surface were scattered ten pages from the pad she'd bought the previous day at the Ben Franklin.

Each page held a separate watercolor image.

But she couldn't imagine these paintings coming from *her* brush. These were dramatic slashes of black paint, rooster combs of crimson, scrawled depictions of carnage beyond imagining—the moonlit figure from her nightmare at play among its ruins at the creek's rim. In some paintings, the iron-toothed monster admired its work; in others, its face was upturned toward the viewer glowing with simpleminded glee.

The face looked vaguely familiar.

Who had painted these portraits of slaughter? Surely not me?

But it was her. It had to be. No one else was here, and even if some artistic savant had wandered into her home while she slept, how could this mystery person have retrieved these images from her dreamscape?

She picked up one of the paintings and studied it in wonder. The artist had employed techniques foreign to her, yet she recognized at once the hand of a genius. She marveled at the brushstrokes, so awe-inspiring, so brutally assured. Strokes bold and relentless. Violence permeated every facet of this study, prodding the viewer with glimpses into the mindset of a killer beast at its grim task. It was obscenely, delightfully voyeuristic.

One by one, she examined every painting and found each to be a memorial to terror tinged in artistic magic. These paintings had to spring from a heart that knew abysmal darkness.

How could they have come from me?

She remembered reading about a Welshman known as the Sleepwalking Artist. Lee Hadwin, who, when awake, had no artistic ability but at night would arise and create artworks in his sleep. It began when he was four or five. With crayons or pencils, he would scribble on walls, creating drawings that, over time, grew more sophisticated. Doctors determined the activity was harmless, so Lee Hadwin began collecting art supplies and laying them out in preparations for his nocturnal creativity.

Today his artwork sold for thousands of dollars.

Is that what happened to me? Did I emerge from the strange nightmare adrift on a gossamer breath of inspiration, take up a palette and brush, and recreate these otherworldly visions on paper? Could I possibly be an artistic sleepwalking genius?

She scanned the paintings onto her laptop computer, emailed the images to a former classmate who worked at a gallery in Chicago, and asked her what she thought of them.

Then she drove back to town and bought three more pads of watercolor paper and a resupply of tints. On her way back, three police vehicles roared past her, sirens wailing. Something was up at Fairview Garden Park. Out of curiosity, she might've followed the squad cars or at least driven home and walked over to catch a glimpse of what the excitement was all about. But on this day, the flashing lights and the sirens barely registered. Her mind was elsewhere, on the mysterious paintings and what they could mean for her life.

She made up her mind to attempt to replicate one of the paintings. She selected her favorite (or rather the one she judged technically superior since none of the images were exactly idyllic) and contemplated it with that critical eye of hers. There was no underlying sketch that she could see, making her think the painting was done entirely freehand, something she'd tried before only experimentally. She set the image down on the tabletop, clipped a blank page to her easel, and began.

The process proved more taxing than she'd have imagined. When studying the watercolor's techniques, she found herself continuously struggling against the hypnotic urge to be pulled into the painting. Into its swirls and slashes of black, into its dynamic crimsons; into the overall morose imagery and chilling mood of the piece. Her creative self yielded again and again to virtual worship of the original's mastery.

It took her more than three hours to complete a thoroughly unsatisfactory reproduction. She wadded it up and tossed it aside. She tried one more time to similar results before turning in for the night.

I'm not good enough to make these paintings, she told herself. *It just isn't possible.*

Still, she laid out fresh watercolor sheets just to see what would happen.

That night she lay in bed reading for a while: *The Moon and Sixpence*, Somerset Maugham's backhanded homage to Gauguin. The novel's protagonist, Strickland, leaves his life in London as a stockbroker, abandons his wife and children, and devotes himself exclusively to painting. Lilly tried to imagine herself making such a sacrifice for her art. Leaving behind Barrytown and all that was familiar and giving herself over entirely to her muse in some far-off place like Paris or Tahiti. Would her nocturnal talents be enough to carry her off this way? Or was last night just a fluke?

These were the thoughts she entertained as her lids grew heavy and consciousness blinked away.

Once again, she found herself at the wooded creek in the dead of night, with moonlit shadows weighing on her. The wind whistled through skeletal trees and up from the surface of the flowing stream. Unseen fauna stirred all around on the blackened ground.

Her monster hunched at its horrendous wet work, its hacking arm casting black driblets of blood. The creature paused in its carnage long enough to turn to her. *You again?* its flecked expression seemed to say, a mild annoyance crossing its countenance. *What do you need that I have not already given you?*

Given me? She remembered the bolt that shot through her the other night, the searing brightness and poison it brought to her core.

The monster gestured with its blade to the writhing form beneath it.

Stepping closer, she saw the face of the prone figure pinned in the pool of blood had no features, like some department-store mannequin. But instead of being molded from plastic, its flesh was real.

The monster bared its pitted and stained iron teeth and shrugged at her as if to say, *They're all like this. Faceless. There are new ones made every day.*

She looked down and saw the blade now in her hand. She peered at it curiously. When she looked up, the creature had vanished, but the faceless victim remained, trembling beside the whispering creek.

It's only a dream, she told herself as she approached. *It doesn't matter what we do in our dreams.*

TRILLING awakened her. In bed, in her pajamas, she reached for the cell phone on the nightstand. The I.D. informed her that the caller was UNKNOWN. Probably a scammer, but you can never tell. She brought the device to her ear. "Hello?"

"Lilly?"

"Yes?"

"This is Terra Bronski. We went to Barrytown Community College together?"

"Oh, Terra. I didn't expect you to call me." Terra sounded so much older on the phone. "You still work at the Addington Gallery?"

"I do. That's why I'm calling. I opened your email this morning and saw those haunting images you sent. Of course, they'll have to be appraised, but I showed them around, and we're all quite excited by them. I didn't know you painted such dark subjects."

She sat up in bed and cleared her throat. "Well ... they just seemed to pop out of me. Must have just been in a dark mood when I painted them."

"That's understandable, given the murder they discovered yesterday in the park."

"The park?"

"Yes, Fairview Garden Park. Isn't that near where your parents live?"

"Yes. I mean, did live. They're both gone now."

"I'm sorry to hear that. It's been a few years."

"Now that you mentioned it, a couple of squad cars went by me yesterday on my way home. You say someone was murdered in the park?"

"Murdered, chopped up, and parts of her were missing. Kind of like the scenes you painted. The police think the Midwest Butcher is responsible."

"The guy from Indiana?"

"He travels throughout the Midwest, they say: Illinois, Indiana, Minnesota...."

"Hmmm. Do you know the name of the victim?"

"Patricia Bates, I think I heard. It'd be in the paper. Did you know her?"

"I don't think so."

"Anyway, we'd definitely be interested in displaying your pieces. We have certain collectors who love the dark stuff. Do you have any more like these?"

She remembered the pages she'd laid out in the kitchen. "Maybe. I'll have to think about it."

"Well, overnight us what you have, and we'll take it from there. I'm so happy for you, Lilly. We think you're going to make quite a splash. You have real talent."

On the kitchen table, eight fresh paintings awaited her. The first five were similar to the images she'd emailed to Terra: dark and rich and oozing with malevolent ambiance. But the other three were different, each markedly lighter than the next, like copies from a printer depleting of ink. The last one faded out to nothing halfway through. She examined it closely.

Why had the images washed out like that? It wasn't because she'd run out of supplies. She had plenty of watercolors, brushes, and paper. Rather, it was as if her artistic vision had begun to fade during the last three paintings.

She turned on her computer and searched Google News for the story of the murder in Fairview Park. There it was: brief and to the point.

BARRYTOWN, Ill. — Police are investigating the gruesome murder of a woman found brutally stabbed inside Fairview Garden Park Saturday afternoon.

Authorities believe Pamela Lynn Bates, 22, formerly of New Hope, Minn., is the latest victim of the serial killer known as the Midwest Butcher.

Bates' body was reportedly found by a Boy Scout troop holding a campout.

According to Scoutmaster Leonid Shevlin, "Several of the boys came running up to me, saying a lady was dead by the creek. I went there immediately, and, sure enough, the troop was gathered around her, staring, some of them crying. Someone had stabbed her countless times. There was blood everywhere. Whole sections of her body were cut away. I dialed 9-1-1, then I told the boys to go back to the campsite.

"I don't know how these boys will ever get over the trauma of witnessing that horrible scene. Some of them were so shaken, it was like they were in a trance. I canceled the campout. Had their parents pick them up when the police were through with them. I'll admit I'm shaken pretty badly myself."

The FBI has been called in to assist in the investigation.

That day at work, everyone was talking about the murder. The victim worked just down the road at the Snuggle Inn. Pamela Bates, that was her name. One of the busboys personally knew her. "You know the one," he said. "Cute with purple hair and a nose ring. She and her boyfriend came in a few times for lunch. A really friendly couple."

Someone knew her boyfriend but couldn't remember his name.

Lilly had trouble concentrating. Luckily, she knew her day work well enough to do it by rote.

Up till then, all her thoughts on the killing had been eaten up by her mysterious artwork and her main subject: the iron-mouthed assassin. If the person she'd painted *was* the Midwest Butcher (and it would be a hell of a coincidence if it wasn't), then the ravaged torso beneath the blade would be that of Pamela Bates.

Perhaps she should show her paintings to the police? See if they could find some clues in them to the killer's identity. But what would she say? "These images came to me in a dream, and I painted them in my sleep." She had difficulty believing this herself.

After the brunch cleanup, she finished out her evening shift.

"What's up, Lilly?" Rich asked when they were alone in the back. "You seem a little out of it today. Is it because of the murder? That happened pretty close to where you live, didn't it?"

"I think the Addington Gallery in Chicago is going to show some of my paintings."

His eyes widened. "Your watercolors?"

"Yes. Some watercolors I painted the other night."

"Well, that's great news. Are they still lifes?"

"Not in the usual sense."

"What do you mean?"

She shrugged but didn't answer him. Finally, she said, "What do you think happens to us when we go to sleep, Rich?"

He shook his head as if surprised by the question. "Where did that come from?"

"Do you think we're another person when we sleep? Is it possible we could become someone else?"

His walrus mustache trailed his lips to one side of his face, and he appeared to nibble briefly at his inner cheek. "I wouldn't think so. Who knows? I guess it's possible. Why?"

Before she left work that day, she collected the Sunday newspapers from where customers left them. She wanted to find out all she could about the killing.

Back home, she added the five darker prints to the previous ten, bound them carefully in several sheets of cardboard saved from watercolor-paper pads, and wrapped these in a brown grocery bag. She addressed the finished product to the Addington Gallery, then set it off to the side.

She'd mail it tomorrow.

THE NEXT SUNDAY was Easter. Not too long ago, her parents would have gathered with her around the kitchen table to celebrate the occasion with a special meal, though by then, the family had become lapse in religious observances. For the Barneses, Easter had become a time of fuzzy bunnies, colorful eggs, a holiday ham (which Lilly would pass on), a vegetarian pasta dish, and a unique coconut lamb cake her mother made each year from a cast-iron baking mold.

Lilly wondered what they would've thought of her dark watercolors. They probably would've offered their typical brand of tepid encouragement, but she'd be able to read in their faces the bewilderment triggered by these stark images.

At first, Dad would be unsure about the gallery, always suspicious of scams. The truth was, though generally supportive, her parents were never entirely sold on Lilly's artistic talents. "And this is a reputable place, you say?" her father would ask.

"The Addington is one of the best galleries in Chicago," she'd reply.

"So you've taken up ... *crime painting?*" her mother would say, looking at her strangely.

Yes, it would've been a difficult pill for them to swallow.

Terra Bronski called from the gallery as Lilly spooned ramen soup from a ceramic bowl.

"We'll need you here for the opening," Terra said.

"In Chicago?"

"Yes. Of course."

It hadn't occurred to Lilly the gallery might require her presence. She shared the squeamishness of many suburbanites when it comes to driving in the big city. She swallowed. "Okay."

"We were thinking May seventh, that's a Friday. How does that work for you?"

Her head was swimming. *Chicago? May seventh?* "That should be fine."

"We were thinking of pricing them in the neighborhood of two-thousand dollars."

"Apiece?

Terra laughed. "Of course, apiece. Maybe we could get more. We'll see how the opening goes. And, I should warn you that the gallery takes forty percent of sales."

Lilly did some mental math. Two thousand times fifteen was thirty thousand. Sixty percent of that was still eighteen-thousand dollars. She whistled.

"Not a bad prospective haul for an unknown artist, is it?" Terra said.

"It's fabulous."

"We're thinking of framing them in black with black matting. Is that alright?"

Lilly paused for a minute. "Sure."

"Were you going to name these images?"

"I don't know. I guess they should have a name. What would you suggest?"

"Hmmm. Well, they seem to follow a sort of progression. Maybe name them all the same but number them, one through fifteen."

"That's a good idea."

They batted around a few ideas that played to the paintings' dark theme before settling simply on *Still Life*.

"Say, you haven't any more of these paintings, have you?"

"Not as good as those," she said.

"Well, if you could work up a few more, you may need them. We may need them. We're thinking of calling the show 'The Macabre Chimeras of Lilly Barnes.' That should draw out the right clientele. Any objections?"

For an instant, Lilly was speechless. Then she said, "No. Call it what you like."

"Great. We'll see you then on the seventh. Bye, Lilly."

The connection went dead.

Eighteen-thousand dollars, Lilly thought. *And I don't even remember painting them.*

Sadly, it looked more and more as if those fifteen paintings would be the first and the last of her lucrative chimera period.

Every night, she left her painting supplies out on the table, hoping to be amazed in the morning by new masterpieces of bloodletting and gore, but, so far, nothing more had happened. She tried sleeping on the couch, hoping proximity was the key. All it gave her was a strain in the small of her back. She tried drinking Lambrusco before bedtime to no avail. She'd even walked to Fairview Park, where she'd found the creek and the blood-slaked spot that marked the demise of Pamela Bates. It looked exactly as she'd dreamt it, and at this recognition, something crawled within her. But, once again, her efforts were in vain.

She drove to Chicago the day before the exhibition.

She remembered when she was young, and her father had driven them to see the Tutankhamen showing at the Field Museum. She remembered that the nearer they got to the city, the more maniacal Dad's driving had become. By the time they entered the city proper, it was as if Mario Andretti were behind the wheel, going full blazes on the curves at the Indy 500. Her father had been born in Chicago, and it didn't take long to acclimate himself to the prevalent driving style of the city's downtown commuters.

Lilly, on the other hand, resisted the norm and got herself honked at and cut off, and became the recipient of numerous unpleasant hand gestures.

She stayed at the Hotel Felix, a vintage brick building at the corner of Clark and Huron streets, a mile and a half from Navy Pier (should she feel adventurous). Inside the Felix was a spacious lobby with glass baubles suspended from the ceiling and two flanks of contemporary armchairs facing each other. A queen-size room there cost her a little over two-hundred dollars a night, but it was comfortable, modern, and quiet. For an added seventeen dollars daily, she got a cup of strong coffee, high-speed wifi internet access, and amenities such as a fitness center that she knew she would never use. She ponied up the extra for three nights anyway, for the wifi and the coffee.

Room service was pricey, but she'd come prepared, stocking her luggage half-full of bagels, granola bars, Twizzlers, and ripple chips. Not necessarily the most nutritious choices but enough to keep her going for a couple of days. Maybe she'd get some takeout somewhere, if she got too famished. *Or wasn't there a Whole Foods just down the street?*

She'd received a bottle of water from the receptionist when she checked in. When she'd emptied that, she'd do something she hadn't done in years: drink from the faucet.

She'd brought along her watercolor supplies on the off-chance the city inspired her. These she stacked neatly on the room's writing desk, not really expecting to use them.

She took a bath, turned on the television for a marathon session of *Hoarders* and *Sister Wives*, and eventually fell asleep in a Felix Hotel robe, munching on a Twizzler.

That night she slept restlessly, drifting in and out of REM, half-awaken by the wailing of police sirens on the streets outside. Her dreams were jagged and jumbled, crowded with stick-thin walking effigies and human-sized juju dolls and House of Wax mannequins-come-to-life, all grappling toward her like zombies in a George Romero movie. *They've come to get you, Lilly.* She tossed and squirmed as their bent fingers reached out to seize her.

Then she had another dream.

In it, a svelte Black man in a gray wool suit stood outside an urban hotel at night, smoking a cigarette. He looked to be in his mid-thirties, a businessman judging from his demeanor, with immaculately trimmed hair and professionally manicured fingernails.

A blue sedan pulled up to the curb beside him. As the window rolled down, the barrel of a rifle came to brace on the door's rubber weatherstrip. Now, through the gunman's eyes, Lilly watched as the svelte man looked up in alarm. The rifle coughed rapid fire. Its bullets bit into the man's chest, leaving spreading blooms of red. The cigarette fell from his hand in a cacophony of sparks. His legs gave way beneath him, and he crashed to the sidewalk.

As the car pulled away, the shooter turned to Lilly, who now sat beside him. The killer, a Mexican man with a busted-up face and a wide, fat-lipped mouth, grinned broadly and gave her a thumbs-up sign.

Then the gunman, the car, and the night street spun from view, and she went somewhere far away from ghouls and guns, where nightmares of the dead and dying could no longer touch her.

IN THE MORNING, once she'd remembered where she was, Lilly sat up in bed, a half-eaten Twizzler stuck to one cheek. She pried it loose.

The television was on, and some celebrity chef was talking about the importance of using *extra-virgin* olive oil (not the less expensive *virgin* kind) in his sweet-potatoes-and-scallions dish. "EVO is healthier for you and has a fruitier taste," the chef, who looked a little like Bobby Flay and dressed a little like Guy Fieri, explained. "It's less acidic and is formed from pressure exclusively, not heat. But when cooking with EVO, it's important to always use low-temperature settings...."

She searched among the covers for the remote and thumbed to a channel with local news.

The anchor guy and the weather woman were bantering about the City Series, which pitted the Cubs against the White Sox. The anchor liked the Sox; the meteorologist was all-Cubs.

"Mark my words," the weather woman said. "The Sox will be hung out to dry."

The anchorman groaned at this.

But Lilly's attention was now off the screen and directed toward the room's writing desk. The packets of watercolor supplies had been broken into and messily upended, and freshly painted sheets of ten-by-fourteen, one-hundred-and-forty pound, hot-press paper lay spread on the table's surface.

She climbed out of bed, chewing on the half-eaten Twizzler.

The paintings were again exquisite. Swirls and thrusts of ominous colors revealed scenes of chilling carnage that featured the svelte character from last night's dream, his dance of death captured from every angle.

She tried to look away from the grisly images, but they kept drawing her back. There was unmistakable beauty in this horror.

She was standing in awe of their artistry when words from the television caught her notice.

"... Rang out in the River North neighborhood just after midnight this morning. A drive-by shooter in a blue sedan shot and killed a twenty-six-year-old man outside the lobby of the Home2 Suites by Hilton at Huron and Clark streets."

Huron and Clark? That's where she was, wasn't it? And wasn't.... She looked out her hotel window. Yes, the Home2 Suites was just across the street.

"A father of three from New Hope, Minnesota...."

On the television, uniformed cops wandered inside a perimeter of yellow crime-scene tape at night. In the background, she saw the Felix Hotel sign.

She sat down on the end of the bed as the newsman moved on to the other seventeen shootings that had occurred in Chicago last night. His voice became a meaningless rumble as she nibbled on the last of her Twizzler and began to suspect how this sleep-art of hers worked.

For her nocturnal muse to come alive, maybe she needed to be physically near actual bloodshed. It was like a weird type of sleep osmosis, to be sure. But instead of learning while she slept, she painted, and she could only do it if actual carnage was close at hand.

She wasn't sure how she felt about this. Had she become some kind of morbid voyeur; a pain painter of the repulsive?

Lilly dressed, gathered up the new paintings, and collected her cup of coffee from the shop downstairs. She splurged on a scone.

The gallery didn't open to the public till eleven o'clock, but the staff would probably be in by now. It was nearly nine.

She dialed up Terra Bronski.

"Terra? Hi, this is Lilly Barnes. Listen, I don't know if you'll have time to use them, but I painted some more images last night and was wondering if I could drop them off for you to take a look at?"

"That would be great. But listen, Lilly, I'm afraid we're going to have to cancel your exhibit tonight."

"Cancel?" A spike of fear rose within her. "What do you mean cancel? I thought it was all set." What would she tell her friends back home who were all so excited for her?

"Yes. Well, you see, we post our pieces for sale on various websites. Usually, we do it after an exhibit, but somehow there was a mix-up on the dates and your works posted yesterday."

"Okay."

"Lilly, they've sold out. Every painting of *Still Life*. All fifteen images."

"Can't you use the ones I painted last night?"

"Hmm. Let me have a look at them. Are you very far away? I could send someone to pick you up."

"I'm less than two minutes' walk from the gallery. At the Felix. I'll be right over if that's okay."

"Give me fifteen minutes to make a few calls on this. To see if the media have been contacted yet."

"Great."

Lilly pressed the hang-up icon on her phone and searched Google News for an update on the shooting. She came to a video of the victim's heartbroken wife, holding an infant and pleading for the killer to come forward.

"Turn yourself in," she begged. "We deserve justice."

Lilly clicked off the news feed and closed the website.

What would this poor widow think of my art?

SOMEHOW, everything came together seamlessly. Terra and her coworkers were suitably impressed with the new paintings. Rather than waste the money already spent on advertising, the new images were quickly framed and hung, and the opening went on as planned that evening.

The original *Still Life* images were displayed as sold, and the new ones, dubbed *Drive By* and numbered one through ten, were exhibited just below these. They were priced at thirty-eight hundred dollars apiece.

About a hundred people turned out for her showing, ranging from suited business-types to academics in sweater vests and rumpled trousers to Goths and free spirits with their tattoos, piercings, and brilliantly colored hair. After a brief introduction by Terra, all eyes fixed on Lilly, who, though unaccustomed to such attention, swiftly warmed to it.

"Thank you for coming tonight," she said. "I'm not sure what to say about my work other than its reflexive in a primal sort of way. These images come to me in my dreams, and I paint them in something of a trance, I guess. I have no recollection of creating them. I've painted in watercolors most of my life, but I've never produced images like these before. It's as if they came hotwired straight from my central nervous system. I don't know how else to explain them."

She took questions from the crowd, including barbed queries from a local art critic in a pointed yellow beard who asked, "Are your images pro- or anti-violence? Or are they strictly objective, left for the viewer to decide?"

"I'm not a violent person. I don't favor hurting people if that's what you mean."

"Then why do you paint scenes of such utter depravity?"

This drew smatterings of protest from the crowd.

"As I said, the images come to me in dreams. Nightmares, if you prefer."

"But why expose the art world to your grotesque visions?" He twisted the point of his beard.

"I'm a waitress in Barrytown. I painted the first series of images after the Midwest Butcher brutally killed a woman in a nearby park. I painted the pictures before I consciously learned of the attack. I guess I picked that event up somehow. The experience left me badly frightened, I assure you. My subconscious reacted in a certain way. I'm only beginning to understand the process myself. I sent JPEGs of the paintings to the Addington and was invited by them into the art world."

"The art world has invited in a wide assortment of deviants, from Adolf Hitler to John Gacy. So what makes your paintings any different from theirs?"

"No one has ever called me a deviant before." She felt slightly woozy. "I guess you're free to characterize me and my paintings as you like."

This response generated hearty applause from the crowd, though when it came to this group, she suspected she was in considerable measure preaching to the choir.

She stayed around to mingle for a while but slipped away after a few hours.

The following morning, she learned that the *Drive By* images had sold out, as well.

No new paintings awaited that morning on the writing desk.

She spent the entire day in bed, watching reality television and mulling over the night's events. Ten times thirty-eight hundred times sixty percent equaled almost twenty-three-thousand dollars. After a night like that, she could even afford pricey room service at the Felix Hotel.

But, while thoughts of all that money and how she could spend it brought her joy, the critic's questions and remarks returned to prick at her. He'd suggested there was something monstrous about her paintings. Something monstrous about *her*. *Was he right?*

Lilly tried to picture what she and these paintings looked like through the eyes of others.

She emerged from her hibernation the following day. Before checking out, she was sipping an espresso in the cafe downstairs and thumbing through the morning's edition of the *Chicago Tribune* when she came upon a brief piece about her exhibit at the Addington in which the reporter described her paintings as "hypnotically grotesque" and alleged to have come to the artist in "some sort of fugue state." *Okay, fair enough.*

The article included a small photo of her surrounded by art patrons, as well as a larger shot from her piece *Drive By: Number Ten*, which featured the svelte Black man lying prone in the night street in a tarn of red, sightlessly meeting the gaze of the painting's viewer. In the corner of the picture, the rear of a blue sedan could be seen speeding away from the curb, its Illinois license plate partly visible. The partial plate number read 519.

She hadn't noticed this detail before. Now she wondered whether this was from the actual license plate or just a number her subconscious dreamt up. *If the number was correct, it could be a valuable clue for the police.*

On the drive back to Barrytown, she considered sharing the number with the cops but knew how crazy that would sound.

"Yes, officer, you see, I saw the shooting in a dream, and when I awoke, I found I'd painted it. In one of the paintings...."

She couldn't imagine any scenario in which she didn't come off sounding like a lunatic.

WHEN SHE RETURNED to work on Monday, she was excited to share with Rich and Namadia the success of her exhibition at the Addington. But they already knew about it, thanks to the newspaper article.

Upon arrival for her morning shift, every seat in the diner was taken, and all the customers and the staff broke out in a spontaneous round of applause.

A hand-printed banner reading "Welcome home, Lilly Barnes, famous painting waitress" hung from the ceiling. Xeroxed copies of the Tribune article were on every tabletop, and everyone's face was aglow with good feelings and excitement.

She was so shocked, she didn't know what to say.

Rich rushed up to her, misty-eyed, and gave her a big bear hug, his walrus mustache tickling the back of her neck. "I'm so proud of you, Lilly." He squeezed her so tight, she almost couldn't breathe.

Namadia, her coworker and friend (and Rich's sometimes girlfriend), joined in to make it a group hug. Namadia, with her big head of permed hair and her tiny eyes, hugged clumsily but sincerely.

"Thanks, guys," Lilly said at last.

The day zipped by smoothly, considering the abundance of patrons. No one complained about slow service or sent food back to the grill for being undercooked. Customers posed with her in photos, and she even signed a few autographs. Tip-wise, it was her best day ever.

Around two o'clock, business slowed a bit. Namadia snuck out for a cigarette, and Lilly followed her to the back of the building.

"So, what's it like to be a big-time *artiste*?" Namadia asked, lighting up.

Lilly thought for a minute. "Part of me is thrilled. But, on the other hand, part of me feels like I don't deserve it."

Namadia squinted as a spiral of smoke from her Marlboro drifted into her eyes. "What do you mean, 'Don't deserve it?'"

"Well, you know. As the newspaper said, these images came to me in my sleep, and I don't even remember painting them."

"Oh, right. Fugue state. And that's real?"

"That's not even the weirdest part. The only scenes I can paint that are of professional quality are scenes of violence. And I'm pretty sure I have to be near these crimes when they're taking place for the whole process to work."

"Near them? That is weird." She drew deeply, a slight tremor to her hand, then blew a plume of smoke from the corner of her mouth. "But there's money in these paintings, right?"

"I made about forty-thousand dollars off them, so far."

"*Forty thousand*? Wow, Lilly, you have to find a way to make this work for you."

Lilly frowned. "So, what do I do? Run around the country living in violence-prone areas? Waiting for the muse to strike again?"

Namadia considered this. With the hand holding her cigarette, she flicked the nails of her thumb and little finger back and forth. Then she said, "That's what I'd do."

After work, Lilly went to the drive-through at Taco Bell, ordered three bean burritos fresco style, brought them home, then camped out on the couch with her laptop and began looking up violent-crime statistics.

SHE AWOKE with a start in the dark of late night on the couch with the laptop precariously balanced on her pelvis. Cold metal had poked at her.

Or maybe she'd just dreamt it?

For a minute, she gathered her wits.

She remembered drifting off, knee-deep in major-city crime stats where the lives of human beings were callously reduced to blood-red charts and bar graphs. She remembered she'd nearly settled on making her next excursion to Detroit but hadn't entirely made up her mind. She'd never been to Detroit, but homicide-wise it had much to offer. She could always go back to Chicago, she'd supposed. Or Minneapolis.

Ambient moonlight from the living-room window filtered into the dark at its edges, reassuring her of her bearings in the unlit house.

She sat up, set the computer aside, and touched the spot on her shoulder where she had felt the icy poke. She must have dreamt it.

But it had felt so real.

She stretched and yawned and was about to stand up when a voice from the shadows said, "Hello, Lilly."

A wild clamor of fear arose. It felt as if a hundred tiny razor blades were digging into her belly. "W-who's there?" she said in barely a whisper, suddenly unable to move.

The corner lamp beside the TV blinked on, flooding the room with sudden brilliance.

Looking at her, down the barrel of a wood-grained, bolt-action rifle—the barrel with which he'd no doubt just poked her—stood the broken-faced Mexican from her drive-by dream: the assassin of the svelte Black man. The one who'd given her the thumbs-up signal.

"You know who I am, don't you?" he asked.

A surge of giddiness mingled with her fear. It was as if he'd stepped directly from her dream: this nightmare man made flesh and now pointing his rifle at her. Corralling some of her swirling emotion, she said tightly, "You're real."

He grinned, his wide, fat lips pulling back from teeth that seemed preternaturally big and white. "Of course, I'm real. Aren't you?"

She nodded uncertainly.

"And you recognize me, too, don't you? I knew it. I understand how you could have seen the car from your hotel window, maybe even caught part of the license plate, but how did you see me inside the car? Did you see the driver, too? He's outside, waiting for me, by the way."

She hadn't seen the driver in her dream, not that it mattered. "You have to understand, I just dreamt it—the shooting, I mean. I woke up in the hotel room and...."

"Save it. I read the newspaper story. I know all about your so-called 'fugue state.' You think we believe that crap? You think we're idiots?"

She shook her head.

"You must have watched through binoculars or something. If you hadn't painted the blue Audi and the partial license plate, it wouldn't have mattered. But if anyone put those paintings together with the shooting, well, the cops may be slow, but you can't always count on them being stupid. They'd eventually come knocking on your door, asking questions. And who knows what you'd tell them?"

"I wouldn't tell them anything." Her voice took on a higher pitch. "I'd tell them what I told you. That the paintings were from a dream."

"The car, well, that's now just a cube of metal at a scrapyard in Aurora. They might still be able to trace it back to the owner, but he'll tell them it was stolen. That leaves us with just one loose end."

His face went slack. His eyes narrowed.

He pulled the trigger.

"ISN'T SHE that painting waitress everyone's been talking about?" asked the first cop, dusting the wall for fingerprints.

"Yeah, looks like her painting days are over," said the second cop, as the EMTs rolled the body bag out the door on a gurney. "It's a shame. Young girl like that."

"Hey, you guys," the third cop called from the kitchen. "Did you see this?"

"The paintings, you mean?" the second cop asked. "I saw them but didn't really pay any attention to them."

"Well, this you gotta see."

They went to the kitchen, and all three of them stood looking down at the tabletop where five paintings were spread out. The images were stark and vibrant and displayed a crime in vivid detail, frame by frame, from the moment the assailant emptied a round into his victim, through the blood spraying on the wall and the ceiling, to the final image where the victim's dead eyes gleamed out of a face vacant and haunting.

It was the face of Lilly Barnes.

Acknowledgments

C an there exist a mystic connection between a gun and its owner? Can dark legends of the distant past reappear to threaten us in the present? Does revenge truly bring relief to those who suffer from a monstrous act by a sinister figure?

Probably not, but I leave that for you to decide. I only tell the stories.

In the Heart of the Garden Is a Tomb is my sixth book and I feel a remarkable sense of accomplishment in finishing it. I think it's my best work so far, but I always think my newest book is my best, so not sure you can go by that. Hopefully, it entertains and satisfies you, the reader.

Once again, much of the book is set in New Hope, Minnesota, which is a real place and not any more spooky than any other American metropolitan suburb. It just happens to be where I live and I'm familiar with the place. Shout out to my New Hope neighbors!

I'd also like to thank my good friend Helen Lloyd-Montgomery, my fearless editor Danita Mayer, and my wonderful stepdaughter Jennifer Thompson for their assistance in putting this book together. And thanks to Attila Orosz, and to Joshua Evans for their help when called upon.

As always, I also thank my wife, Debbie, for allowing my dreams to come true, and my many friends and relatives for their support and encouragement. A special thanks goes out to my buddy Keith Peterson for his enthusiasm, validation and friendship.

If you enjoyed *In the Heart of the Garden Is a Tomb*, consider recommending it to your friends and family on social media. Also, reader reviews are the lifeblood of modern publishing, and posting a brief review on Amazon, Goodreads or your favorite readers' blog would help a struggling author immeasurably.

For updates on my work, and other readings on dark fiction, check out my website at: www.joepawlowskiauthor.com. You can follow me on Facebook @ Joe Pawlowski, Author or on Instagram @ joepawlowskiauthor.

Let the Terror Continue

OTHER BOOKS BY JOE PAWLOWSKI

Why All the Skulls Are Grinning

A shaken teenage girl, lost and abandoned at the gateway to another realm. A man driven mad by isolation who believes he's built an automaton to lead him back to open skies. A car salesman whose girlfriend winds up a sacrificial offering to a rock god's dark deity. The stories contained in Why All the Skulls Are Grinning look into these tortured lives and many others.

Why are all the skulls grinning? Could it be because they have to smile to keep from shrieking?

Available from Amazon in paperback and ebook. Free on Kindle Unlimited.

The Cannibal Gardener

A gardener with a secret life, a Goth woman with a morbid fascination, a serial killer who leaves a trail of bodies across the Midwest: they all come together at a Minnesota lakehouse in a transformation as evil as it is shocking.

The Cannibal Gardener combines out-of-this-world horror with a love story and a touch of grim humor from a master storyteller.

Available from Amazon in paperback and ebook. Free on Kindle Unlimited.

The Vermilion Book of the Macabre

From author of *The Cannibal Gardener* and *Dark House of Dreams* comes this highly anticipated collection of 16 spellbinding tales of supernatural suspense.

Readers call it "a blood-chilling collection" and say of Pawlowski "he paints his dark tales so realistically you will have nightmares."

Available from Amazon in paperback and ebook. Free on Kindle Unlimited.

The Watchful Dead

A 12-year-old boy housebound all his life, a conjure woman who speaks to the dead, an evil slave trader driven ruthless by greed and a war hero whose greatest battles take place in his own mind: all are about to have their lives shaken to the core by powerful forces from beyond the grave.

Readers are calling it "a ride right off the bat" and "nicely written, with a lyrical quality that kept me turning virtual pages," and the author "possesses the talents of a classic great writer."

The Horror Review says *The Watchful Dead* is "a gutsy, ambitious, skillful exploration of cosmic/epic dark fantasy."

Available from Amazon in paperback and ebook. Free on Kindle Unlimited.

Dark House of Dreams

In a city overrun by ghosts, fear lurks around every corner.

Add a murder plot, a devastating earthquake, a missing mother, a gang of outrageous villains, and a young boy tormented by demons both real and imagined, and you have an epic quest through the hidden places of monsters and gods.

Readers say it's a "well-written and creepy" journey that begins with a secret revealed in a charnel cave and ends with a hard-earned lesson learned in a *Dark House of Dreams*.

Available from Amazon in paperback and ebook. Free on Kindle Unlimited.

Made in the USA
Middletown, DE
07 August 2022

70358001R00125